Money
Never Sleeps

Money Never Sleeps

A *Millionaire Wives Club* novel

Tu-Shonda L. Whitaker

ONE WORLD TRADE PAPERBACKS
BALLANTINE BOOKS NEW YORK

A One World Books Trade Paperback Original

Copyright © 2011 by Tu-Shonda L. Whitaker

Published in the United States by One World Books,
an imprint of The Random House Publishing Group,
a division of Random House, Inc., New York.

ONE WORLD is a registered trademark and
the One World colophon is a trademark of
Random House, Inc.

Title-page illustration: © iStockphoto

ISBN 978-0-345-52512-3
eBook ISBN 978-0-345-52513-0

Printed in the United States of America

www.oneworldbooks.net

9 8 7 6 5 4 3

To Melody Guy, for your patience,
your talent, and for the richness you
have brought to my literary career!
I could never thank you enough
for all that I've learned from you.
God bless and may we meet again.

"Money *can't* buy you love; it *is* love."

—Tu-Shonda L. Whitaker

Welcome to
Millionaire Wives Club

Season Two

The Club

The evening sun settled over Manhattan's Lincoln Center as the three reality stars of *Millionaire Wives Club* walked the red carpet at Jacque Chanel's premiere fashion affair. The ladies' hips swayed as they passed paparazzi, and millions of dollars in rare jewels, ultrachic sheath dresses, and diamond-encrusted Stewart Weizman dream stilettos graced their bodies.

They each thought *fuck last season*. To hell with the way the audience reveled in what the camera revealed: that beneath their posh facades lay emotional bag ladies, dressed in a collection of heartache, uncertainty, and decades of bullshit.

This was a new season, a new script, and a renewed chance to prove to the world that they'd finally gotten it together.

"Ladies!" An *E! News* reporter rushed over to them, hoping to snag a quick interview before they entered the fashion show. "You all look lovely tonight," he said as they stopped and faced him.

The ladies smiled and their eyes shone at the flattery. "Thank you," they said simultaneously.

"Can you tell us what to expect from the second season of

Millionaire Wives Club?" He pointed the mic toward the woman to his right. "May we start with you—?"

"Milan Starks!" A voice rose above the buzzing crowd and caused everyone's eyes to dart in search of its origin. Before their eyes could find the source, two women appeared before the cast, grabbed unexpected hugs from each of them, and then grinned as if they were all long-lost relatives. The women were dressed exactly alike, from their matching fire-red and curly lace-front wigs to their red sequin short sets. The only difference between them was that one appeared at least ten years older than the other.

"Look at these bitches here!" The older woman snapped her fingers in a z-motion, as the short set she wore glimmered in the fading sunlight. "You know y'all stay sharp as shit." She popped her lips. "But y'all crazier than a motherfucker." She looked into the camera and nodded for emphasis. "Are we on TV?"

"Ah, yes," the reporter said. "Yes, we're live."

"Oh, shit." The woman bounced her shoulders. "I'm Trena and Uptown's in the hiz'zouse!" she said into the camera. "And this is my daughter-in-law, Roz!" She pulled the other woman close.

Roz smiled and shouted. "Hey, Money! I miss you, baby. Thank you for always holding it down! Don't even sweat those C.O.s! You got three hundred months left on your stint, and you'll be home soon."

"Where is security?" Milan mumbled to her costar, Chaunci Morgan, who stood next to her.

"Excuse me," the reporter said. "Do you two ladies know the cast of *Millionaire Wives Club* personally?"

Roz answered. "Hell, yeah, we know 'em personally. Every Thursday night at ten, we get to know 'em very, very well."

"So you're fans of the show?"

"Absolutely! We love it!" Trena said. "And ever since we spotted them getting out of the limo, we've been following them and trying to get their attention."

"What?" Milan said, taken aback. "You've been following us? Can somebody please find security?"

The reporter continued, "Would you like to tell us who your favorite is?"

Roz popped her lips. "Milan is my favorite." She draped an arm over one of Milan's shoulders, forcing her to look into the camera with a plastic smile.

"Why?" the reporter asked.

"'Cause *honnnneeey,* this trick don't give a damn!"

"Excuse you?" Milan blinked.

"Dat ass," Roz continued, "was scandalous. How you gon' sleep with that girl's husband like that? What was her name, ummm . . . ?" She snapped her fingers.

"Evan," Jaise volunteered. "Yes, um-hmm, my dear friend Evan."

Milan elbowed Jaise, her other costar. "Are you starting again this season?"

"What?" Jaise flicked her hand. "They asked, and Evan was my friend. Oh, and make a mental note of this: Don't elbow me again."

"Look at you, Jaise," Trena sassed. "Finally learning how to stand up for yourself and stop being so damn high sadity and weak. My girl. But *annnnywaay,* that chick, Evan, was a crazy-ass train wreck! What kinda ho-bag walks into the ocean? She wasn't Moses. Hell, she had to know she couldn't part the motherfucker. Damn shame."

"Tell it, Trena. That trick was twisted. Poisoning her daughter and shit. And Kendu, he couldn't see that coming? Oh, wait." Roz looked Milan over. "He was too busy doing you. But you know what they say: 'How you get 'im is how you lose 'im—' "

"Amen," Jaise signified.

"Oh, really, Jaise?" Milan said in disbelief. "Really?"

"Are we gon' see somebody beatin' ass this season?" Roz asked anxiously. " 'Cause I don't care what you say, you three are a buncha hood rats." She winked. "My kinda girls. But wait, stop the press." She held her hands up. " 'Cause I have got to know: Who the hell is the new chick?"

Trena gasped. "I forgot about the new chick."

"How you gon' forget the new bird? You know the new bitch is supposed to be here tonight. And speaking of pigeons, where's Al-Taniesha?"

"We don't keep up with Al-Taniesha," Jaise snapped.

"I bet you don't," Trena said. "Especially since your son knocked up her daughter."

"Now, the new girl," Roz interjected. "Who is she? Everybody's been so hush-hush about it. Is it true she's Denzel Washington's jump-off or R. Kelly's ex-wife?"

"R. Kelly?" Trena's eyes bulged. "Oh, that would be fiyah. 'Cause I know she was tired of his ass makin' rounds on the playground! Now tell us." She looked back at the cast. "Who is she?"

"I don't know," Milan sucked her teeth.

"Me either," Chaunci and Jaise said.

Roz and Trena laughed.

"These heifers know how to lie." Trena snickered. "Like they really don't know. *Surrrrrre* you don't. I just hope she's somebody who'll let y'all asses have it, 'cause you three can get *waaaaay* outta control! So anywho, back to you, Milan." She pointed. "What you did last season was real fucked-up. You might even be the real reason why Evan killed herself."

Milan's eyes bugged. "What?"

"Okay, ladies," Chaunci interjected. "Nice meeting you. But we need to get going before the show starts."

"Wait," Trena said. "I just have to know—Chaunci, did you ever get with your daughter's father? Puhlease say yes, 'cause yo' ass was so damn uptight you needed to be whipped with the dick—"

"Beat down by the ding-dong!" Roz held up a black-power fist.

"Hallejuah!" Trena waved her hand to Jesus. "'Cause that Idris was a fine-ass black man—" She turned to Jaise. "Not finer than your husband—but he was fine."

"Thank you." Jaise blushed. "Bilal is rather handsome."

"You bet he is." Trena slapped Jaise a high five. "But you better hope he doesn't leave you. As insecure as you were, I don't even know what he saw in you. Plus, it looks as if you put on a few pounds."

"Say that again?" Jaise parked her neck one way and twisted her lips in the other direction.

"I know you don't have an attitude." Milan shook her head. "No, not you."

"Jaise, girl," Trena carried on. "I was happy for you when you finally found the one, 'cause I spent most of the season wanting to slap you! I thought for sure you would've been the one to kill yourself. *Annnnnnd thaaaaat* son of yours."

"Whew!" Roz shivered. "You should've kicked his ass! 'Cause if you would've put your foot down he wouldn't have had you on all the gossip sites when he got arrested last season for underage drinking. And all the reports said he was drinking Old Milwaukee. Who in *da hell* still drinks *Old Milwaukee*? Jaise, he had yo' ass lookin' real bootleg."

Jaise quickly moved her head from left to right and snapped her fingers. "Let me tell you something, you don't talk about my child!"

"Security! Security!" Chaunci yelled and snapped her fingers in a panic. After she made eye contact with one of the officers she quietly mouthed "help," then slyly nodded her head toward the overzealous fans.

The reporter's face gleamed in excitement as Jaise continued to lose it. "I'm not the one!" she spat.

After confirming that Roz and Trena didn't have press passes or tickets to the fashion show, two armed security guards stretched out their arms and said, "Back it up, ladies. This area is for press and guests only."

The three cast members rushed toward the entrance.

"We love you!" Roz and Trena shouted as the women entered the private marquee. "We never missed an episode!"

The lights were dim inside the exquisite tent. The walls were covered with flowing crisp-white drapes, and the designer's name illuminated in lights around the room. A sleek black runway was in the center of the floor, and the guests' linen-covered chairs were aligned in rows along both sides of the stage. The women eased into their front-row seats, with Chaunci sitting in the middle and Jaise and Milan to her left and right, respectively. A few seconds after they were situated—with their legs crossed and their Devi Kroell handbags and clutches resting in their laps—Milan leaned in and whispered, "What. The. Fuck. Was. That?"

"Some bullshit," Chaunci said, as they waited for the fashion show to begin.

"Exactly," Jaise agreed. "A moment longer and I would've really lost it. And as long as security took, you would've thought we were a bunch of Celebrity Rehab D-listers."

"Oh, no!" Milan gasped. "Well, I'll just have to clutch my pearls at the thought."

"I have worked too hard!" Jaise carried on, oblivious to Chaunci's laughter. "I have sacrificed too much . . ."

Chaunci snickered and said low enough for only Milan to hear. "Clutching your pearls?" She wiped tears of laughter from her eyes. "Would you stop fucking with that chick before she gets mad and we have to whup her ass?"

"Let me inform you," Jaise ranted. "If it weren't for the cameras I would've whupped the jungle out of their asses."

"Don't let the cameras stop you," Bridget, the show's producer, whispered unexpectedly over their shoulders. "Don't *ever* let the cameras stop you."

Each of the women paused. They hadn't seen Bridget since last season's reunion show a year ago. And since she wasn't at the entrance to greet them when they arrived, they'd hoped that the rumors of her moving on to produce another reality show were true. They couldn't stand her last season. She was obnoxious and unreasonable, she constantly invaded their privacy, and she took reality-show production to new heights—or lows, depending on how you looked at it.

It was just like Bridget to lay in the cut and then spring forward when everyone least expected it.

"Bridget." Jaise smiled. "How are you?" she said as they all turned quickly toward Bridget and air-kissed her on both cheeks.

"Oh, doll faces, you all missed me?" She grinned.

"Of course," Jaise said.

"Well, I quit another show to be here."

"How lovely." Jaise shot her a Barbie-doll smile.

"Truly," Bridget agreed. "And Milan, no need to thank me for bringing you back for another season. Who knew you'd be the breakout star?"

"So, Bridget," Chaunci said. "Where's the new girl?"

"She isn't here yet." Bridget smirked. "But Al-Taniesha and Lollipop just arrived." She pointed.

Jaise closed her eyes tightly as if she were having a bad dream, while Chaunci and Milan shook their heads. "Oh, already, y'all asses tryin' to get it crunked?" Al-Taniesha smacked her lips. "How you not gon' share a limo with us?"

"Did somebody say it was prom night?" Jaise looked from side to side. "You should've hired a driver."

"Jaise, don't make me take it to the streets on your ass!"

Al-Taniesha looked over at Bridget. "I'm not gon' tolerate attitudes and shit. So consider this a warning. Al-Taniesha Chardonnay Richardson beats bitches' asses, okay? And this entire cast will go from starring on *Millionaire Wives Club* to *The First 48*!"

"And that's what's really hood." Lollipop popped his lips as he and Al-Taniesha slid off their identical mink coats and revealed their pink leather catsuits and rainbow leg warmers.

"What the hell is this? Twin night?" Chaunci said as Milan drew in a deep breath and Jaise blinked in disbelief.

"I won't even touch the outfits," Jaise commented. "But why do you have on mink coats? It's eighty degrees. Did you miss the memo that it's still summer?"

"Let me tell you something," Al-Taniesha said as she wiped sweat from her brow and sat beside Jaise. "We paid fourteen thousand—" She held her fingers out as if she were counting on them. "—seven hundred eighty-two dollars and seventy-nine cents for this fuckin' farm of fur, and we don't care if it's a hundred degrees outside. If we wanna sport this, we gon' rock the motherfuckers, okay? So handle your damn scandal and we'll handle ours."

"And there you have it!" Lollipop snapped his fingers as the first model appeared at the top of the stage.

Jaise simply shook her head as everyone leaned back in their chairs and watched the show. As the models worked the runway Jaise noticed Al-Taniesha and Lollipop snickering.

"What are you laughing at?" she asked them.

Al-Taniesha did her best to compose herself. "What kinda Walmart bullshit is this? Who inna hell would wear that?" She pointed at the models.

"Excuse you," Jaise said. "That is haute couture."

"Puh-lease." Al-Taniesha frowned. "That is haut-mess. K-to-da-mart. Straight blue-light special."

Jaise was thoroughly disgusted. "The outfits are artistic," she whispered.

"Artistic? That shit is straight out the ten-dollar spot."

"Shhh . . ." floated through the air.

"You don't shush me," Al-Taniesha retorted.

Chaunci looked at them and said in a stern whisper, "Would you stop it?"

"So sick of y'all asses," Al-Taniesha mumbled, leaning back in her chair.

The show continued. Al-Taniesha and Lollipop cracked up at the models and even laughed until they cried at some of the outfits. When the designer walked out on the runway and took his bow, he rolled his eyes at Al-Taniesha, then resumed smiling at the rest of the audience.

"Did that mofo just roll his eyes at me?" Al-Taniesha spat. "Did he?" she demanded. " 'Cause I will beat the breaks off dat ass. Okay! This was a complete waste of my damn time! I've seen better shit on QVC."

"Would you have some couth?" Jaise said, tight-lipped.

"Would you mind your business?" Al-Taniesha retorted. "I sure hope I can get along with the new chick, 'cause y'all bring out the hood in me, and since me and Lollipop hit the lottery, I'm really tryin' to be a fuckin' lady and have some goddamn class, but you're pushing me. Now, where is this new trick?"

"Good question," Chaunci said. "I guess she decided to stand us up."

"Seems so," Jaise said, slightly disappointed.

"No need to sound disappointed, Jaise," Milan said. "I heard the bitch was straight ghetto anyway."

Jaise blinked. "That's what you heard? Seriously?"

"I heard that too," Al-Taniesha interjected. "Someone told me the new bitch moved her ass from the west side of the projects to the east side and she suddenly thinks she went somewhere. Imagine that. On second thought, this skeezer just might be a problem."

"And I don't need drama, honey." Chaunci shook her head. "So to hell with her."

"I'm going to give her a chance," Jaise said. "She might turn out to be okay."

"Oh, puhlease." Milan rolled her eyes. "You are so damn phony."

"I'm not phony." Jaise looked Milan over. "I just don't judge people."

"What?" Milan said, shocked. "You've been judging me since the day we met. And besides, your nonjudgmental ass is the one who called me to make amends and then in the same breath said we didn't need to film with Al-Taniesha. That it wouldn't be a good look."

"Oh, no, you didn't!" Al-Taniesha spat. "That's why I haven't had any camera time today? I was wondering why no one showed up to my crib!"

"I never said that," Jaise insisted.

"Oh, yeah, you did." Milan frowned.

"Look," Jaise said. "*What I am saying* is this: I believe in giving people a chance, but if she's hot trash, we sell her out to the tabloids."

"Well," Chaunci said. "I'll say this. If the bitch wasn't coming, she could've sent a message to let us know!"

"Excuse me," said a woman. She had flawless mahogany-colored skin and exquisite makeup done to Cover Girl perfection. She held marble-black, bumblebee Chanels in one hand and a platinum clutch in the other. She batted her mink lashes and spoke with perfect diction. "Obviously, the gossiping whores were too busy being pimped by made-up bullshit to realize that *this bitch* arrived two hours ago." She flipped her hair behind her shoulders and looked them over.

They all paused and sized her up. She had perfect size-eighteen hips, perky round breasts, and presence that spoke volumes, and she was dressed like a million dollars. Her glove-fitted black knee-length Yves Saint Laurent dress was from a private collection, and her four-inch platinum-colored Christian Louboutin stilettos with sapphire heels were a limited edition. Everything about her said she was about her business.

The women all stared at one another. Then, as if they'd tele- pathically communicated and come up with a plan, they looked at her and burst into pleasantries such as, "Hey, girl, it's wonderful to finally meet you!"

Bridget clapped her hands together. "Vera Bennett, meet your costars: Milan, Jaise, Chaunci, and Al-Taniesha." She let her intro- duction linger in the air for a moment, then said, "Now welcome, Vera dear. Welcome to *Millionaire Wives Club*. The place where money never sleeps, reality is never what it seems, and love—" Bridget draped her arms over Lollipop and Al-Taniesha's shoul- ders. "—is a whole 'nother story."

Lights . . .

Vera

Vera sat, thick thighs crossed, four-inch python pumps swinging from the tips of her well-manicured feet, as Miles Davis's horn eased through the surround sound of her Upper East Side rooftop terrace. Behind her, the early morning sun glistened over the Manhattan skyline like an amber diamond as she watched the chef prepare a breakfast of turkey bacon, scrambled eggs, buttered toast, and sliced fruit in the outdoor kitchen.

Vera hoped that the cameraman, Carl, would pan out enough to provide a glimpse of her 5,000-square-foot penthouse, especially since she lived on New York City's most exclusive street: Fifth Avenue.

She knew that all eyes would be on her as the newest cast member on *Millionaire Wives Club.* And she welcomed it. Because two things were for sure: She loved a challenge, and she never *ever* brought a knife to a gunfight.

Vera looked into the camera lens and scanned her reflection. Everything was in its place: hair, makeup, cleavage. She cleared her throat, batted her extended lashes, and eased her orange juice—

filled flute to her lips, leaving the imprint of a glossy kiss along the rim. "I hope everyone's doing well. Welcome to my home."

"Cut!" Bridget yelled, waving her arms. "Cut!" She shook her head.

"Why?" Vera grimaced.

"Vera, my dear," Bridget said as stoically as she could. "Show the camera who you really are. You'll be a natural at this, I'm sure. You just have to remember that everyone wants to get to know you and what you're about. Especially your costars, who by the way have been all over New York digging up dirt and selling you out."

"Selling me out?" Vera said, taken aback. "They don't even know me."

"You really think they need to know you?" Bridget squinted. "Wow. Okay."

"What the hell are you talking about?" Vera said, as if she were throwing in the towel.

Bridget looked concerned as her eyes met Vera's. "I really like you, Vera." She hunched her shoulders forward. "And I want to see you succeed on the show. But from where I'm standing, you'll never make it if you're underestimating rich, catty women who waste money and have too much time on their hands."

"One thing I know is how to handle a bitch." Vera waved her hand dismissively. "And a bitch is a bitch, no matter her bank balance."

"Oh, no, my dear." Bridget smirked. "I have to stop you there, because now you're wrong. A rich bitch is a whole other level of bitchery. And since you're richer than all of them, you need to remember that. These women will dig up dirt on you, pour piss on it, and auction it off to the highest bidder."

And money or no money I'll bust a cap in their asses, Vera thought.

"Well, Bridget," Vera said, struggling to hold on to her perfect diction and not let the edginess of her Brooklyn accent slip between her lips. "I'm bigger than that." She managed to say with perfect enunciation, "And I try my best not to behave that way."

"Oh, well, pardon me, Vicki Buchanan. Apparently I'm on the wrong soap opera; I could've sworn you were Alexis Carrington. So continue." She snapped her fingers. "Roll tape, Carl."

"Funny, Bridget. And since you yelled 'Cut,' I completely forgot what I was saying."

"You were getting ready to tell us that you're married to a world-renowned oncologist. And how he developed an 89.99-proof medication that will kill certain types of cancer without radiation and patented it for the next ten years, and how the zeros in your bank account defy infinity—"

"That's not all I was going to say."

"Oh, yeah." Bridget yawned and patted her lips. "You were also going to tell us about your seven-year-old daughter, Skyy, and your snow-white Maltese puppy, Fluffy."

This bitch. "And what's the problem with any of that? I didn't sign up to show my ass."

"Of course you did," Bridget said. "But I understand you being hesitant and not wanting to address your costars because you're intimidated by them."

"What?" Vera said, taken aback. "Who told you that?"

"Well." Bridget tapped the center of her lips with her index finger. "That has to be the case. Otherwise, why wouldn't you want to address their—how do I say it—?" She snapped her fingers. "Talking greasy about you?"

"Greasy? They don't know me well enough to say anything *greasy* about me."

"And while you're believing that lie, they're off feeding the tabloids." Bridget reached for her briefcase and eased out *Star*, a weekly gossip paper. She took a seat in a director's chair and leafed through a few pages. "I guess this is no big deal."

"What's no big deal?" Vera asked.

"Ummm, nothing." Bridget's eyes continued to scan the paper. "Abandoned in the trash."

"Bridget, what are you reading?"

"If you insist on knowing—" Bridget pointed to the paper. "—let's start with this page."

"Yeah, let's." Vera cocked her neck.

"Well, on page six, it reads: 'Jaise Asante, of *Millionaire Wives Club*, declares that her newest costar, Vera Bennett, is nothing more than a hot-comb-front-porch-hair-braiding-beautician from down the hall.' "

"Oh, no, that bitch didn't." Vera sat up at attention.

"Yeah, she did." Bridget rattled the page.

Vera spat, "I own three very lucrative salons: one in Brooklyn, one in Manhattan, and one in Milburn, New Jersey. What does Jaise have? An online business selling a buncha rusty shit that wouldn't even make it on *Antiques Roadshow*!"

"Pretty much," Bridget agreed.

Vera continued, "*And* I make my own hair products."

"Oh, wait." Bridget's index finger scrolled the page. "Jaise is quoted here as saying that your hair products are nothing more than a dressed-up can of sulfur 8."

"Really?" Vera said, completely taken aback. "This trick likes to chat? Then we need to talk about how her dumb ass is so busy running around wiping up her son's shit that word has it she better watch her husband before the cleanup woman runs off with him." Vera snapped her fingers in a z-formation. "Next."

"Oh, my." Bridget pressed her hand into the base of her neck. "I didn't mean to get you so worked up. I'm sure Jaise meant no harm. She really is a nice woman. Now, Milan, on the other hand, her quote—" Bridget rattled the paper. "—is really below the belt."

"Milan? That gold-diggin' whore-ass bird? And wait, didn't she kill somebody?"

"Well," Bridget smiled. "She didn't exactly put a gun to dear ole Evan's head, but I believe that when Evan found out Milan was sleeping with her husband it pushed her out to sea."

"Exactly. A murderous, gold-diggin' whore-ass bird and this bitch had something to say about me? Puhlease." She waved her hand, her eleven-karat solitaire gleaming.

Bridget went on to read, "Milan says here that she was contacted by your former boyfriend, Bryce, and that he told her you were a crack baby who still suffered from tremors, and were raised by a loudmouthed barmaid and her country-ass boyfriend of 30-plus years. But never mind any of this." Bridget closed the paper. "We both know you're above the drama. So go on, finish welcoming us to your home." She arched one brow. "Would you like to talk about the square footage now?"

Vera moved to the edge of her seat and slid her shoes completely onto her feet; as she stood up, she spotted her husband, Taj, from the corner of one eye. Taj stood on the threshold of their French doors, his rich chocolate skin complemented by his freshly twisted dreads, and his white lab coat and scrubs lay perfectly over his athletic frame. His calming presence was the only reason Vera didn't rise from her chair, grab her Hermés bag, and charge out the door to sling a bitch.

"Tell me something," Bridget said, recapturing Vera's attention. "Before your father hooked up with your then-teenage mother, was he already hooked up with your grandmother? Just asking. Chaunci's quoted as saying that. Her source was a cousin of yours named Biggie who said you left him in the projects."

Vera bit her bottom lip, a nervous habit she'd had since childhood that only kicked in whenever her level of pisstivity rose above ten.

Shit was just beginning and already was too much. Taj had warned her that this cast didn't seem like the type of crew she could swing with for long. Nevertheless, she'd insisted that reality TV was the last piece of rich-bitch candy she needed. She'd promised Taj it would be like filming a summerlong infomercial.

But her childhood wasn't what she wanted to advertise.

It wasn't that she was ashamed of who she was or where she'd come from. It had more to do with her having already moved past having a drug-addicted mother. Who, by the way, had been sober for the last five years. And so what if her dead father was a pimp. Was that her fault?

And Bryce, her ex-boyfriend, was it her problem that he felt jilted? Or that her cousin, Biggie, couldn't understand that she didn't want junkies around her daughter?

Who could blame her for that?

And as far as the barmaid and her country-ass boyfriend, they'd saved her life by picking her up from social services when she was nine and rearing her as if she were their own biological child.

So if these TV bitches wanted to give interviews to tabloids without even knowing the real deal, then fuck them. They weren't her friends. She'd had the same three friends since childhood and she didn't need even one of these bitches.

Vera looked directly into the camera and said, "Let me tell you something: I don't know why those li'l cartoon puppies, Bryce and Biggie, are running around telling my business or why these media whores are buying into it, but this just lets me know who I have to handle.

"So trust that I will be stepping to *Millionaire Wives Club*, stiletto to stiletto, and welcoming them to the life and times of the new bitch, Vera Bennett." Vera's Brooklyn accent had completely taken over. "I don't tolerate bullshit. Now, if they're looking to get it crunked, then I'm their woman, because I'll strut into their personal space and sting them to their faces."

"Was any of what they said true?" Bridget shrugged. "Just asking."

Vera paused. "I am the epitome of rags to riches."

"What does that mean?"

"It means I can rock with the best and the worst of them." She paused again. "I was born in the trash and raised in the gutters of

Brooklyn. And not in a swanky brownstone either, but the piss-filled hallways of hell: Lincoln Projects. A newborn junkie is what I was, courtesy of Rowanda, my mother, a teenage dope fiend. So, yeah." She nodded. "I was a drug baby. And from the time I was nine, my shero, Cookie Turner, raised me and loved me, and she didn't give a damn that her brother was a pimp and had me with his bottom bitch's daughter.

"Now, I'm all for giving motherfuckers a chance, but I will bring the ruckus and I don't need *anybody* injecting me with camera balls to do it! And you can bet your life on that."

"Cut!" Bridget yelled. "Cut! Now that's what I'm talking about." She shot Vera a high five. "That was beautiful, Vera. Ab-so-lute-ly beautiful."

C lusters of multicolored balloons and silly string floated through the foyer of Jaise's Brooklyn Heights brownstone as she stood in narrow four-inch pencil heels and leaned from one aching foot to the next. She tried desperately to keep a smile on her glistening MAC-covered lips as she held an overflowing tray of Mickey Mouse cupcakes that attracted a rambunctious group of children who waved their hands and chanted, "Gimme cupcakes!"

"Okay, sweeties, but first let's get back to the party." It was Jaise's attempt to gently shoo the children away, but they didn't move and she was forced to stand there or risk dropping the treats.

Her eyes scanned her living room, where she'd brought a Disney ball to life. Mickey Mouse, Minnie Mouse, Princess Tiana, and Donald Duck danced about and played with the children, who were all dressed in Disney costumes. There were antique popcorn stands around the room, a cotton candy booth, and an area for face painting. There was also a live band, three clowns, and two magicians. Needless to say no one—not even the staff she'd hired for the party—noticed that there was a ring of excited children around her, forcing her to wonder when all this had become her responsibility.

Her son was grown.

Nineteen.

She was supposed to be done with giving birthday parties, not be the host of her year-old grandson's shindig. Hell, she wasn't even supposed to *have* a grandchild, let alone be his goddamn surrogate daddy. She was only thirty-seven, and her son, Jabril, should have been a college freshman at Morehouse who came home for summers and holidays, and at most they were supposed to argue about his major and graduating on time.

Not babies.

Not how he spent little to no time with his son.

Not how his baby's mama, Christina, needed to stay off Jaise's phone crying and complaining about his ass.

This plight belonged to the low-grade down the street. The irresponsible mother who had kids with different daddies and dumped her children on other people. Children who were abused and expected to be fucked-up.

Not Jabril.

Not when she'd prayed endlessly that what she went through with men—his father kicking her ass, cheating men making her cry, disappointment causing her to scream, and humiliation causing her to ache and lie in bed for days—didn't affect him.

Not when she knew for sure that when the worst things happened to her he was too young to understand. And when he became old enough to understand, she put him in his place by telling him, "I'm the mother and you better mind your business."

And especially not when she'd specifically *told him,* "You do what the fuck *I say* to do. Not what *you want* to do!" She meant take his ass to college, graduate, get a damn job paying at least six figures, *then* get married, and *then* have babies. He was supposed to become the man she envisioned, because she surely didn't rear her only child to be a fuckin' mess.

But he was.

He liked hood rats. Not good girls.

He didn't make it to college . . . because he barely graduated from high school.

He lied.

He treated his girlfriend like shit.

He cheated on her. Cussed at her.

He was a horrible father.

He was lazy.

He couldn't keep a job.

He didn't want a job.

He wanted to be a rapper.

He couldn't rap.

He could sing.

He hated singing.

And no matter what she said he always did the opposite. To think she'd once believed in fairy tales and had held her breath until she'd met a six-foot-three, honey-colored, fine-ass Superman, who wanted his own baby and for a brief moment—a split second of insanity—she wanted to give it to him.

But the longer she stood with her feet aching, her patience wearing thin, and a sudden realization that motherhood was something she'd already fucked up once and had no need to try again, she figured screw Superman and his futuristic baby. She was done.

"Are you gon' give the kids cupcakes, or are you gon' eat 'em?"

Jaise glared into the eyes of the cameraman, but before she could figure out if the curt, raspy voice belonged to him, Al-Taniesha walked over and stood behind the chanting children. "I know you got an attitude," she spat at Jaise. "And no, my sister shouldn't have dropped her five kids at the door and left, but I don't appreciate you making them beg you for cupcakes."

One day I'ma fuck this bitch up was one of a million thoughts that ran through Jaise's mind as she looked into Al-Taniesha's face. She shoved the tray of cupcakes into her hands. "You give 'em to 'em," Jaise said as she spun on her heel, stormed past the partying guests, and strode into the kitchen. She slid the double mahogany pocket doors closed and leaned against them.

An iron fist wedged its way into her throat as waves of pissed-off anxiety washed over her.

I need to get out of here.

Just for the hell of it she clicked her heels together, but when she opened her eyes and realized that she wasn't in Kansas, she was still in Brooklyn dealing with the same downtrodden bullshit, she took a deep breath, freed it from the side of her mouth, and whispered to no one in particular, "Fuck it."

She rose and moved off the doors, and as she turned to slide them open she heard the knob on her back door twist. She turned back around, leaned against the counter, and watched Jabril slowly stick one Timberland over the threshold and then the other. He eased in through the doorway and looked directly into her face. "Ma." He shot her a nervous smile. "Wassup?"

Jaise dipped one brow and arched the other. "Wassup? Good question. Wassup with yo' ass and where *the fuck* have you been?"

He hesitated. "Ma, I, ummm, had to get a kit replaced on my Beemer."

"A who on your what?"

"I had to get some work done to my car."

"That's my damn car and who paid for that?"

"I paid for it."

Jaise stared at Jabril as if she could've smacked the shit out of him. "Shut up telling lies. You don't have a job." She flung invisible sweat from her brow. "Jabril, if some li'l girl is spending her welfare check on you—"

"Why does she have to be on welfare?"

"Because that's what you like. Down-and-out. Destitute. Downtrodden. That's the shit that turns you on. Now, back to the matter at hand: It makes no sense that you're late to your son's party."

"Look, I know I'm late. My fault."

"Your fault. You're right. You should've been out buying your son something for his birthday."

"I *did* get him something. He *is* my son."

"Where is it, Jabril?"

"In my car."

"You're a liar." She walked up close to him.

"I can't win. If I didn't buy him a gift you'd cuss me out. I bought him a gift and you're still cussing me out!"

"Jabril, you already knew that I bought him gifts." She pushed her left index finger into his chest. "And you also knew that I put your name on the motherfuckers. So don't give me that!"

"You need to stop cussing at me and let me buy what I want to for my son."

"But he deserves more than your slop, Lawrence—" Jaise stopped in her tracks, realizing she'd just called him his father's name.

"My name isn't Lawrence!"

"Well, you act just like the motherfucker," Jaise snapped. "As soon as I put hope and faith in you that you'll change or that *you've changed,* you fall right back into the trap of same-ole-same-ole. It's liked being fucked-up is in your DNA! Damn, I need a cigarette." She snatched a drawer open and searched frantically through it. After coming up empty she slammed it shut.

"You're going a little to the left. And I don't appreciate that. I think you owe me an apology," Jabril said.

"Really?" Jaise blinked in disbelief. "An apology? An apology?" She tapped the ball of one stiletto. "An apology? Really. Well, how about you owe me an apology for the hours and hours of labor to deliver you and nineteen years later you're still a pain in my ass! Have you even seen your son today? Christina dressed him in sagging-ass jeans, boxers over his Pampers, Tim's, a wife beater, and a blue bandanna wrapped around his head. I didn't know whether to kiss him or be scared he was going to rob me. I mean, really, is he a Crip now? I give him a Disney ball, and he comes dressed as a gang member!"

"You should've come at her like you're coming at me. *She* dressed him like that!"

"It's inappropriate."

"I didn't do it, so why are you yelling at me?"

"Because this is what happens when you don't spend time with your child!"

"I spend time with him."

"When, Jabril? When? Because you're never here and Christina is always calling me crying, complaining, and looking for your ass! You know what it's like not to have a father, and this is the shit you pull? Do you know how it looks that everyone else is here but you?"

"That's all you're concerned about! How things look to everybody else! Just like this ridiculous party is for everybody else! I didn't want to be a part of this! Damn. Why you always sweatin' me? Can I breathe? Got Christina sweatin' me, 'Come get your son, do this, he needs that,' and then you steppin' on my jugular. A man needs a break, not a nag."

"A man?" Jaise took a step back. Now she knew for sure she was in the Twilight Zone. Hell, she wanted him to be a man, but his manhood had yet to manifest itself. And certainly manhood went beyond beauty. Yet beauty was all Jabril had. He stood five eleven, with sparkling hazel eyes, and a single dimple in his left cheek. He was naturally cut, and his chest had delicious definition. His skin was the color of milk chocolate, and he had a smooth, seductive deep voice.

Jabril was more pretty than handsome, and not only did he know it, but every girl who laid eyes on him knew it too. But what the girls didn't know, while his mother clearly did, was that Jabril being so fine only complicated things.

Clouds filled Jaise's eyes. "I'm soooooo sick of you!" Her heels stabbed the wooden floor as she stormed over to the refrigerator. "What you better do is get in there and act like this is the best goddamn party you've ever been to in your life! You understand me?"

She opened the refrigerator, took out the Mickey Mouse–shaped birthday cake, and placed it on a small rolling cart. "Why am I always sweatin' you?" she mocked. "I should've been sweatin' you to do better in school! Sweatin' you to get a better fuckin' attitude!" She tossed two candles on the cart.

"Sweatin' you to put a condom on when you were out there dickin' these goddamn hood-hoes in the street! Then I wouldn't be a grandmother before the age of forty." She reached for a bottle of wine on the counter, uncorked the top, and took a sip. "Sweatin' you to be a fuckin' man, because right now—" She took another sip. "—you're driving me to fuckin' drink! I'ma put your ass outta here! That's what I'ma do for you since I'm sweatin' you!"

"What the hell is going on in here?" Jaise's husband, Bilal, stomped into the kitchen.

Usually his six-foot-four, beautifully honey-colored presence, with Egyptian eyes etched into his clean-shaven face, was enough to calm Jaise down, but at this moment she didn't give a damn. "What's going on in here," she screamed, "is that I'm tired of being the mad black woman and the pissed-off black bitch!"

"You need to calm down," Bilal said sternly.

"No, what I need to do—" She spat with such venomous rage that a spray of saliva flew from her mouth. "—is leave y'all motherfuckers alone!"

Bilal scolded. "Do you realize that everyone can hear you? You need to save this argument for later! Not in the middle of a party!" His chiseled jaw tightened and his lips were stiff. He turned to slide the doors closed, but before he could Bridget ran in.

"Pause!" Bridget said to Jaise and Jabril. "You—" She pointed to one of the cameramen. "Stand by the back door. And you—" She pointed to another. "You stand here, in case she hauls off and slaps one or both of them! Now, Jaise." Bridget nodded. "Continue."

Jaise was stunned. She was so engulfed in disgust that she'd forgotten about Bridget, the cameras, and the microphones. She stood frozen in her spot as Bridget smiled and mouthed, "Go ahead, continue."

This was not how today was supposed to unfold. Bilal had warned her before the party to rein in her temper and keep her cool no matter what. Because the last thing she needed was for life and its unpredictable malfunctions to come along and fuck things up.

But it had.

And now in nine months when this episode aired she was sure she'd have to defend herself from half of America slandering her ass . . . again.

Damn.

She shot Bilal a plastic smile, then turned to Jabril. "Sweetie." She placed two candles on the cake—one for the baby's age and one for good measure—lit them, and said, "I want you to roll out the cake while you sing 'Happy Birthday' to the baby."

Jaise wrestled with the knot in her throat. She entered the living room while Jabril rolled the cake in behind her. Her legs felt like willow branches as Jabril began to sing "Happy birthday to you" in a baritone voice that was a dead ringer for Johnny Gill. A voice that could easily melt the sun. Jaise soon found herself genuinely smiling. His beautiful voice was the one thing she knew for sure he'd gotten from her.

Jabril rolled the birthday cake to the center of the room, where Christina held the baby. The guests gathered around and everyone fell silent as Jabril continued his stunning performance.

When he finished his tune, the crowd erupted into cheers and applause. Christina held the baby over the cake and helped him blow out the candles.

Jaise proudly cut the cake and handed the first slice to Christina, who smeared a smidgen of icing on the baby's nose, causing everyone to chuckle. Jabril slid his arm over Jaise's shoulder. "Thank you, Ma," he whispered.

Before Jaise could respond, a heavy pounding on the front door startled her. "Who's that?" Jaise looked around and directly into Al-Taniesha's face.

"Oh, hell, no," Al-Taniesha spat. "That sounds like the po-po." She looked into the camera. "This is the part where Al-Taniesha gets her fam and leaves."

"I can't stand that hussy," Jaise mumbled as she walked toward the doorway with Bridget and one of the cameramen on her heels. "And you'd think us having a grandchild in common would somehow make her tolerable." Jaise turned to the camera. "Next season if she comes back I'm done!" She snatched the door open to see four uniformed police officers standing on her brick stoop. She thought one of them looked familiar but wasn't sure. After all, she'd invited some of Bilal's co-workers with small children to come and celebrate, but none of these officers had children with them, and none of them seemed like they were here to party.

"Yes?" Jaise looked them over.

"Ma'am," one of the cops said. "We're looking for Jabril Williams."

"Why?" Jaise asked defensively.

"Is he here, ma'am?" The officer stepped closer to the door and looked behind Jaise.

"Why are you asking for Jabril?"

"What's your name, ma'am?"

"Why?" she asked again.

"Is Mr. Williams here?" the officer persisted.

"Why do you need Mr. Williams? Bilal!" Jaise tossed over her shoulder. "Bilal! Come here, hurry!"

"What's wrong?" Bilal said in a panic as he rushed to the door with Jabril and a few guests behind him.

"Ma, you aight?" Jabril asked.

Bilal walked to the door and stood in front of Jaise. "Hi, I'm Lieutenant Asante of the 66th precinct. Can I help you officers with anything?"

"Sir," the lead cop said. "I'm Officer Bryson and we're from the 84th precinct. We have a warrant." He handed the warrant to Bilal. "For the arrest of Jabril Williams."

"A warrant?" Jaise turned toward Jabril and he stood frozen.

Bilal looked at Jabril and said, "You didn't take care of this?"

"He didn't take care of what?" Jaise snapped at Bilal. "You knew about this?"

"I knew he had a warrant, and I told him to take care of it. He told me he did."

"And you didn't tell me? I'm this child's mother!"

"He's a grown man!"

"It takes more than a hard dick to make a child grown!"

"Back up and take it down." Bilal gave Jaise a warning look.

Jaise snatched the warrant out of Bilal's hands and quickly read it. "Child support?" She looked over at Christina, who stood next to Jabril. "You took him to court for child support!" Jaise screamed. "How fuckin' dare you!"

"You don't speak to my goddamn daughter like that!" Al-Taniesha spat.

Tears filled Christina's eyes. "I didn't do that! What is this about, Jabril?"

"This is about my daughter!" A five-foot-three, petite woman stormed up the steps, stood in front of the door, and pointed behind Jaise and Bilal. "This is about my daughter needing to be taken care of and instead of being a father, this motherfucker—" She pointed to Jabril. "—is over here throwing birthday parties and shit with this trick!" she yelled at Christina.

"Hold this, Chrissy." Al-Taniesha took one earring off. " 'Cause I'm 'bout to cut a bitch! Who the fuck are you talking to?"

Jaise couldn't believe it. For a moment she thought she was dreaming. But no. She was still here, with police at her door, her

son stood behind her with no place to run, and a woman screaming about a baby—another baby—that Jaise knew nothing about.
"Who the fuck are you?" Jaise asked the belligerent woman on
her stoop.

"Nicole," the woman spat. "And I'm his worst goddamn
nightmare! My girlfriends told me not to fuck around with no li'l
young boy—"

"Young boy?" Jaise said, taken aback.

"Young . . . boy," Nicole said. "And I don't have time for this
playground bullshit he's trying to pull!"

Jaise's mouth fell open. She walked over to Jabril, looked him
directly in the face, and said, "Who the hell is this old bitch, Jabril?"

"Old?" Nicole said. "I'm only twenty-nine!"

"Twenty-nine!" Jaise screamed and rushed back to the door.
"He's only nineteen!" She spun back around to Jabril. "You
fuckin' wrinkled pussies now, Jabril?"

"Wrinkled pussies!" Nicole tried to pass the police, but they
wouldn't let her in, so she shouted, "This pussy wasn't wrinkled
when he was eatin' it!"

"I will beat your fuckin' ass!" Jaise headed out the door, but
Bilal pulled her back in.

"You cheated on me with this chick, Jabril?" Christina
screamed. "Oh, this is who you're choosing over me?"

"I know you didn't just say no dumb shit like that," Al-Taniesha
said to Christina. "I told you he was a sorry sack of shit. And all
you could say was how much you loved him. Well, you see what
love has got you? You see? It's got you standing here looking stupid, while Li'l Wayne is over there being a goddamn asshole and
not saying shit! So, yeah, that's who he wants to be with." She
pointed to the door. "Another trick, and after that trick it's sure
to be another and another—"

"Wait a minute—" Jabril said.

Nicole interjected, "I'm no trick, and I don't want his ass. He ain't shit. You can have him." She looked at Christina, "'Cause I don't wanna babysit—"

"Then why the hell are you here?" Jaise snapped.

"Because he has a daughter and he needs to take care of her!"

"A daughter," Jaise said, as if a lightbulb had just gone off. She walked back over to Jabril and said, "You have a daughter?"

He didn't answer.

"Say something!" Jaise screamed, and smacked him on one side of his head. "You're standing here with another fuckin' baby, and you weren't going to say anything? You think I'm supposed to keep taking care of motherfuckin' babies? Have you lost your fuckin' mind?" She turned back to Bilal and spat, "And you knew about this and didn't say anything to me?"

"Listen to me," Bilal said sternly. "I knew about the warrant, but I thought it was dealing with J.J., not some new baby. I didn't have the details of the case."

"That's not his fuckin' baby!" Jaise screamed at Nicole. "You're just a triflin' get-money old bitch who wants his trust fund. That's not his goddamn baby!"

"Puhlease, that blood test came back 99.999, okay? As a matter of fact, your granddaughter looks just like you! So think of something else! Now, I don't know what's going on here, but this niggah has a warrant and he needs to be arrested. Unless," she said to the officers, "since you found out his stepfather's a lieutenant and his mother's on reality TV showing her ass, they don't have to abide by the law. And if that's the case, maybe I need to get some street justice for their asses and Internal Affairs for yours!"

"Listen," Bilal said quietly to the officers, "is there any way I can have him turn himself in? I'll drive him to the station."

"I'm sorry, sir," the officer said, "but we can't do that."

Bilal swallowed, turned to Jabril, and shook his head with regret.

"He's not going anywhere!" Jaise blocked the door.

Bilal looked at her as if she'd lost her mind. "You are way out of line," he said.

"Ma," Jabril said, "it's cool." He walked to the door. "I got this."

Jabril stepped onto the stoop and Jaise watched the officers cuff him and read him his rights. She felt like someone had taken a knife, sliced her heart out, and stomped on it. Everything was spinning. Everything was fucked-up. Nothing and no one were as they seemed. She watched Jabril be escorted to the patrol car and pushed into the backseat. She wanted to scream, but nothing would come out. She knew she needed to do something, she just didn't know what. She turned away from the door as the patrol car and Nicole disappeared into the distance. She walked into her home office, grabbed her purse, and headed back toward the door, where her husband and most of her guests remained.

"Where are you going?" Bilal grabbed Jaise by one forearm and said in a low yet stern tone, "We need to talk and you don't need to be running behind him!"

Jaise snatched her arm away. "That's *my* son! And you don't tell me what to do with him, you understand? Now get the hell out my face!" She started toward the door again.

Without thinking twice Bilal aggressively twirled her back around toward him. "Stand. Your. Ass. Right. There."

She tried to wiggle away. "Get off me!"

"You testing me?" Bilal said as a thousand creases etched his forehead.

Jaise hesitated, then halted.

Bilal turned toward the crowd and the camera crew. "Everybody get the fuck out!"

What did he just say? Jaise knew he had to be beyond overheated, especially since he rarely even said "damn," let alone telling everyone to get the fuck out. And then it hit her that he was tossing all her guests into the street.

"Bilal—!"

"Out!" he screamed. "Baby mamas, their grandmamas, camera crews, kids, Mickey Mouse, ev-er-y-body get the fuck out, right now!"

"Bilal—!"

He shot her a look. "Umm, listen, everyone." Jaise swallowed and forced a smile on her face. "Thank you for coming."

"I don't believe this shit," Al-Taniesha said as she collected her nieces and nephews.

"Believe it," Bilal snapped. "Now leave."

The guests' heels clicked against the brick steps as they hurried out the door, some of them toting their gifts back out the door with them. Christina cried and Al-Taniesha said, "I don't know what you expected from shit. Now, stop that damn crying. We've been thrown out of worse places by worse people."

Once the house was completely empty—Bridget and the camera crew included—Bilal turned toward Jaise and backed her up into a corner. His nose flared. "Let me explain this to you—you have got shit completely twisted. Don't you ever in your fuckin' life speak to me like that again! You understand? And you better say yes."

"Yes."

He continued. "Jabril needs to learn a lesson and you need to let his ass be a man. If you really want to help him, pack his damn clothes and tell him to find his ass another home. Enough of him doing whatever he feels like and not thinking about the consequences. Enough! When the warrant was brought to my attention I asked him what it was about and he never once mentioned another baby. I told him he needed to take care of it—"

"He doesn't have a job, and you know his trust fund is tied up until he's twenty-five!"

Bilal tossed his arms in the air as if he couldn't care less, "Tough. He can get a job and keep it."

"If he was your son you wouldn't be saying that!"

"You're right! 'Cause I would've bust my son's ass years ago.

Not at nineteen with two kids. Let his ass go and let him stay in jail until it sinks in that the world doesn't abide by his rules and that when you make babies you have to take care of them." Bilal backed away and grabbed his car keys. "You're so busy paying attention to Jabril's problems that you haven't even realized today's our anniversary."

Jaise's heart raced. *Did I really forget?* "Bilal—"

"Save it." He slammed the door behind him.

Chaunci

"One day I'll outrun the sky." Lalah Hathaway sang live and electrified the small upscale Harlem club where Chaunci nervously waited for Idris. She circled the rim of her frosted wineglass with the tip of one finger.

Her thick mane of hair rested beautifully over her shoulders, and her mahogany skin glistened in the subdued light where she sat, eyes closed and shoulders slowly rocking to the music.

She hadn't seen Idris in seven months, two weeks, and four days. And, yeah, she'd counted the time. Hell, she'd waited with bated breath as the months had passed, especially since eight months ago was the last time they'd made love and Idris had surprisingly asked her to marry him.

She'd said no. She couldn't.

She wasn't ready for marriage.

Emotionally she'd only signed up to fuck him.

Be his friend. Coparent with him.

But marry him?

Everything was fine the way it was. And she didn't have time for anything else. She was too busy having it all. She was independent, and she'd proven to the world that she was an editor-in-chief extraordinaire. A force to be reckoned with. She'd taken her writing talent and her passion for fashion and created *Nubian Diva,* a magazine that competed with and was compared to the likes of *Vogue* and *Glamour,* and became publishing royalty. And at the time Idris had asked her to be his wife, her career was all she could handle. At least until he retired from basketball—courtesy of a knee injury—and moved to L.A. Now, with the exception of checking up on their seven-year-old daughter, Kobi, he no longer dealt with Chaunci.

And she missed him.

Missed everything about him, from the way his lips curled to the right when he laughed to the way they curled around her clit whenever they made love. And there was no way she could outrun the sky for a moment longer. She had to sit still, strategize, and come up with a plan that would legally make him her man.

"Here's the script." Bridget interrupted Chaunci's thoughts, placing sheets of paper on the table in front of her. "And there are your lines." She pointed.

"Lines?" Chaunci looked bewildered as she flipped through the pages. "What are you talking about?"

"Yes." Bridget snapped her fingers. "Lines. This is reality TV, and we have to push things to new heights. None of that uncooperative shit you pulled last season."

"You can't be serious."

Bridget continued. "So, here's what you'll do. Go sit in your car, and when Idris arrives I'll come get you. That will give you time to rehearse your lines and it will also look like he's been waiting on you since last season. You know, waiting on the top bitch."

Chaunci's eyebrows dipped toward the bridge of her nose. "Have you lost your mind? You're taking things too far. I'm not letting you script my life."

Bridget clenched her lips and leaned in. "What life? We've

been struggling to create a story line for you! Work with us here. Last season Milan and Evan were the breakout stars. Now Evan's dead and Milan is, well, Milan. And after the showdown that just popped off over at Jaise's house a few hours ago, I won't have you lagging behind and dragging the ratings down."

"You're going too far."

"No, you're not going far enough! And this season, I'll make sure you sing for your supper. So you better run along to your car and rehearse those lines—"

"You don't tell me—"

"What to do," Idris said, totally surprising Chaunci and catching Bridget off guard too. "Chaunci's famous last words in any argument." He paused and looked Chaunci over. She was a dead ringer for Lalah Hathaway, and all night people had given Chaunci double takes, including Idris—initially. Standing there, his eyes began to make love to Chaunci's smooth skin, nursing her perfect D-cups, and caressing her size-twelve hips.

"You look lovely." He kissed her on one cheek—a place he'd never kissed her before. Her neck, yes, her forehead, yes, her lips, absolutely, but her cheek, never.

"Thank you." Her eyes nervously roamed over him, from the stress lining his forehead to the Gucci loafers on his feet. Quickly she wondered how to get to the meat of the matter so they could end this awkward shit, go home, and make love. She'd been craving his touch for too long, which is why when he called her and said he'd be moving back to New York for the summer and wanted to spend time with Kobi, she'd insisted they have dinner—to sort things out—the moment he arrived.

"Sit down," she said, as Bridget and the cameras faded into the background.

"I think I'll do that," he said, wiping invisible sweat from his brow.

"Thank you for coming." Chaunci smiled, but before she could continue the waiter came over.

"Welcome to Lucille's Blues, sir. May I start you with a glass of wine this evening?"

"Actually, I'll have a Heineken." Idris gave the waiter a half smile.

After a few moments of pregnant silence, the waiter brought over a frosted glass of beer and took their food orders.

More silence.

The food came. Before either of them took a bite, they simultaneously said, "I've been wanting to talk to you—"

They both chuckled nervously. "Can I start, please?" Chaunci asked as she grabbed one of Idris's hands and held it between hers. She chewed the inside of her cheek, then slowly released a deep breath. She wasn't sure how to begin. She just knew she had to lay it all on the line. "Idris," she said, with a sigh, "I don't even know where to start."

"You're at a loss for words?" he joked.

"I guess."

"Just say it." He shrugged.

"I love you," she said without hesitation. "And I never thought I'd allow myself to feel love, let alone put myself and my feelings out there—"

"Chaunci—"

"Let me finish." She paused. "This is hard enough. I just want you to know that I've never stopped thinking about you or wishing I could redo that night when you asked me to marry you—"

"Everything happens for a reason."

"You're right, and I know now that the reason is because I needed to learn to let go and not be stubborn. And so—" She paused.

"Resistant—" he completed her sentence.

"Yeah." She agreed and took another deep breath. "Resistant. And now I'm ready." She pulled out a red velvet ring box and popped it open, revealing a platinum wedding band. "I want you to be my husband. Will you marry me?"

"Marry you?" The words practically tumbled out of Idris's mouth. "Are you serious?"

"Yes." Chaunci's eyes lit up. "I love you—"

"Really?" His voice continued to reveal his surprise. "But what changed? I mean, what makes you think now is the time for us to be married?"

"Because I've grown."

"Really?"

"Yes, Idris. I missed you. And while you were gone I was miserable, and I never want to feel like that again. I couldn't stop thinking about what you were doing, who you were with, and what was happening with you. I didn't like that feeling. And I want you here with me all the time. I really, really missed you."

Idris hesitated. "You missed me?"

"Yes."

Idris shook his head, then looked at Chaunci as if his thoughts were suddenly clear. "How did we get here, Chaunci? To this space where we're proposing to each other and both times end up saying no?"

Silence.

Did he just say no? I knew he was pissed, but not pissed enough to do this. "What do you mean, no?" She did her best not to sound frustrated, though she really wanted to lose it. "I asked you to marry me and you're telling me no? Is that what you're saying?"

"Yes, I'm saying I can't marry you."

Chaunci turned toward the streaming light of the cameras. She could swear fucked-up shit always had a way of showing up and showing its ass onstage. "I see what this is about," she said with as much certainty as she could. "You want to embarrass me because I wouldn't marry you when you asked me to. It wasn't the right time for me then, but it is now."

Idris laughed in disbelief. "You have a lot of goddamn nerve. I don't live my life around your timing."

"Idris, you have to understand that I wasn't ready for marriage then. I was just getting my life where I wanted it to be. Feeling good about myself and my situation. And I wasn't sure I wanted to give that up."

"No, you just wanted me in your bed every night. You wanted to fuck and play house but you didn't want that shit transferring over into real life."

"It wasn't the time."

"And it is now?"

"I love you!"

"You don't fuckin' love me. When did you rehearse that line? Chaunci, spare me."

"We have a child together. You're a great father."

"We will *always* have a child together, and I will *always* be a great father, but that doesn't have shit to do with being your husband."

"I missed you!"

"You didn't miss me." He steadied his tone. "You missed me not being all up in your fuckin' face. Missed me not begging you to be my wife every five minutes! Missed me not being a sucker for your ass—"

"Idris—"

He snapped, "You missed me being out of your damn control. You didn't love me. You don't love me. When it comes to anybody other than Kobi, you don't know what the fuck love is." He slammed his fist onto the table, causing some of the club's other guests to shoot looks their way.

As Chaunci tried to speak she realized she'd lost her breath. Was he right? Or were the nights she tried to force passion to linger long after sex a clear sign that they weren't meant to be? Or maybe it was simply fear.

But what was she afraid of?

She desperately wanted to want Idris forever. He was the type of man she knew every woman needed to have: caring, kind, good credit, big dick, loved children. She wanted to love him—to be in love with him. But all she could seem to handle between them was a few good times, laughs, and memories. Nothing more and nothing less. And so, here they were . . .

"Is everything okay?" Idris and Chaunci looked up as a caramel-brown woman with an asymmetrical bob, a beauty mole in the center of one cheek, and size sixteen hourglass body invaded their conversation.

Idris looked at the woman, surprised. "I thought you were going straight to the apartment." He stood up to greet her and she kissed him on the lips.

"I would've done that, sweetie. But when I got to the airport I realized you didn't leave me any keys."

"And you are?" Chaunci looked into the woman's eyes.

"I'm Shannon." She smiled. "Idris's wife."

Milan

The clock struck midnight as Milan tripped out of her custom "Cinderella" Manolos, leaving one somewhere behind her. The hem of her plum-colored gown had snagged beneath the five-inch heel and practically tossed her to the floor, forcing her to grab the hand of a passerby to halt her fall. She'd just returned from the powder room and prayed that not many people had noticed her mishap, especially since this was Kendu's big night. He was celebrating his retirement from football and his new career as an ESPN sports commentator.

This was the moment for which Kendu had been waiting. For weeks, they'd chatted endlessly about it and made love in the midst of dreaming up this night's possibilities. Milan was just as excited as Kendu, if not more, and here she stood in the back of the dimly lit ballroom, off balance and doing her all to calm the butterflies in her stomach as her eyes scanned the floor in search of her missing shoe.

"Milan," a whisper slipped into her ear. "I'd give you my hand but I think I may need it."

Caught off guard and realizing she'd been holding the hand of a stranger—who oddly enough knew her name—Milan quickly hobbled a little to the right, spotting her shoe. She slipped it on, then stared at Mr. Unknown. She thought he looked familiar but she couldn't place him.

He smiled. "You don't even know who I am, do you? Damn shame." He laughed slightly.

Milan sucked in a sip of air and a full smile filled her face. "Samir?" she squealed. "Is that you?"

He confirmed her suspicion with a one-sided grin.

Milan hugged him. "Oh, my God. I haven't seen you in forever!" Her eyes inspected him. He was a far cry from the kid next door whom she used to babysit. He was now a man. A beautiful and exquisite black man, with skin the color of smooth, rich coffee with a splash of cream, warm chestnut eyes, and a well-put-together body that only a blind woman could miss.

Damn. "I can't believe this." Milan smiled. "I haven't seen you—"

He interjected, "Since I was eight and asked you to be my girl."

"I was your eighteen-year-old babysitter." She playfully curled her lips and put her hands on her hips.

"So what's the problem now?" He stepped directly into her personal space.

"I'm taken," she said without thinking twice, placing her left hand in his.

His eyes dropped to her ten-carat Tiffany solitaire. "By whom?"

She pointed toward Kendu, who'd just stepped onstage after being been introduced by his former NFL coach.

"Kendu? Really?" Samir looked toward the stage. "Damn, I had no idea. Hmph, life is funny. He's going out." He looked Milan over. "And I'm stepping in."

Milan eyed Samir and he winked. She hated that her dimples glowed. "Is that so?" She arched one brow.

"Number-one draft pick, baby. New York Giants starting quarterback."

"Congratulations," she said. "But my man's a legend. Remember that." She returned his wink, turned to the stage, and smiled at Kendu's presence. He was beautiful beyond words: the prettiest deep chocolate skin with Senegalese eyes. His lips were full and were framed by a sexy box beard with a few sprinkles of premature gray. He stood six-three with a chiseled body, a thick neck with his daughter's name tattooed in script on the right side of it, broad shoulders, large hands, matching feet, and a swagger that let anyone and everyone know that he handled his business and handled it well.

"I wanna thank everyone for coming out tonight. I know it's late." Kendu chuckled. "But since this is the last party of my playing career, I figured you all could swing a little past midnight with me."

Light laughter floated through the crowd.

Kendu continued. "I'm from the streets, as most of you know. I don't know my biological mother or father. All I knew growing up was the system and foster home after foster home after foster home. But all that changed when I turned ten, because I met a man by the name of Coach Reid." Kendu pointed into the audience. "He coached a small neighborhood team, and he encouraged me to join. Of course, that's when they started winning."

The crowd erupted into laughter.

"Shortly after I joined the team I had to leave my foster home but Coach Reid took me in." Kendu cleared his throat and Milan could tell he held back tears. "I didn't think I was worthy of shit, and here this man loved me unconditionally. Loved me enough to adopt me and make me his son. He didn't even care that once he became my dad, I continued to call him Coach Reid."

Milan could feel tears building in her throat, especially knowing how much Kendu's coach and adopted father meant to him.

"Stand up, Coach Reid," Kendu said and the coach complied, wiping tears from his eyes. The audience clapped and gave him a standing ovation. "I love you, man," Kendu said. "Thank you for making me your son; without you I wouldn't be here today."

"I love you too." Coach Reid nodded.

Kendu continued. "I also want to thank Jocelyn Carmichael, Johna James, Susan Richardson, and Michaela Jones. My boys from the playground days in Brooklyn. My NFL coach, Coach Johnson. We've been through it all, Coach. Five championships. Hell, he's my daughter's godfather. He was even the best man at my wedding."

Milan wasn't sure why but she felt like a knife had pinged her jugular. She continued watching, nervously biting her bottom lip.

Kendu went on. "I love you, man, and I couldn't have made it this far without you. And, umm, last but not least." Kendu's eyes filled and Milan watched as he struggled not to become emotional. She knew this was her tribute, the one part of his speech she hadn't heard him rehearse, and she hadn't wanted to hear it. She'd wanted to be surprised.

She could feel her throat trembling as one of the cameras zoomed in on her. She swallowed and hoped her makeup and hair were intact.

Kendu collected himself. "I want to thank my baby. We've been through everything together; I'm a better man because of her. The moment she came into my life she changed it."

Tears streamed down Milan's face. Finally the guess factor had been removed from their relationship. She didn't have to assume that he loved her as much as she loved him. Now she knew.

"To my *number-one* girl," Kendu said. "My daughter, Aiyanna."

"Aiyanna." Milan lost her breath.

"I love you, baby girl." He continued. "It's me and you against the world." He looked straight ahead into the live television camera. "Now go to bed." The crowd laughed and applauded Kendu with a standing ovation. "Thank you all," he said above the cheers and well wishes.

"His number-one girl, huh?" Samir boldly stroked Milan's cheek, wiping a single tear away. "You sure the legend's your man?"

Milan inhaled deeply and exhaled quickly. She pushed past her fucked-up and fucked-over pride and embarrassment. "Stay in your lane." She shot him a quick grin.

"Then I'd never win."

"Yeah, sure," Milan said, not knowing if her response was appropriate to whatever Samir had just said. She knew he'd said something, but her heart was still reeling from being sliced into pieces. She wondered if Samir could hear the cracking in her chest.

He didn't thank me . . . he didn't thank me . . . I can't believe he didn't fuckin' thank me . . .

"Excuse me, Milan." Kendu's publicist cut through her thoughts. "Kendu asked if you would step over here, please." She pointed to the other side of the room, where Kendu stood in the spotlight of flashes.

Milan gave Samir a quick smile. "It was nice seeing you again." She tossed him a small wave as she walked over to Kendu and slid into his embrace.

She did her best to smile, but it was a struggle.

"Milan," a reporter's voice rose above the crowd. "What are you wearing?"

"The dress is Gucci and the shoes are Christian Louboutin." She poked out one heel, showcasing the famous red bottom.

Another reporter jumped in. "Milan, what do you think of Kendu's retiring?"

"I think it's fabulous and about time." She kissed him softly on the lips. "Now I get to have him to myself."

"So when is the wedding date?" a reporter tossed.

Milan's face gleamed. "Well, we—"

"—haven't set one yet," Kendu cut her off. "It was hard

enough to get me in this tuxedo." He chuckled. "I'm not ready to get into another one just yet." The reporters laughed, while Milan could've sworn that Kendu had drawn a gun, placed it to her head, and pulled the trigger. She looked directly into the *Millionaire Wives Club* camera and could see Carl smiling from ear to ear.

Tears snatched her voice from her throat as she swallowed and Kendu answered the remaining series of questions.

"Okay, okay," his publicist interrupted the press. "We want to thank everyone for coming. But now my clients would like to mingle with their guests a little more before the night ends."

Kendu intertwined his fingers with Milan's as they walked toward their table.

"Knott," Milan said, calling him by his childhood nickname. "Were you serious just now?"

"About what?" He waved and smiled as someone quickly took their picture.

"About what you just said about the wedding. That was—"

"It was a joke, Milan. Relax." He kissed her lightly on the lips. "I meant to tell you how beautiful you look tonight." He looked her over. "Absolutely stunning. You like the dopest chick I know," he said, giving her the same compliment he'd been giving her, in the exact same way, since they were kids.

"Umm-hmm, listen, I really didn't appreciate—"

"That's not what you're supposed to say." He frowned, then kissed her again. "You're supposed to say what you've always said since you were nine—"

"Knott—"

"You're supposed to say, 'The dopest chick? Like the hottest? Like, real super-fresh-funky-fly-dope? Or you just a lyin' nig-gah?'"

She didn't crack a smile. "We need to talk."

"Kendu," someone called for his attention.

"Give me a minute, baby." And before she could protest, he left her standing there.

Milan drank in a deep breath.

She went to the bar and ordered. "Moscato."

The bartender handed her the drink. She walked over to their table and sat down. For an hour she watched Kendu do at least three rounds of the room. He floated from one person to the next, smiling and paying her absolutely no attention. And for the first time since she was nine, chewing pop rocks, and he was ten breakdancing the worm on a cardboard box in the middle of the playground, she thought that maybe she loved him too much.

Fuck this.

She rose from the table and walked over to Kendu, who was now talking to a group of smiling young women. "Excuse me." She shot them all an annoyed grin. "I'm leaving," she said to Kendu, then turned to walk away.

Surprised, he quickly grabbed her by the forearm and pulled her back to him. "You're what?"

"Leaving," she said tight-lipped. "I'm ready to go. It's late and I'll meet you in the car." He let her go and her heels clicked toward the door.

She could feel the cameras flashing and the reporters chatting as she walked out the hotel to the valet parking lot. A few seconds later Kendu and Carl walked up behind her.

"What's your problem?" Kendu asked as the valet pulled his onyx Bentley up to them.

After a few swallows and attempts to push back the iron fist in her throat and not succeeding, Milan decided to be quiet. She knew if she spoke she was bound to rear her hand back and boom-bop this motherfucker.

The valet opened the door and Kendu waited for Milan to enter. He closed her door. He and Carl then slid in, and a few minutes later they were out of the parking lot and on the street.

"What. Is. Your. Problem?" Kendu said again, his patience obviously strained.

The soreness of Milan's bruised feelings spread from her throat to her chest. *Stay calm.* "You stood up there in front of all those people and you couldn't remember to thank me?"

Kendu hesitated. She could tell that his thoughts drifted, and when he brought them back he said, "Milan, seriously, you're mad about that shit? You of all people know I had a million things going through my mind. I meant to say your name, but I got swept up in the moment. My fault, baby." He lightly tapped her knee.

She blinked. "Your fault? That's it, your fault?"

He sighed. "Okay, I apologize. Feel better?" He made a left turn and raced up the street. "And besides, I thank you every day."

"Wow, you thank me every day," she said in utter disbelief.

"Yeah, I do. Now, did you see my high school coach?" he said, moving the conversation along. "I think we should have him over for dinner."

"Have. You. Lost. Your fuckin' mind? Have you? Really? You are out of control."

"What?" he said, caught off guard and pissed. "What did my high school coach ever do to you? Are you still mad because he didn't want you cheerleading? Baby, let's face it, you were a little thick, and most of the cheerleaders back then were a size two, not twelve."

"You are so selfish." She shook her head. "I don't give a damn about your coach or cheerleading!"

"Milan—"

She snapped. "Milan, my ass. You think I want to talk about a coach, when not only did you not thank me, you left me at the table sitting by myself for more than an hour tonight? And, oh, let's not forget about that slick shit you said to the reporters about us getting married—"

"It was a joke."

"That wasn't a fuckin' joke!"

"Milan," he said steadying his tone, his eyes scanning a hungry Carl in the rearview mirror.

"What?" Tears danced in her throat.

"I've already apologized. Now drop it." He whipped into their Westchester driveway and put the car in park. "I don't want to hear this shit anymore." He slammed the car door behind him and stormed into the house.

Milan choked back tears. She entertained the thought of dropping the argument for a moment. Especially knowing that if she pressed forward the round they were gearing up to have would end in a T.K.O.

This was what she hated about being on reality TV: The best-laid plans went to hell. She turned toward Carl, and although her thoughts told her to pretend like she was ready to call it a night and head straight to sleep, she couldn't do that. Instead she stormed inside and followed Kendu into the kitchen, where he took a frosted Heineken from the refrigerator and twisted off the cap. He turned around and to his surprise she was pointing in his face. Before she could say anything, Kendu rested his beer on the counter and grabbed her around the waist. "I'm sorry." He kissed her on the lips. "Don't be mad. I just want you to get over that shit. I'm ready to go upstairs." He pressed his hard dick into her thigh. "Can't we deal with this another night?"

She snatched out of his embrace. "No. We can deal with it right now!"

"Goddamn, Milan." He was pissed. "You can't be serious." He looked over to the camera.

"Does it look like I'm playin'?" She turned to Carl. "Carl, am I laughing?" She pointed to her chest. "No, I'm not *fuckin'* laughing."

"You being real extra right now."

"Extra?" she said as one brow arched. "Extra?" The other brow dipped. "Extra is you thanking all those motherfuckers tonight and leaving me standing there looking stupid and shit. Dumb-ass fuck! I'm being extra and you were cracking every corny-ass motherfuckin' joke you could think of, but I'm being extra? You thanked every-*goddamn*-body but me, when I was the one who laid up with you *every goddamn night,* and you couldn't even thank me? But I'm being extra! Ain't this some shit." She waved her hands.

Kendu paused. "Yeah, extra, and you're being real silly right now. I've apologized, and I'm not saying it anymore! This was my goddamn night." The veins in his neck stuck out. "And I had to leave because of you and your selfish ass. If anything, you owe me an apology!"

"Owe you an apology?" she said in complete shock.

"Yeah, you owe me an apology! *And* you're selfish as hell!"

"Are you kidding me?!"

"Everything is always about you, Milan. You know how I fuckin' feel, but you gon' get an attitude because I didn't say thank you?" He took a step back, curled his lip, and looked her over. "Didn't I say thank you when I proposed to your ass? When I bought you that fuckin' Aston Martin you're profiling in? Bought your fuckin' clothes? Investments? Stacked you some goddamn bills in the bank?" He screamed. "I even thanked your fuckin' ass when I agreed to do this fuckin' show that ruined my motherfuckin' life last year, as a matter of fact." He looked at Carl and pointed his hand like a gun. "Get the fuck out!"

Carl didn't move.

Kendu pushed Milan to the side and walked closer to Carl with every word he said. "Do. I. Need. To ask you to leave an-other way?"

Carl quickly gathered his things and rushed out the door.

Kendu turned back to Milan. "I say thank you all fuckin' day, every fuckin' day, and the one goddamn time the shit slips my mind you in my motherfuckin' neck! Shit is never good enough for your ass! You ain't never happy!" he said, bits of spit flying angrily from his mouth. "And you wonder why I don't wanna get married—" He stopped in his tracks. His tirade instantly ended, and Milan could tell by the look in his eyes that he knew he'd gone too far.

He reached for her but she walked backward until her head hit the wall.

"Milan, I'm sorry." He sliced through her silence and reached for her again.

She jerked away and pushed him back. "Fuck you!"

"Listen to me." His body crowded the corner she stood in.

"No! I don't want to hear shit you have to say! I've heard enough. You don't wanna marry me?" She took her ring off and tossed it at his chest. "Fuck you, Knott. You stood up there tonight, chest all poked out." She pounded his chest. "And you thanked every-motherfuckin'-body from the towel boy to the motherfuckin' waitress tonight and you forgot me!" She held her fingers out as if she were counting on them. "You were up there thanking bitches named Jocelyn Carmichael, Johna James, Susan Richardson, Michaela-the-fuck-Jones, and all I could think was, 'Who are they?' "

"Milan."

She pushed him in his chest again. "But you forgot me? I knew you before any of those motherfuckers, including your goddamn father! I'm the one who told you he had a neighborhood team! But I'm not important enough for you to remember? If it wasn't for me, you wouldn't have a goddamn career! I'm the one who testified for you when you were sixteen and got the bright idea to join a motherfuckin' gang." She threw up a gang sign in his face. "And pulled a fuckin' drive-by. Don't you think I knew your ass was guilty, Loc? Considering I helped you come up with an alibi? And you gon' forget me?"

"Milan—"

"You thanked niggahs you played ball with on the goddamn playground in Harlem!" she screamed in his face. "But did those motherfuckers feed your ass when your umpteenth foster mother tossed you out? Hell, no, 'cause that was me and my family. We fed you. But I slipped your motherfuckin' mind? Are you serious?"

"Milan—"

"I've. Loved. You. All. My. Fuckin'. Life. And I don't get a thank-you? I love your daughter as if she was mine, hell I love her as if she were really yours motherfucker, and I'm reduced to nothing? I nursed your punk ass through three knee injuries." She pushed him as hard as she could.

"I wiped your snotty-ass nose when that doctor told you you'd never play football again, and you cried like a baby! I'm the one, the only one, who *knows* why you really fuckin' retired!"

"Milan, baby. I'm sorry." He pulled her to him and held her so tight she couldn't wiggle away, so she resorted to pounding his chest until her heavy punches grew weaker with each tear. He pressed his forehead against hers, her tears streaking onto his cheeks. "I'm so sorry. I fucked up."

"I'm done." She tried to twist out of his embrace. "It's over."

"You don't mean that." He held her close. "I love you more than you'll ever know. You're the only one who knows me, I mean really knows me. Everything I do and everything I am is because of you. You complete me, every part of me, and I fucked up. I love you more than anything in the world. I have to marry you, because you're my better half."

"You don't mean that. Just let me go. It's okay. I get the shit now."

"It's *not* okay, because I can't lose you," he whispered against her neck. "Because if I do, how will I breathe? How I'ma live if my air is gone?" He peppered her lips and neck with kisses. "I need you to forgive me, please. I don't know how to live without you."

Tears streamed quietly down her cheeks as Kendu's whispers of "I love you" turned into kisses against her neck. Then he slid his tongue between her lips. She accepted it. "I fucked up." He set her on the counter and lifted her dress over her head, revealing her pasties. He peeled them off, revealing her breasts.

His tongue flicked one nipple, while his thumb pinched the other one. "I really fucked up."

Silence.

He sucked. His lips wrapped her nipples with a seductive force she'd never felt before. She wanted to fight against her body's tremors and her sugar walls' desire to give in, but she couldn't. She had no choice but to moan.

"I love you so much." He pulled her thong off and spread her legs across the kitchen counter. He slid down her belly and lapped her juices. "I know I gotta get my shit together." He dipped his index finger in and sucked her milk from his tip. His tongue curled like a straw and moved in and out of her pussy, until she screamed his name. "Knott!" She rubbed his face into her wetness, her cream glistening on his face like lotion.

"Damn, look at this shit." He admired the diamond puddy sliding between her thighs. He palmed her pussy and rubbed his entire hand over it. And then he slid, one, then two, then three fingers in, spooned out more of her wetness, and lapped it like it was a liquid breakfast.

His tongue returned to tap dancing on her clit as he buried his entire face between her thighs. "Sssss," he hissed. "Damn, I even love the smell of this shit. Sweet pussy . . . sweet, sweet, pussy . . . tell me you love me, Milan. I need to hear that shit. I need to hear it."

She warred with keeping the truth inside, but as his tongue did her pussy's favorite dance, she could no longer contain the obvious. "I love you."

"I know you do," he said, seducing her pussy to churn more of its butter into his mouth. "That's why we gon' get past that bullshit, you gon' put your ring back on, and we gon' be all right. Now promise me you'll love me forever." He looked into her face, continuing to finger her wetness.

"Knooooottttttt!"

"Promise me!" He looked into her eyes.

"Forever. I'll love you forever."

"You better." He lifted her from the sink and carried her to their master suite. They lay on the bed, both now completely naked. Kendu lifted Milan's legs in the air and placed his tongue at the base of her ass. He licked a creamy trail that ran between the slit, and then he opened it, making certain to leave nothing but tongue tracks behind.

After he literally kissed her ass, he slid his steel into her heated sex, forcing her to gasp. No matter how many years she'd experienced his ten inches, each time felt like the first time. "I love you," she whispered against his neck.

"And I love you." He pounded, his dick creating just the right rhythm. "Listen to that shit." He moaned. "Listen to that pussy. That pussy loves me."

Milan couldn't respond. Shivers tangoed from her belly to her spine over and over again. His penis made loud splashes through her heated river as waves crept up her back. She wrestled with him a bit and flipped him over. He proudly lay back and watched her ride him. "I'ma give you whatever you need," he said and she reached down and bit his bottom lip.

"Fuck." He hissed from the pain.

"Don't say shit you don't mean." She bucked.

"I never say shit I don't mean." He gripped her ass and pushed her double Ds into his face, and she fed him her nipples like grapes. He sucked them as if they were the sweetest he'd ever tasted. Milan could feel Kendu's pelvis contract and the muscles in his six-pack clench. His face contorted and at the exact moment that his liquid gift exploded between her thighs, her sugar walls melted and coated him.

With vanilla icing between them, Kendu pulled Milan to his chest. "I'm sorry, baby. I love you so much, and I want nothing more than for you to be my wife."

She cradled his face between her hands. "Are you sure?"

"You the dopest chick I know," he said.

A smile crept onto Milan's face and pushed past her bruised heart. "The dopest chick?" She twisted her lips to one side. "Like the hottest? Like, real super-fresh-funky-fly-dope? Or you just a lyin' niggah?"

Chaunci

Chaunci leaned against the glass wall in her living room and stroked her index finger down the center of her reflection. She was dressed in a beige camisole, fitted jeans, and a navy Gucci blazer. She wondered what had possessed her to unpack her vulnerability and display it before Idris. She couldn't figure it out.

All she knew is that an aged sore spot weighed down her chest; and for the first time in her life she couldn't push it to the side. And now the iron fist that she'd grown up with had risen and was too stubborn to leave her throat.

That fucked with her.

And the longer she stood there and stared into the ghostly eyes of her image, the more fucked-up and fucked-over she felt.

Her feelings had nothing to do with silly-ass love and its consequences. This was about escaping meekness and weakness, and plain and simple being independent, strong, an anti-damsel in distress.

She'd always prided herself on being whoever she needed to be: a mother, a friend, a lover, a boss, a bitch . . . and she'd never slipped. Ever.

Until now.

Chaunci swallowed and said to no one in particular, "I can't believe he did that shit to me. And I know I wasn't perfect . . ." The lump in her throat swelled and forced her voice to rise. "I had my faults. But for him to run off with some bitch as if we didn't have an unspoken agreement that he was my man—ring or no ring. He was *my* goddamn man . . . in ways she will never understand. This is just—" The lump threatened to explode and she began to scream, "Is just. Fucked. Up!" Chaunci's eyes became cloudy, and she did all she could not to drop a single tear.

She lost and tears slid between her lips, filling her mouth with salt.

Knock. Knock! "Chaunci!" Bridget yelled and pounding on the door, crashing Chaunci's pity party. "We're here! Open up."

Chaunci stood frozen. Bridget and *Millionaire Wives Club* were the last things on her mind. She wiped her eyes and sniffed.

Bridget pounded again.

I need a drink.

Chaunci walked over to the refrigerator, took out a bottle of wine, and poured herself a drink. "Here's to . . ." She held her glass in the air. "letting go . . ." She sipped and returned to her living room, eased onto her chenille sofa, and crossed her legs.

"I know you're in there!" Bridget banged. "Now open up!"

Fuck that. She sipped again.

"We have to get footage!" Bridget slid an envelope under the door. "And you need to let us in, while you have a chance to be a breakout star!"

I don't give a damn about that.

"We've been trying to reach you for two days now. Two days too many!"

Then take your hint and leave.

"That's a copy of your contract in the envelope. Now, we can do this nicely or we can play another way. But either way we'll get in the sandbox. And we'll get in there today!"

Bitch, please. Before Chaunci could finish her thought her telephone rang. She leaned toward the end table and peeked at the Caller I.D. It was her mother.

Don't answer.

The phone continued to ring and a moment later Chaunci sucked in a sharp breath and placed the receiver to her ear. "Hello."

"Hey, Honey." Her mother spoke in a soft, steady southern drawl that flooded Chaunci's mind with too many memories and with the reasons her visits home to Murfreesboro, North Carolina, were next to nonexistent. "I'm just calling to check on you."

Chaunci cradled the phone to her ear and resumed staring out the window. "I'm fine."

"You don't sound fine," her mother said.

"Mama, what did I just—" Chaunci stopped herself. Hearing her mother's voice—especially at a time like this—unnerved her. She was already at war, but now the battle had switched from Idris's bullshit to her mother's, neither of which she wanted to deal with a moment longer. "Mama." She drew in a deep breath. "I'm fine."

"Well, I didn't mean to upset you, Chaunci. I've just been worried about you."

"I said I'm fine." *Why do I keep repeating myself?*

"Chaunci!" Bridget yelled as she steadily pounded against the door.

Chaunci ignored Bridget as her mother continued. "You know yesterday was the pastor's birthday. Your sister called, but you and your brother didn't bother at all. He's always been a nice man to you all."

I've never called on his birthday. "Mama, please drop it."

"I'm just saying that it would be nice if you and your brother called him. He's always been there for you three. He baptized you, and he helped raise money in the church when you all went to college, so the least you can do is call him on his birthday."

Chaunci snapped. "Why, Mama? He's your man and his wife's man. Not mine! He's not my father—"

"Your father didn't stick around! He went to the store when you were a baby and never came back."

"That's the same story you told all three of us about our fathers. All three of them did not go to the store when we were babies and never come back!"

"Chaunci," her mother said calmly, but with an annoyed edge. "I am trying very hard not to hang up this phone but you're pushing me. And I wish you and your brother would stop bringing up your fathers."

"I can't!" Chaunci screamed.

"Why not?"

"Because I keep looking for him in every goddamn thing I do and I'm pissed off about it."

"You never wanted for anything. I did my best, and Pastor treated you three like his own children, and what he is to me is none of your business! I can't believe you just said that."

"It's the truth. And I have too much on my mind to pretend otherwise."

"Nobody's perfect, Chaunci. I've made mistakes. That's what I was trying to explain to you about Idris, you have to learn to give people a chance."

"What?" Chaunci said, taken aback, "Idris?" She paused. "I'ma ask you this last time to please stop." She paced from one end of the room to the other.

"I'm not calling to fuss, Chaunci Renee. I'm only checking on you. So you need to stop getting so upset."

"No." Chaunci stopped in her tracks. "You need to *start* getting upset. And start demanding more for yourself. Stop letting everyone run over you!" Tears filled her eyes again. "My God, Mama. I love you, but I'm tired of running away from anything that looks or makes me feel like you."

"And I don't want you to be like me. I want you to have a husband. Now you need to talk to Idris and marry him. You're not getting any younger. And in case you didn't know or didn't learn from my life, pretty girls get lonely too, Chaunci."

"I'm only thirty-four, I'm not desperate, and I can't marry Idris because he's married to someone else! And there's nothing I can do about it!"

Her mother gasped. "Chaunci!" She gasped again. "I can't believe you were so stubborn and let that man get away from you. You better hope she doesn't keep him happy and maybe he'll be willing to keep you company at night."

Chaunci was pissed. "What kind of thinking is that? I'm not accepting that."

"It's the truth. And I don't understand how you could do something like that. You need to stop looking at men's flaws and start looking at the goodness in their hearts. God provided you with a man, and not just any ole man, but a good man and you just spat on him. I don't know where you get this." She sighed. "You and your brother. You two could not have come from me. He's on his third wife, and you're so set in your ways you'll never be a wife. I swear, I swear, like Pastor said, all I can do is get on my knees and pray for you."

Chaunci felt as if a jagged knife had ripped its way up her face and over her skull.

To most people—church folks, neighbors, distant relatives—her mother was a saint, always kept her cool, did no wrong, and Chaunci was the problem. The mouthy child, the rebellious teen with impractical dreams, who grew up to be the ungrateful adult-child who moved to the city, made it big, and forgot where she came from—mama included.

"Mama, I gotta go." She hung up.

Bridget continued to pound. "This is crazy!" Bridget screamed. "Do you know how many people want to be reality stars? Do you?"

"What are you doing?" Chaunci heard Milan's voice mix with Bridget's tirade.

"You need to talk to her!" Bridget yelled at Milan. "This is ridiculous. She's acting as if we don't have to script her a story line! As if she's a natural!"

"Milan." Chaunci cracked the door. "I didn't expect to see you."

"I know. I was just dropping by."

"Come in."

Milan walked swiftly into the apartment. Bridget and the camera crew tried to push past her, only to be greeted by a forceful shove and the door slamming in their faces. "Now stay out!" Chaunci screamed as she and Milan pushed the door completely closed with their backs and behinds. The automatic lock clicked into place and Chaunci looked at Milan, who held a bottle of merlot in one hand. After a moment of staring at each other they burst into laughter that shook their entire bodies and caused them to slide down the door, to the floor, with tears falling from their eyes.

"What the hell are we doing?" Milan asked, as she kicked her stilettos off. "How did we end up on the floor, locking Bridget out? This is bullshit. You know this is bullshit." She cracked up.

"And I'm tired of it—"

"Me too." Milan smirked. "Hell, Kendu and I had the biggest argument the other night. We made up, though, which is part of the reason my ass is sore. I need to get in shape, truthfully. But no matter how I try to get Kendu to build a gym in his house, he looks at me like I'm crazy. He doesn't give a damn . . ." her voice drifted.

"This faking the funk bullshit isn't for me. It's like I'm strong for everybody—everybody—and when *I* need to steal a lean—"

Milan fanned her face. "Nobody gives a shit. Don't give a damn that I need to get this weight off of me—"

"I feel like a bag lady." Chaunci bit her bottom lip. "Like I'm constantly dragging shit—"

"Me too."

"And dragging shit . . . and dragging shit. When at the end of the day, all I want to do is drop this defense and learn to love."

"What?" Milan whipped her head toward Chaunci and blinked. "Are we talking about the same thing? I'm talking about losing weight."

Chaunci continued as if she were oblivious to Milan's last statement. "It's like no matter how I try to get it right with men, I keep seeing my mother and then I falter and screw up—and now I've really messed up."

"What happened?" Milan wiped the tears steadily slipping down Chaunci's cheeks. "No judgment."

Chaunci picked at a thread on her jacket. "Well, girl, when Idris first came back to town, I asked him to meet me for dinner."

"Did he?"

Chaunci hesitated. "Yeah."

"What happened?"

"I asked him to marry me." She paused.

"You did what?" Milan said shocked.

"I asked him to marry me." Chaunci shrugged. "He said no."

"Did he say why?"

"Because." She swallowed. "He's already married."

"What?" Milan screeched.

"What's going on in there?" Bridget yelled.

Milan continued, "Why are you just telling me this? We're girls, I would've cut that motherfucker and wiped your tears the same night."

"Milan, I'm just realizing that this isn't a dream. That something has happened in my life and I wasn't able to control the shit. Like, he really married this bitch? Did he really do that, without talking to me, without asking me if I was sure we didn't need to be together."

"You can't control everything, Chaunci."

"But I need to, because when I don't, I lose."

"It's not about losing, it's about letting go, letting some shit ride."

"And how do I do that? If I'd let shit ride, I'd still be stuck in that damn country-ass town, barefoot and nursing goddamn babies. I have never been the type to let anything ride, because I knew I had to take what I wanted out of life, otherwise I'd be stuck."

"But it's not that simple, you can't take everything. You can work for it, work at it, but in the end you have to let the chips fall where they may."

"Fuck that."

"You need to take the *S* off your chest and just learn to be a woman."

"I did, the night I proposed and now I'm sitting here a damn wreck." Tears fell from her eyes.

"Have you spoken to Idris since then?"

"Yes and no. He called for Kobi and I dropped her off. He asked me if he could speak to me and I told him no."

"You can't hold everything in."

Silence.

Milan hesitated. "I just can't believe that he did that." She wiped Chaunci's tears with the back of her hand. "If you want we can drop the maturity, go high school and whup both of their asses."

Chaunci laughed.

"Dumb motherfucker," Milan said.

Bridget yelled. "Open. Up. This. Door!" She pounded.

Milan flicked her wrist dismissively at the sound of Bridget's voice. "I'm so sorry that happened to you, Chaunci. But think about this: you weren't exactly sure if you two needed to be together . . . forever."

"I keep telling myself that and it hasn't made me feel better yet."

"You're in shock."

"That's an understatement. Anyway," Chaunci steadied herself on her feet, dusting her clothes. "Let's turn off this sensitive shit and get back in character. How does a diva look?" She ran her hands along the sides of her body.

Milan stood up and looked her friend over. "We can't always be in character. Sometimes we have to be the mess we really are."

"Can you save the deep shit for another time? Now let Bridget in, please."

Milan twisted the knob. The moment the door was ajar Bridget and the camera crew rushed through it, causing Milan to stumble and the door to swing wildly.

"Don't you ever do anything like that again!" Bridget pointed her finger and admonished Chaunci. "You know we have to get footage and here you are acting crazy and without the camera there to witness it. Oh, no, we will have none of that!"

Milan looked at her diamond encrusted watch. "We need to get going."

"Oh, no," Bridget said. "She's not going anywhere until we interview her about the other night." She pointed to Carl. "Roll." She looked at Chaunci. "Now, tell us about when Idris dumped you and surprised you with his new bride."

Chaunci swallowed and pushed past her emotions. "Pretty much, Idris has lost his mind. I told him I couldn't marry him a few months back and he was so distraught that he ran out to L.A., hit Skid Row, and married the first stripper who'd have him."

"She was a stripper?" Bridget giggled and gasped. "Continue Chaunci." She clapped her hands.

"Of course, she was a stripper. What else would the cheap bitch be? Did you see her shoes?"

"Pay-to-the-less," Milan added. "I ain't sayin', but I'm just sayin', that Idris went to the bottom of the sea with that one."

"Did you expect something like this from Idris?" Bridget asked.

"I expect anything from a man," Chaunci said.

"Especially a bitch-ass one," Milan added.

"True, indeed," Chaunci agreed. "And this move he made, just proved I was right the first time. My mistake was second-guessing myself. Which is why, when this ho divorces his ass and takes half his damn money, he cannot come back to me!" She cocked her head to the side, flipping her hair behind her ear.

"Are you ready?" Milan asked. "You know the bitches are waiting."

Chaunci tucked her Hermès clutch beneath her arm. "Well, my dear, in that case we should leave." She batted her lashes. "It's never been my style to keep any bitch waiting."

The Club

An evening rainbow of amber and indigo danced in the sky, casting its beauty over Vera's exclusive yacht. It was a diamond of the water, filled with heated marble floors, three bedrooms, an all-white living room, original artwork, hand-carved wooden trim, a formal dining room, an infinity pool, and three decks.

Vera placed small tokens—beauty baskets containing Volume, her line of hair products, as well as sugar scrubs and satin lotions—in each of her guests' chairs.

She stood back and admired the way her staff had filled the table with oysters, clams, shrimp, lobster, caviar, yellow rice, spinach salad, and chilled bottles of wine. Light jazz provided a mellow backdrop as she walked onto the front deck and looked toward the pier.

"So what do you ladies think of Vera inviting you onto her yacht for dinner this evening?" Bridget asked Milan, Chaunci, and Jaise as they rode in the limo sipping Pinot Grigio.

"I really don't know what to think of it," Chaunci said. "I mean, we just saw her two days ago and already she's extending dinner invites?"

"I think she's trying a little too hard," Milan added.

"She's *trying* to be friendly," Jaise said.

"I only came to be polite." Milan sipped her drink.

"Yeah, really," Chaunci said. "I was so surprised when my assistant brought me this formal invitation and it read 'Dine on the Hudson with Vera Bennett' as if this was supposed to be an exclusive event." She pointed out the window toward Vera's yacht, which was only a short distance away, "And, I mean, it's . . . okay."

"But it's not all that." Milan refreshed her drink.

"Wow," Jaise said, impressed. "And when's the last time you two ladies went yacht shopping? Just curious."

Silence.

"That's what I thought," Jaise said as she pulled her compact from her purse and checked her makeup.

"Jaise, why do you *always* disagree with *everything* we say?" Chaunci asked.

"That shit is such a pain in the ass." Milan lifted her eyes toward the heavens, as if she were searching for patience.

"*My opinion* is a pain in *your ass,* Milan?" Jaise snapped her compact shut. "Well, your *truth* is a pain in *my ass*. Every time I see you with Kendu, I think about how he was married to Evan and you couldn't respect that. Every time I see my godchild, Aiyanna, and she thinks you're the best replacement mommy in the world, I get pissed off. So it seems to me that we just may be even."

"Honestly, Jaise, I don't give a damn what you think," Milan retorted. "You don't know my or Kendu's story, so stay in your lane."

"Stay in my lane? And what does that mean?" Jaise said. "Is that some South-Bronx hood lingo?"

"Would you like me to get South-Bronx hood on your ass, Jaise?"

"Milan," Chaunci interjected. "Don't feed into that. You know she'll jump ship in a minute. Pun intended. First she wanted to be nice and make up with us, and now she's BFF with the new girl."

"Whatever." Jaise waved her hand as if they could be easily dismissed. "And how high school are you? I don't know Vera. And anybody who was born a drug baby I'm a little hesitant of. But she invited us here and the least we can do is be respectful. Hell, she realizes there's a pecking order and she's on the bottom. She's trying to make an impression. Let her do that. That's all I'm saying."

"All I wanna know, Carl," Al-Taniesha spat as she and Lollipop stormed up the pier and onto the yacht, "is why you ain't been at my crib taping me and Lollipop?"

Carl didn't respond.

"You hear me, Carl?" Al-Taniesha pointed at him. "I know you hear me!" She placed her hands on her hips, causing her one-shoulder dress, with dollar bills printed all over it, to rise and reveal the ripples in her thighs.

Al-Taniesha looked at Lollipop, who rocked a cherry-red cat-suit, designed with flames that rose from the crotch and burned up to the V-neck. "Stay calm, Niesha," he said. "Stay calm."

"Oh, I'ma stay calm. I'ma calmly go the fuck off." She wiggled her neck. "Carl!"

No response.

"When. The. Hell. Are. Y'all. Comin'. To my mo'fuckin' spot?"

Nothing.

"Oh, you a mime now?" Al-Taniesha moved her hands as if she were climbing a wall. "Do you understand I'ma hook your ass if you don't tell me something?"

"You have to talk to Bridget," Carl whispered.

"Don't put this shit off on Bridget. She's the one who told me that the next time I saw your ass I needed to call you out on camera because then you wouldn't have a choice but to be honest."

"I told you it's 'cause we live in the projects, Niesha," Lollipop said, clearly pissed. "I told you we needed another crib."

Al-Taniesha spun on her heel toward Lollipop. "Is you trippin' on dumb shit again? Didn't I tell you I wasn't giving up my rent-subsidized apartment? Didn't I? Fuck that. Motherfuckers too busy 'round here with their priorities fallin' out their asses, buyin' houses and boats." She waved her hands in the air. "A buncha retarded shit, yet they on antidepressants. Buncha unhappy hoes who've fucked their kids all up." She pointed to where Jaise, Milan, and Chaunci were walking up the pier. "Just like Jaise's son is running around being led by his dick like he's stupid as hell."

"Dumb," Lollipop signified.

Al-Taniesha carried on. "Which is why at the end of the day, what do any of them have? Nothing. So busy trying to keep up with the Joneses."

"Why do you have to bring up the Joneses?" Lollipop growled. "Fuck the Joneses. I used to whip the Joneses's asses in high school. Hmph, especially after they walked the halls calling me sensitive and shit. Rafique 'Lickin' Lollipop' Gatling is a lotta things but sensitive is not one of 'em." He dabbed at the corners of his eyes.

"I told you to ignore those bitches, Lollipop." Al-Taniesha rubbed his back. "Fuck 'em."

"You're right, Niesha. You're right."

"I know I am. Just like I'm right about these tramps who think they're so much, spending a fortune to own an apartment."

"That's what we need to do, Niesha. Buy an apartment."

"Excuse me, Mr. Sensitive?" Al-Taniesha said, pissed.

He wagged his finger at her. "Don't call me that!"

Al-Taniesha continued. "Our rent is five hundred fifty-five dollars, and thirty-nine cents, heat and hot water included. What exactly do you think we're gonna pay for a mortgage in New York City? Hell, we already live on the top floor, got a view and a balcony, and our shit is decked. Now what's the problem? This is a reality show and we keepin' it real."

Lollipop snapped, "I wanna keep it real over at a condo on Madison Avenue."

"And who gon' pay for that? You spent your half of the money on catsuits. Yo' shit is done. I'm trying to start me a megachurch. I told you I gotta damn calling for my life and you playing games. And besides, that was *my* lottery ticket!"

"Hear this calling, Niesha, I gave you the damn dollar for that ticket. Now don't get it twisted."

"You the king of twisted, want everybody to call you 'Lick' all of a sudden."

"I told you that was my stage name for the show!"

"But they didn't cast you for RuPaul's Drag Race, so I don't understand the name change."

"Don't get to showin' off!"

Al-Taniesha looked him over. "And. What. In. The. Hell. Is you gon' do?"

Lollipop walked behind Al-Taniesha and spoke against her neck. "I'ma bend dat ass over." He gripped her hips and growled against her neck. "And I'ma knock er' single cobweb out yo' ass." He pumped her twice.

Al-Taniesha shivered and turned toward Lollipop. She slid her arms around his neck. "Oh, baby. I swear this is why I'm so glad me and my mother signed up to be prison pen pals and I found you and she found her a lifer."

"My baby came to see me every Sunday." Lollipop squeezed her.

"And I was at those gates when they released you, baby."

"And we've been riding ever since."

"Good ole Lollipop." She stroked his crotch and they started to kiss.

"Oh, my God," Jaise said as she walked past them. "Throw. Up. In. My. Mouth."

"Why is he always around every time we get together?" Milan asked.

"Seriously," Chaunci added.

"What those bitches say?" Al-Taniesha asked, breaking away from her and Lollipop's kiss.

"Welcome to the *Skyy Bennett*," Vera's assistant said, then smiled at the ladies, welcoming them onto the yacht, which was affectionately named after Vera and Taj's daughter. "Mrs. Bennett is putting some finishing touches on a few things," she continued. "And while she does that I'd love to offer you ladies a tour."

"You can tell this bitch is new money," Jaise mumbled to Chaunci. "She couldn't come out and greet us herself?" She smiled at Vera's assistant, then said, "I'd love a tour and I'm sure the other ladies would as well."

Afterward, the women were escorted into the dining area. Their expressions revealed how impressed they were.

"This yacht—" Jaise walked over and kissed Vera on both cheeks—"is absolutely stunning."

"And you are absolutely two-faced," Chaunci said softly.

"What was that, Chaunci?" Vera asked. "I didn't hear you."

"I was just saying," Chaunci said as she greeted Vera, "that the yacht's maintenance must be a pretty penny."

Jaise rolled her eyes and looked toward the camera. "Only new money would talk about money. My God."

Al-Taniesha placed her hands on her hips. "This shit here is like the floating B.E.T. awards. Looks fly, presents well, but there are still some ghetto motherfuckers in the audience."

"Amen," Lollipop said.

Choosing to ignore Al-Taniesha, Jaise said, "Thank you for inviting us."

"Thank you for coming," Vera said. "Sit down, ladies and let's have some drinks and dinner."

"Oh, this is cute." Milan picked up the basket from her chair.

"Thank you," Vera said. "That's for you ladies to take with you. It's from my hair-care line, Volume."

"Oh, the dressed-up sulfur 8." Milan looked toward Jaise. "Isn't that what you called it?"

"Yes," Jaise nodded. "And I meant it in the nicest way."

"Hmph," Vera said. "I was going to wait until we at least had dinner, but since we're on the topic of what you all have said, let's discuss."

Jaise picked up her fork and ate a shrimp. "I think we should just let the past be the past."

"It will be. Right after I set a few things straight," Vera assured Jaise. "Now, Bridget read an article to me." Vera placed the tabloid on the table. "And it seems you ladies had a few interesting comments about me."

"That had to be Jaise's." Chaunci stabbed her finger into the paper. "I don't deal with tabloids."

"Don't put that shit off on me," Jaise spat. "They called all of us and we all commented."

"Except me." Al-Taniesha waved her hand. "So don't get me mixed up in your bullshit."

"I can't help it if people come looking for me," Milan said. "I mean, your ex-boyfriend called my publicist."

"And what exactly do you need a publicist for?" Jaise snapped. "How to gold-dig?"

Milan spat "Bitch—"

"Look," Vera interjected. "Let's stick to the matter at hand."

"Which is what?" Chaunci asked.

"That you three talk too fuckin' much. Period." Vera paused, giving the women a chance to respond. When they didn't, she continued. "Now, I'm not one for a buncha cackling behind other people's back. TV didn't invent me—"

"Or me either," Chaunci said. "I have my own shit."

"Then we understand each other," Vera said. "Don't gun for me and I won't have to shoot you."

"You're way out of line," Chaunci insisted.

"I know you didn't get us in the middle of the Hudson to start an argument." Milan shook her head. "You're being really messy right now, Vera."

"Oh, puhlease, every bitch here is a mess," Vera said, pissed. "Now, like I said, my intentions were to speak to you ladies over dinner, maybe have a decent discussion and hash this out, because I realize that you don't know me and I wanted to give you that opportunity. But since you're bringing it to me all willy-nilly rah-rah style, then that's how we're gon' handle it." Vera's Brooklyn accent had completely taken over. "So get this—watch what the hell you say. 'Cause you don't know shit about me. You don't pay my bills, you're not my man, you can't match my money, and you're not my homegirls or my goddamn family, so keep my name outcha mouth when I'm not around. 'Cause where I'm from, chicks get their asses beat for shit like that."

"A thug in a cocktail dress," Al-Taniesha spat. "This is my type of motherfucker right here." She reached across the table and slapped Vera five. "On the blackhand side." She turned her palm down.

"Yeah," Lollipop added. "She handling that shit."

"I don't take kindly to threats," Chaunci said.

"I haven't threatened you," Vera said. "Stop putting words in my mouth. I'm just letting you all know that you need to watch *what the fuck* you say. That's all I'm saying." She waved her hands. "Watch. What. The. Fuck. You. Say. Now, I can be your best friend or your worst enemy. You choose."

"Pow!" Al-Taniesha said as she pulled a large jar of Vaseline from her purse and slammed it on the table in front of them. "Just in case." She looked at Vera and flung her head to the side for emphasis.

"Now are we cool?" Vera asked. "Or is it a problem?"

"How about this," Jaise said. "I know that sometimes we all say things we don't mean. And I am definitely one for being the bigger person. So if I said anything to offend you, Vera, I'm truly sorry. Because I really would like to get to know you and move on."

"You are such a fuckin' punk." Al-Taniesha shook her head.

"I agree with Jaise." Milan rolled her eyes. "We do have to move on. And maybe I said a few things that I shouldn't have, and if what I said offended you, then I apologize as well."

"I just think this was really uncalled-for." Chaunci crossed her legs. "I don't have a problem with moving on, but I do have a problem with some of the things you said, Vera."

"My sentiments exactly," Vera added.

"Let's just call a truce," Jaise said, picking up her glass of wine.

"Sounds like a plan." Vera held her glass in the air. "Truce."

"Truce," Milan, Jaise, and Chaunci said simultaneously as they clinked their glasses.

"Uhmm-hmm." Al-Taniesha twisted her lips and looked at Vera. "I'm all for a truce. But all I'ma say is this." She pointed to the other women. "Watch 'em. That's all I'ma say. Watch 'em. 'Cause it's only a matter of time before one of these heifers shows her ass again."

A Week Later . . .

The smell of sweet potato pancakes, cheese and eggs, grits, country bacon, maple ham steaks, and apple turnovers filled Jaise's kitchen as she leaned against her lava countertop and proudly inhaled the scents.

A nervous smile made its way to her face as she felt the ship that had taken up residence in her stomach sinking. In an effort to help it move along, she reached for her vintage mirrored cigarette case and tried to open the clasp. She fumbled.

Fuck.

The ship sank further.

She closed her eyes.

Get it together.

Slowly she slid her thumb over the cigarette case's clasp. After a few tries it finally popped open and revealed a full tray of Virginia Slims. Jaise slid one to her lips and lit it. The seductive taste of nicotine mixed with the food's aroma and made her feel lighter. Smoking while she cooked was not a habit; it's just that when things were fucked-up she had to cling to her vices: cigarettes and food. And in that order.

How the hell am I going to tell him this shit? Jaise took a few steady tokes and then flicked the half-smoked cigarette into the brick fireplace. Before she could answer her own question, Bilal's keys were rattling the backdoor and he was stepping over the threshold.

Showtime . . .

"Good morning, Mrs. Asante." He walked up behind her and tapped wet kisses softly along the violin curve of her neck.

"Good morning, baby." Goosebumps rose on her skin as she melted into his kisses. "How was your night at work?" she asked him as the last kiss was placed below her right earlobe. Her eyes scanned the stove's clock: nine a.m. "I know you like to have a hot breakfast before you hit the sack." She did her best to sound sincere.

"Not really. I like to hit the sack before I go to bed." He slapped her on the ass. "Why don't you cut the stove off and we can head upstairs?"

Jaise blushed and turned toward her husband. She draped her arms over his shoulders. "You are so fresh." She did her best to sound bubbly.

"And you love it."

"That I do."

Bilal kissed Jaise lightly on the lips and ran his hands up her thighs. "Seriously, though, when I came in from work this morning my intention was to make love to you." He placed one of her hands on his hard dick. "I even called you to tell you that, so you'd be upstairs waiting for me, but you didn't answer the house phone or your cell phone. Where were you?"

Jaise hesitated and looked Bilal dead in his eyes. *Should I tell him?* She stared at him a moment too long. *Not yet.* She ran the back of her thumb across his lips and did all she could not to sound mechanical. "Look at all this food. Now where do you think I was? I had to go to the grocery."

"Really?" Bilal said more to himself than to Jaise. He took a step back and looked her over. "What's up?"

She pointed to the kitchen table. "All your favorites: pancakes, grits, cheese and eggs, apple turnovers—"

"Not the food. With you. You seem a little . . . I don't know." He paused. "Is everything okay?"

"No." She landed a peck on his lips. "I feel like I really don't show you enough how much I love you. And you are such a good man, so understanding. I know we have our times but I feel like I can tell you anything—"

"You can."

She gave him a half smile that barely rose above the corners of her lips. "I know, sweetie. I'm just blessed to have you in my life." She began to fix his plate.

Bilal sat at the table. "Did something pop off that I should know about?"

Jaise quickly turned back to him. *Does he know?* She read his face. *No, he doesn't.* "Lieutenant Asante, can't your wife just shower you with love?"

"Or is it guilt?"

"Guilt about what?" she said a little too quickly.

"Missing our anniversary. I accepted your apology. I know you've had a lot on your mind—"

Jaise rolled her eyes. "Are you going to toss that shit in my face forever?" She gave a hard flick to her wrist as she set his plate before him, causing some of the food to shift and the plate to slide a few inches to the side of him. "Please, I have apologized a thousand times and all you really need to accept is one of them." Jaise felt her shoulders tense. "I really don't want us to argue."

"I wasn't trying to argue," he said, baffled. "And what's with the attitude all of a sudden? Were you even listening to me? I said I accepted your apology."

Did he say that? "Good, because we've been arguing too much lately." She struggled to collect herself. "Besides, I go through enough with the bitches of New York." She handed Bilal his cutlery. "These women cause me so much grief and havoc, especially when there are cameras around." She poured two cups of coffee. "It's like they become mean girls, nasty and self-inflated, bougie bitches, when there's TV involved." She handed Bilal his coffee.

She sat directly across from him. He reached for her hand, said a simple blessing, and began to eat.

"Truthfully," Jaise said, "it makes no sense. We're all successful women and you'd think we'd all get along. And have a nice, you know, family show filled with our husbands and children. But we, well, not *me*, but *they* don't know how to get along for five minutes."

"Taping just started and already it's a problem?"

"Exactly."

"Well, they're not the only ones who lose their minds when you all get together," Bilal said, lifting a fork full of eggs to his mouth. "*All of you* add to the reason TV is mindless brain candy."

Jaise carried on. "I try to tell them to calm down." She sipped her coffee. "That we have enough shit that jumps off in our lives that we don't need to be amped up all the time. Wait a minute . . ." She swallowed. "What did you say?"

"I *said* they're not the only ones who lose their minds. You lose yours too when you're on camera. You become somebody else." He sipped his coffee.

"What?" she said, taken aback.

"Someone I don't always like."

"Oh, really? And how long have you thought that?"

"I've wanted to talk to you about it for a while."

"And say what?" she snapped.

"That we, well, *you, really,* no longer need to do the show."

"No longer need to do the show?"

"I know Bridget will threaten you with a lawsuit, but we can speak to an attorney about our options."

"So you have it all worked out?"

"Yeah." He nodded. "I do. We have other things to deal with."

"Like?"

"Jabril. And we need to work on our life together."

Jaise was completely shocked. This was not the way she'd planned or needed their conversation to go. "What's wrong with our life together?"

"Right now this whole 'lights, camera, action' bullshit is tearing us the hell up. I didn't sign up for this—"

"I was already signed up when you met me, and the show's only for the summer."

"But it's a summer of being fucked-up," Bilal said. "We have other shit to do."

"You can't just decide on your own without consulting me that I should leave my show, excuse me, my job, because you think it's mindless brain candy."

"It is."

"Well, the stupid-ass candy means something to me!" she spat.

"Apparently it means more to you than I do."

Jaise paused and tried to regroup. "You know that's not true. You know I love you."

"Then listen to me, baby." He reached for her hands. "I love you so much," he said softly, stroking her face. "And I want us to have a long life together, but we have some things we need to work on."

"I don't like the way this conversation is going. Are you trying to tell me something? Are you thinking about leaving me?"

"No, Jaise. What I'm thinking about is being with you forever. But I need you to trust me and to follow my lead with some things. We're young, baby. You're only thirty-seven and I'm forty-one. We need to live, or did you forget?"

"No, I didn't forget. It's just that I've got Jabril, and this girl accusing him of fathering this baby."

"That's his problem."

"And he needs my help!"

"No, I need you!" He let her hands go. "Can you be there for me? Be my fuckin' wife?"

"Since when did you start cussin' so much?"

"Since I got pissed off. This shit is crazy. I don't like living my life on TV. I don't like my wife becoming this high sadity, money-over-everything big-mouth. And I especially don't like and can't stand the fact that I'm laying up in the house with another grown-ass man, taking care of his ass, while all he does is skip off and make babies for you to take care of. That's why I'm glad you left him in jail, because he needed to learn a lesson—"

"Daaaaaang." Jabril's bare feet slapped against the floor as he dragged himself into the kitchen. He wore a white wife beater and a loose pair of boxers as he stretched and yawned in the doorway. "I can hear y'all all the way upstairs."

Jaise gasped. Her eyes quickly read the disbelief in Bilal's eyes. She shouted at Jabril, "Didn't I tell your ass to stay upstairs until I told you to come down here?"

"I was getting hungry." He looked around the kitchen and his eyes landed on the food. "You cooked my favorite, Ma. Apple turnovers." He walked over and began to fix himself a plate. "I haven't eaten like this in days. They serve some real messed-up food in Rikers. I hate that place." He turned toward Bilal. "Law enforcement needs to fix their jails before they start running out to men's houses and arresting them for nonsense."

Bilal continued to stare at Jaise and she could've sworn that he'd stopped blinking. "Is this why I couldn't reach you this morning?" Bilal clenched his lips tightly.

Silence.

"Yeah, this is exactly why." He pointed. "Because you took your ass and bailed him out after I told you not to." He arched his brows and his nostrils flared. "Cigarettes and food. I should've known."

"This is not the time," Jaise whispered to Bilal. She looked toward her son. "Jabril, don't touch my food without washing your hands."

"What do you mean, this is not the time?" Bilal yelled and

pounded his fist on the table. "This is definitely the time! I'm sick of this! And you and your son need to get your shit together."

"Whoa." Jabril spun on his heel, holding his full plate of food. "Bilal, you know I respect you, and I usually don't get in y'all's business—"

"Bruh, you all up in our business. All the time."

"Whatever, man. All I know is that lately I don't like the way you've been coming off on my mother, and I'm definitely not gon' stand here while you talk to her crazy, coming all out the side of your neck and shit. Now, what you need to do—" Jabril poured syrup on his pancakes and stuffed a piece in his mouth. "—is lower your voice or you gon' have a problem." He chewed. "And that's on my word."

"A problem?" Bilal said, shocked. "A problem?"

"A problem," Jabril assured him.

"Jabril!" Jaise sprang from her seat. "You need to mind your business. You don't speak to Bilal like that! Now apologize."

"Apologize?" Jabril said, surprised. "You trippin'. I'm up here standing up for you—"

"You don't even know how to stand up," Bilal barked. "Up here with babies and shit all over the place."

"And what, you mad 'cause you don't have one?" Jabril asked.

"Jabril!" Jaise screamed.

Bilal smirked. "You know what, Jabril? When I married your mother you became my son, which is why I really should be reaching across this table and fucking you up."

"Bilal," Jaise said, "you're going too far."

"Somebody needs to pick up where you drop his ass off. But don't worry, I'ma let him live." He looked back at Jabril. "Because I realize that you're stuck. You don't know how to be a man because nobody ever taught you. You don't have a job, or any skills, and apparently the only thing you know how to do is make babies and live off somebody else's money. So I'ma place the ass-whippin' that you really deserve on reserve. But if you ever—"

He stepped over to Jabril and stood so close that his breath blew into his eyes. "—and I mean ever, tell me how to speak to my wife, call yourself checkin' me, or threaten me, then I'm gonna bust yo' ass, youngblood. And that's on *my* word."

"Bilal, stop." Jaise slid in between them. "Leave him alone!" She then turned and screamed at Jabril, "I said apologize!"

"Apologize? Did you just hear what he said to me?" Jabril asked.

"You were wrong!" Jaise insisted. "As much as Bilal has been here for you!"

Jabril shook his head. "Know what?" He walked to the cabinet and grabbed the roll of aluminum foil. He wrapped his food to go. "Let me just get my shit and bounce."

"Yeah, do that," Bilal said. "And make sure you take enough to last a while."

"Jabril!" Jaise yelled as he stormed out of the kitchen. "Come back here!"

"What the hell are you screaming after him for? Really, where the fuck is he going?" Bilal said, pissed, as Jabril ran up the stairs and slammed his door.

"You shouldn't have spoken to him like that!" Jaise spat at Bilal.

Bilal stroked his chin and said, "You're right. I shouldn't have. I shouldn't have had to, because you should have taken some time out from your glitz, Gucci, and glamour to teach him how to be a man. Because I can't clean up after you anymore. Fuck it, let his ass fall and fade to shit! I'm done with him! And if he gets in my face again you'll be putting him the hell up out of here or I'll be leaving!" Bilal walked out of the kitchen. As he reached for his car keys, Jaise snatched them and held them to her breasts.

"Oh, hell no, motherfucker," she said, fuming. "You think you're going to say that to me and then run out the fuckin' door?"

"I'm not about to argue with you." He reached for his keys and she snatched them away.

"Well, then, you will fuckin' listen. How dare you say some crab ass shit like that!"

"Give me my keys!"

"I'm not giving you anything but a piece of my mind. My son is nineteen, goddamn it! Haven't you ever done anything fucked-up?"

"This is not about me. This is about Jabril and where he's headed!"

"Who died and left his future in your hands? How dare you look down on my son! I know he's not perfect but he's mine." She pointed to her chest. "And so what if he's a teenage father? Shit, I had him when I was seventeen! Had my mother put me out and turned her back on me like you want me to do, where the hell would I be? Fuck that."

"So the solution is to coddle him? Oh, that makes a lot of goddamn sense."

"Don't you worry about it! That's my child. You weren't there when he was born premature, weighing a goddamn pound. Or when he was nine and was diagnosed with leukemia. I don't remember seeing you at his radiation treatments or when he was losing his hair. And you damn sure weren't there when I cried every night and begged God to let my baby live. And now that he's cancer-free and has survived nineteen years, I should just abandon him, 'cause you said so? Fuck that."

"That's not what I'm saying!"

"No." She shook her head. "You're not saying shit!"

"You better watch who you're talking to."

"And who would that be? Because from where I'm standing I don't even see Bilal Asante, the man I married. What I see is a rotten asshole who's worked my last fuckin' nerve!" She tossed his keys at him, hitting him in the chest. "From this moment on, *my son* is off-limits." She picked up her purse and stormed out the front door.

Milan

Milan snaked her tongue lightly over Kendu's pecs and through his chest hair, working her way down his stomach. She dipped her tongue in and out of his navel, before making her way below his pubic bone.

She took him into her mouth, softly caressed his scrotum with her thumb, and French-kissed his dick. The taste of him was so sweet and so exquisitely rich that Milan was certain that she was receiving a gift. His manhood was more than filling; she actually had to use a special technique in order to deep throat him without gagging.

He pulled her hair gently, yet rough enough for her to feel his grip as she jaw broke him, forcing his cream to explode between her lips, some of it oozing from the corners of her mouth.

She swallowed. Then smiled.

They kissed, she eased up on his dick, and for the next hour he guided her hips until his pelvis contracted and he filled her vulva with more creamy gifts.

"Sssss . . ." he hissed as his sticky candy flooded between her thighs.

Milan came twice before collapsing and rolling over to his side. He cradled her in the crook of one arm. She tossed a thigh over his waist and wiped sweat from his brow. "I think you're pussy-whipped," she said proudly.

Kendu gave Milan a playful smirk. "The pussy is good." He caressed her thigh. "It was always good, from the moment I first popped that cherry—"

She rolled her eyes. "You are so crass—"

Kendu continued, "But it ain't like that."

"What. Ever."

"If anything"—he pointed to his middle—"Double Barrel got you going."

Milan's eyebrows rose. "Who the hell is Double Barrel?"

"My dick."

"Oh, puhlease. Get off your sack." She laughed. "Who names their dick Double Barrel?"

"What you want me to call it? Johnson? That shit is corny." He cupped his dick. "And besides, look at all this dick, what would you call it?"

"Damn," Milan said as she suggestively stuck one index finger in the corner of her mouth and ran the wet tip down the spine of his dick. "That is a lot of dick. Alright, since it's your birthday, I'll give you Double Barrel for the day."

"Oh, you'll give it to me, or is Double Barrel gon' give it to you?" Kendu said and Milan noticed that every time he looked at her his eyes lit up.

"You love me, don't you?" she asked.

"What you think?"

"I think I can't wait to be Mrs. Malik." She cupped his face and kissed him on the forehead. "I was thinking." She straddled him and stroked his box beard. "What if our wedding color was black?"

"Black?" He frowned. "It's not a funeral."

"Okay, what about coral?"

"Orange." He frowned. "Nah."

Milan sighed. "So then what's your suggestion?"

"I really don't care what the colors are."

"Yeah, right." Milan chuckled.

"I don't. What I care about is the budget. No more than ten thousand."

"You're getting high, right? Ten thousand? Are you kidding me? My dress is more than ten thousand."

"More than ten grand? Who the hell is the seamstress? Jesus?"

"Funny."

He placed his hands on her waist. "Why can't we have something simple? We go downtown, tie the knot, I give you my last name, and be out."

"You are so cheap."

"You weren't saying that when Double Barrel was freaking you." He softly bit her chin. "I was the man then."

"That's because you *were the man,* then, but now you're being a cheap-ass."

He laughed. "You know you're fly, right? Like the dopest chick I know."

"The dopest chick?" She twisted her lips to one side. "Like the hottest? Like, real super-fresh-funky-fly-dope? Or you just a lyin' niggah?"

"Nah," he said seriously. "I'm not lying. And I know I act crazy, but you and my daughter are my world."

"Are you sure about that?"

"Yeah." He placed a soft kiss on her lips. "I'm more than sure."

"Have you talked to Aiyannah since she left for Orlando?"

"Yeah," he smiled. "She called me and said that they were having a ball. My stepmother has a granddaughter Aiyanna's age so I'm sure they will have fun this summer."

"I'm sure they will." Milan said as she stroked the center of Kendu's chest with one of her index fingers. "So umm . . . your birthday is coming up soon and I was thinking that we should have the engagement party/birthday celebration."

"What?"

"You know, celebrate the engagement and your birthday on the same day."

"Hell no." He frowned. "I don't want a birthday party. Have the engagement party on another day."

"Why don't you ever want a party, Knott? Most people celebrate their birthdays."

"Most people have something to celebrate on their birthday."

She looked at him, confused. "And you don't? Do you know how blessed you are?"

"Look," he said, on edge. "I'm thankful to be alive. I'm grateful. Really, I am. But my birthday is not some international holiday and shit. It's the day my junkie-ass mother left my ass in the hospital and never came back."

Milan paused. Out of everything she knew about him, she never knew he hated his birthday. Tears filled her eyes. "Oh, Knott." She caressed his face. "I didn't know you felt like that." Tears wet her cheeks. "How come you never told me that before?"

"'Cause I knew you'd be doing just what you're doing now?" He wiped her tears.

"It's not about me. This is about you." She hesitated. "Maybe you should look for your mother."

Kendu stared at Milan as if she'd lost her mind. "Where did that come from? I would never look for her."

"Why?"

"Because I don't allow myself to want somebody who doesn't want me. Fuck her."

"Don't say that."

"Bitch is dead to me."

"You don't mean that." More tears clouded her eyes.

"Would you stop with the tears?" he said, clearly agitated.

"I'll help you look for her."

"Listen to me, I'm not motherfuckin' Antwone Fisher. I don't give a shit."

"Yes, you do."

"I just said *I didn't*." His jaw clenched. "And you're pissing me off. Maybe when I was a kid, I cared. When nobody wanted my ass, and I was shuffled around from place to place, I cared. Hell, I used to look at my teachers and shit, my neighbors, the local fuckin' fiends and wonder, 'Is that my mother?' Maybe I cared then." He lifted Milan off of him, and rose from the bed. "But I no longer give a fuck! Now if you want an engagement party, then plan it and I will be there. But no birthday celebrations."

"Knott."

"You heard what I said." He got off the bed, walked into the ensuite bathroom and slammed the door.

"What the hell just happened here?" Milan whispered to no one in particular as she lay in the center of the bed, staring at the vaulted ceiling.

"Vera, we need to talk." Taj said as he leaned against the closed bathroom door and spoke from behind it.

Vera's eyes scanned the digital clock on the wall. "Taj, baby." She struggled hard not to release a deep and aggravated sigh. "Can we please talk later tonight? I have an appointment this morning."

"You always have an appointment."

"Because I have businesses to run!"

"Right now I'm your business!"

Vera opened the door and stepped out fully dressed in a navy Armani pants suit. She smiled at the camera and then looked back to Taj. Now was not the time for a serious conversation. She walked into her closet and slid on her navy stilettos. "Taj, tonight. I promise."

"I've been trying to talk to you for a fuckin' week."

"And all I keep hearing you say is how long you've been try-ing to talk to me." She grabbed her makeup bag and sorted through it. "Just say it!"

"We need to talk about our family. Children."

Vera paused. She hated talking about children and babies, pregnancy, and staying home and expanding their family, which is what she knew Taj wanted to talk about, especially since that's all he ever wanted to talk about. But there was no way she wanted another child. One was enough, at least for right now.

She had other things to do.

Chances to take.

New discoveries to make, and having a baby would destroy her plan of kicking Susie Homemaker's ass to the curb. Vera had to claim her independence. She had to. Or else she would die . . . and death wasn't an option.

But he wanted a son, and she had promised to give him one . . . and she did, well almost.

"Taj, I'm bleeding," Vera said, as she lay in bed seven months pregnant with blood running between her legs.

"What?" he said, groggily stretching as he sat up.

Vera screamed as warm blood soaked into the sheets and spread like a spider's web. "Taj!" She panted in pain. "Help me!" She doubled over as her stomach cramped.

"Okay, baby, just relax." Taj's doctor voice kicked in, but she knew he was panicked. He called the ambulance. They came just as she passed out, and when Vera awoke, she was in the hospital and Taj's head was buried at the side of her thigh.

She rubbed her swollen stomach. She knew it was empty. "Taj." Her eyes peeled open.

"I'm here." He stroked her hair. "How are you feeling?"

"How's the baby?"

He stared at her. Hard. Deep.

"Taj."

He hesitated. "Vera, baby, you had toxemia . . . and your blood pressure was so high, Vera—"

"Where's my baby, Taj?" Her voice cracked, and her head felt like a chisel had stabbed through it.

He wiped her tears and held her hands. "The baby didn't make it."

Vera took a deep breath. *Count backward . . . ten . . . nine . . .* She sucked in another breath, held back tears, wiped her face, and quickly peeked in the mirror at her reflection. *Relax.*

Vera walked into the kitchen with Taj behind her. "How about I come by one of the salons, where are you, in Brooklyn today? And we have a late lunch before Skyy's recital this evening?" Taj asked.

Vera turned to face Taj. "Recital?"

"Her ballet recital? I know you didn't forget, Vera. It's tonight at seven." She could tell he was two seconds from losing it.

"No. No, I didn't forget. I'll meet you there, though. I can't do lunch." She looked back at the clock, and as she walked swiftly toward the front door Skyy shouted, "Mommy!"

Damn. I'm going to be late. She turned to face Skyy, who was standing with her arms folded and pouting. "What's wrong, baby?" She walked toward her daughter.

"I have an annountament to make." She placed her hands on her hips.

"It's announcement," Taj corrected her. "And wassup?"

"Yeah, tell us whatcha workin' wit, baby girl." Vera's Aunt Cookie stretched as she walked into the kitchen with her boyfriend, Boyden, following behind her.

"Mornin'," Boyden, who everyone called Uncle Boy, said as his red rabbit slippers slapped against the floor. He tied back the strings of his matching fur do-rag and smiled, his gold crowns shining. He walked over to Cookie, slid his hands around her waist, and looked into the camera. "Allow me to introduce myself. My name is Boyden and I'm Vera's daddy. Well, almost, considering I've never hit Rowanda off. Not that Rowanda isn't hot. I mean since she left crack alone she's not looking so ashy. But she's in Chicago and married, and besides she's not my type, 'cause Cookie's my boo."

"Oh, my God!" Vera snapped. "Aunt Cookie, please get him."

Cookie smiled into the camera. "Okay. Ver-ra." She said with perfect diction. "I shall get thy Uncle Boy." She turned to Boyden. "Would you sit yo' ass down?" She said tight-lipped. "Vera told us we could only spend the night if we acted as if the cameras weren't around, and your ass is up here profiling."

"I know how to act on TV," Boyden insisted.

"Divorce Court doesn't count," Cookie snapped.

Boyden spun around. "Like hell it doesn't. We got a free trip to L.A. and I went off so bad, the judge never knew we weren't really broken up."

"I knew you two looked familiar," Bridget said. "How lovely." She smiled at Vera. "I smell a spin-off coming on."

"Vera," Cookie said, calling for her attention. "I think you need to talk to your daughter." She pointed to Skyy who was still pouting.

"What's the problem, Skyy?" Vera felt as if she were being pulled in a million different directions at once. Out of habit she quickly fixed Skyy a bowl of cereal. "Tell mommy what's bothering you."

Skyy hopped into a seat next to her father at the island. "I'm dropping out of the dance recital, and if Ciara returns to my school in September, then I'm going to drop out of school too."

"What?" Vera and Taj said simultaneously.

"Skyy," Boyden said, "you can't get a G.E.D. in second grade."

Vera shot Boyden the evil eye. "Skyy, why don't you tell us what happened, because dropping out of school or the dance recital isn't an option." She placed Skyy's breakfast before her.

"Your mommy's right." Taj stroked Skyy's cheek. "So talk to us."

Skyy popped her lips and stuffed cereal into her mouth. "Nothing really happened, except I don't like Ciara anymore. She's not my best friend."

"Hell wit' her then," Boyden volunteered.

"Would you be quiet?" Vera said sternly.

"You don't tell me to be quiet," Boyden scolded Vera. "I raised you."

Vera ignored him and turned back to Skyy. "Why are you mad at Ciara?"

"Because she said I was playing with Sasha more than her. So she got mad and told me that I looked like Kermit the frog's dog."

"She said what?" Cookie said pissed. "You should've talked about her big ass—"

"Aunt Cookie," Taj said. "Don't tell her that. Skyy, you should've told the instructor."

"It's not nice to call names," Vera added.

"That's what I told her," Cookie said.

"*Shiiit*," Boyden attempted to whisper. "I wish a mothersucker would call me a damn dog."

"I tried to tell the instructor," Skyy said. "But she didn't listen to me. So I had to handle it."

"Handle it?" Taj said, taken aback. "And how did you *handle* it?"

"I told Ciara I'd rather look like Kermit the frog's dog than smell like a Puerto Rican whore."

Cookie and Boyden fell out laughing. They laughed so hard tears fell from their eyes.

"What?" Taj said. "Skyy, you need to apologize."

Vera looked toward her aunt and uncle. "Would. You. Stop?"

"We're sorry, Vera," Cookie said, doing her best to compose herself. "You're right. Skyy, that is unacceptable."

"Yeah, baby girl," Boyden added, "Leave 'Puerto Rican' off the next time. And besides, you have to go to school. Dropping out ain't cool."

"That's right," Cookie added. "And plus, two wrongs don't make a right."

"Now," Vera kissed Skyy on her forehead. "I want you to apologize to Ciara, and I'm sure you two will be friends again before you know it. Now Mommy has to go." She rushed toward the door.

"Mommy!"

"Yes, Skyy," Vera said annoyed. "What?"

Taj looked at Vera, surprised, and she instantly changed her tone. "Yes, honey."

"I love you and I can't wait for you to see my moves tonight!"

"And I'll be there with bells on!" Vera blew Skyy a kiss. "I love you, but I have to get going."

"Going where?" Taj asked. "And why are you in such a rush?"

"Bye, baby." She waved at Skyy.

"Vera," Taj called.

"Damn," she said, exhausted.

Taj walked up behind her. "Let me speak to you for a minute." He followed her into the hallway, with Bridget and Carl a short distance behind him.

"What the hell is going on? And don't lie!"

Vera sighed. She looked from the camera crew to him. She didn't have five minutes, but she had to find a way to give it to him. "Taj, I'm not lying to you about anything. I just have an appointment this morning and I can't be late."

"I *need* to talk to you. Today."

"Tonight. Please. I can't do lunch. And I really have to go," she said without taking a breath. She pressed the button for the elevator. It opened and she stepped on.

"Bye," she said as the doors closed.

Vera practically broke a heel as she hurried outside to where her driver waited. "Good morning, Richard," she said as she slid into the car with Bridget beside her. Carl sat in the front passenger seat and turned the camera toward Vera.

Bridget grinned. "I take it Taj doesn't know you're headed to Florida this morning?"

"No, he doesn't."

"And when are you going to tell him?"

"After HSN and my lawyers have inked the deal."

Five o'clock . . .

Vera looked at her cellphone as she paced back and forth from her seat to the ticket counter. There was a rainstorm in Florida, and she'd been waiting for her flight to be cleared for takeoff for over an hour. If she didn't leave soon, she'd miss Skyy's performance.

Fuck.

She took her seat, anxiously crossed her legs one way, then quickly crossed them the other. She looked at the time. *Five thirty.*

Her heart raced, and every time she looked at Bridget, who she knew loved the drama of her life falling apart, she wanted to smack her.

Six o'clock . . .

As Vera stormed over to the ticket counter, her heels stabbed the tiled floor and the loud clacking seemed to announce that not only was she on her way, but that she'd be pissed once she arrived. "Listen," she said to the ticket agent. "I know you're just doing your job, but I really need some answers. I need to be back on a plane right now to New York City, and I need you to tell me how you can make that happen."

"Ma'am, we're truly sorry about the inconvenience but safety comes first—" She paused. "Excuse me," she said to Vera as her desk phone rang. "Yes," she said into the phone. "Thank you." She placed the phone on the receiver. "Ma'am," she looked at Vera. "All first-class passengers can board now."

"Thank you." Vera smiled, relieved.

By the time Vera made it through bumper-to-bumper New York City traffic, grabbed a bouquet of flowers from a street vendor, and rushed into the recital, the children were taking their bows and the curtains were closing.

"Don't even try to explain this shit," Taj said, his jaw clenched. "Just act like you've been here all night."

"Mommy, Daddy!" Skyy ran over to them. "Did you see me, Mommy?" she asked excited. "I was so good."

"Yes, you were, baby."

"Skyy, where's your dance bag?" Taj asked.

"I left it backstage."

"Come on, let's go get it." He grabbed her by the hand and left Vera standing there.

"Where the hell were you, baby girl?" Boyden asked.

"I . . . umm, had something to do and I ran late," Vera said biting her bottom lip.

"You need to start making time for something besides yourself," Cookie added.

"Would you please?"

"Please what?" Cookie said aggravated. "I'ma tell you like my mama used to tell me. Idle hands is the devil's playground."

"What the hell are you talking about?" Vera said, frustrated.

"Slow down, baby girl." Cookie eyed Vera. "You know what I'm saying to you. You have been running around doing all kinds of shit other than what you need to be doing. You need to be around for your husband and your child."

"I resent that. I'm here for both of them!" Vera looked at the camera out of the corner of her eye. "And can we discuss this later?"

"Hell, nawl." Cookie said. "Where you do it at is where you get it at. I don't give a damn about those cameras. The truth is the truth and the truth at this moment is that you need to check yourself."

"Before you wreck yourself," Boyden added. "Now be quiet,

Vera. Because I haven't pulled up and tapped that ass in years—but don't push me."

"I don't need the guilt trip," Vera said, pissed.

"No," Cookie said. "You need your ass kicked! Coming up in here when the baby's dance is over. If I didn't know better, I'd say you just left a short stay."

"You're going too far," Vera warned. "I am not cheating on my husband."

"Really?" Taj said from behind Vera, causing her to jump. "Because I was damn sure wondering what the hell is really going on."

"Taj—" Vera turned toward him but before she could say anything more he'd grabbed Skyy by the hand and mingled into the bustling crowd of proud parents and gloating children.

The Club

Vera and Jaise were at the Setai Spa on Wall Street, waiting for Chaunci and Milan to arrive. They lounged in the full-service room, which had walls made of white grass cloth and blond-colored soapstone, bleached bamboo floors, chocolate-brown woven chairs, and candelabras hanging from the ceiling.

Warm towels were wrapped around their necks as they sat in reclining chairs dressed in white terry-cloth robes with their feet soaking in honey-scented water and rose petals.

A harpist strummed a soft melody. Vera closed her eyes and Jaise said, "It's so typical of these two hood buggers to be late." She looked at the camera, smirked, and turned back to Vera. "Last season, they were late every time we got together, and a few times they didn't even show up. They have the worst manners, I swear."

"Jaise, didn't we agree on a truce?"

"Girl, please. A truce among this clique means I won't call you a bitch to your face. I'll let you hear about it."

"Damn." Vera chuckled. "Well, when I start calling bitches"—

she swished her feet around in the water—"it will not be behind your damn back. And what the hell is a hood bugger?"

"We've arrived," Milan announced as she and Chaunci walked into the room, also dressed in white terry-cloth robes.

"You still want me to answer that?" Jaise mumbled. "Ladies," she said as Milan and Chaunci entered. "Glad you could make it."

"We were stuck in traffic," Milan said as she and Chaunci took their seats and dipped their feet into the water. "You know New York City."

"Where's Al-Taniesha?" Chaunci asked.

Bridget, who stood next to Carl, answered. "She said she didn't have time to be here today."

"Why?" Jaise pried.

"Said something about she and Lollipop are opening up a Chinese food/nail salon."

"What?" Milan laughed. "Are you serious?"

"You know Al-Taniesha," Jaise said. "Somebody probably taught her how to say chicken wing and full set in Chinese and she lost her damn mind."

All the women laughed until tears formed in their eyes. "I get so tired of that bitch," Jaise continued. "I swear she was placed on this Earth to haunt my ass."

"You do know she's not going anywhere," Chaunci said. "Especially since your son has a baby with her daughter."

"Tell me about it," Jaise said as the spa's host served each woman a glass of champagne.

Milan sipped. "Speaking of babies, Jaise, I heard from this little birdie that your son had another one. Seems he has a thing against using protection."

"And what does that have to do with you?" Jaise asked, annoyed.

"Well, since we agreed on a truce I figured I'd ask you and not pose the question in a tabloid." She chuckled. "I'm only kidding about the tabloid."

Jaise paused. She crossed her ankles in the water and did away with her first thought, which was to tell Milan to mind her own fuckin' business because last she checked, the weeds in her garden needed tending to. But instead she remained silent.

As far as Jaise was concerned Milan was ignorant. She had to be, because there was no way she understood the gut-wrenching turmoil her flip comments caused Jaise. Because if she did, she'd shut the fuck up and realize that the hurt and anguish Jaise felt behind not having a stellar kid and having failed as a mother was enough for her to snap at any moment, get up out of her chair, grip Milan by the roots of her hair, and drag her ass.

Jaise cleared her throat. "I think you better stick to discussing your engagement and leave my son alone."

"I only asked a question," Milan said. "I mean, you were the one bragging and everything at the reunion about how great Jabril was doing, headed to Morehouse and all."

"What's he doing now?" Chaunci asked. "Community college, at least?"

Jaise looked toward Vera whose eyes clearly said, "Handle 'em." And then she looked toward the camera and decided that she would check them, but she wouldn't stoop to their level to do it, she'd drop even lower.

"I was upset." Jaise admitted. "But you know he's only nineteen, not thirty-plus acting as if he's a man. And hell, it's not like these girls are as old as you two." She pointed to Chaunci and Milan. "I mean, Jesus, according to what I heard, you were crying, Milan, about Kendu not thanking you at his retirement dinner, and all I could think was, 'Why would a man thank a woman who's always available to be used?' Last I checked jump-off was a thankless position."

"Checkmate." Vera laughed as she lay back in her chair and the aesthetician placed cucumber slices over her eyes.

"You're going too far," Milan warned.

"Oh, my goodness, am I really?" Jaise clutched her chest and said in an exaggerated southern drawl. "And you, Chaunci. I mean, my goodness, how did you feel when you proposed to a man and hadn't even checked to see if he already had a wife?"

Chaunci was completely taken by surprise.

"Seems we have the same birdie," Jaise said as the aesthetician began to paint her face with a vanilla scrub. "Oh, that scrub smells delicious."

"Truthfully, Jaise," Chaunci said. "As far as I'm concerned the busted bitch can have Idris."

"Damn, he left you for a busted bitch, oh, my," Jaise said. "That's even worse."

Vera laughed as she lifted a cucumber slice from over one eye. "I could've sworn we said we were going to move on from the pettiness."

"Touché," Jaise agreed. "But hey, all's fair in love and bitch-slaps."

"Look, I didn't come here to start drama," Milan said. "I came here to have a relaxing time. And I just figured I'd ask you to your face, Jaise, what I wanted to know."

"Exactly," Chaunci said. "But Vera's right. Let's end this before it turns into a war."

"Yeah, let's," Milan agreed.

The women were silent for the next half hour. The harpist's melody was the only sound in the room until Jaise turned to Chaunci and said. "Honestly, Chaunci, I know how you feel. I mean, last year when I caught Trenton with that trick he was sleeping with, you were there for me, so if you need anything, advice, whatever I can offer, just let me know."

"Thanks, Jaise," Chaunci said, as she lay on the massage table with her arms crossed under her chin, and the therapist kneading her shoulders. "I'm trying like hell to let the shit go. But it's soooo hard."

"Do you still love him?" Jaise asked.

"I think so," Chaunci said. "But I'm confused. When he was with me, I wasn't so sure, but now that he's with that bitch Shannon, I feel like I did love him. And I feel like she took my man from me. And I know it sounds crazy and immature, but I truly feel like this heifer kidnapped his ass and now this motherfucker has Stockholm syndrome."

"Which means you really *didn't* love him," Jaise said. "You just didn't expect him to want anyone else."

"Maybe you have a point," Chaunci admitted.

"Or maybe your time was up," Vera squinted. "Nobody has to wait for you to get it together."

"Obviously so," Chaunci said. "Because Idris is Mr. Happy with his new wife, her son, and my daughter."

"Does Kobi like her?" Jaise asked.

"She just met her the other day," Chaunci said. "And when Shannon and Idris introduced her son to Kobi they introduced him as Kobi's brother. 'We don't use the term "step,"' Shannon said. 'We're a family.' I wanted to scream, 'No, bitch you're not family! I'm family. You're nothing.' Honestly, I wanted to kick her fuckin' ass!"

"Baby mama isn't quite standing up next to wife." Vera interjected, taking the cucumber slices off of her eyes. "So she was right. They are a family."

"Yeah, pretty much," Jaise said. "They are a family and if she's anything like my ex-husband's new wife she's going to remind you that she's his wife every damn chance she gets. Bitch."

"And furthermore," Vera said. "You should be happy she wants to embrace your child. Any mature woman who marries a man with a child is going to love the child as if it were her own. And second of all, it really pisses me off that women always want to fight one another. But I have yet to hear a woman say she wants to kick a man's ass. Shannon doesn't owe you anything. And I mean, really, if you didn't love Idris, or if you did love him, but you blew your chance, then you should understand that life will go on—with or without you."

"Oh, please," Milan said. "How the hell is he going to ask her to marry him and seven months later he shows up with some skank on his arm? Give me a break."

"Listen, that's a question that Chaunci needs to ask him," Vera said. "But Shannon didn't ask him to marry her. It was the other way around. Hell, maybe he was seeing her before Chaunci crept back into his life. I watched the show last season. Don't you think he had a life before he met back up with you? Shit, it's not your world and things happen without you."

Chaunci looked Vera over. "Well, you seem to know a lot more about the situation than I do. You wanna tell me why you're getting so upset, you act as if you know the bitch or something."

"Actually," Vera leaned forward. "I do."

"What?" Chaunci said shocked and the other women fell silent.

"Yes, I do. Shannon is my childhood friend and I mean, you seem cool, but all that rah-rah you're talking, you need to bring that down, because where I'm from bitches get their asses beat for talking too much."

"Ding!" Bridget said as she snickered.

Chaunci was shocked. "So all of this time you listened to me moan and complain and you and Idris's wife are best fuckin' friends! You should've told me that!"

"I don't owe you any explanations!" Vera spat. "I know how to be cordial to you and be best friends with my best friend. The only difference now is you know not to come out the side of your mouth about Shannon."

"Well how about this?" Chaunci rose from her chair.

"You can stand up," Vera said. "But I don't advise you to bring your ass over here."

"Now, ladies," Jaise said. "Let's remember our truce."

"Fuck a truce," Chaunci spat. "Here I am thinking perhaps I can build a friendship with all of you and all this time Vera's friends with Idris's wife. That is so fucked up. You should've told me that from the jump and then it would've been my decision how much of my life I wanted to share with you."

"Like I said," Vera stressed. "I don't owe you any explanations. Now if you want to be friends, then cool, let's be friendly, but if you want a war, I'm letting you know upfront, don't bring any knives to gunfights."

"And make sure you take your own advice." Chaunci looked toward Milan. "I'm leaving because I need a drink."

"I'm right behind you."

Milan and Chaunci switched out the room and as they stepped through the door Jaise and Vera looked at each other and fell out laughing. "Betchu they learn to shut the fuck up now," Jaise said.

Chaunci

The day's sun faded into Manhattan's evening sky, streaking the air with highlights of gold and fire red as Chaunci stood on her terrace and held a wine glass in the air. "Honestly," she said as she looked into the camera. "I didn't like the bitch from the first hello. So that little spa date did nothing more than open the coffin shut . . . shut the coffin . . . nail it open." Her words slurred slightly. "You get my point."

I better give the wine a rest.

Bridget smiled. "You all have the same terms of endearment for one another so please tell the camera which bitch you're talking about."

"Vera." Chaunci sipped and lifted her eyes above the glass. "And it has nothing to do with Shannon. And by the way I read a blog the other day that claimed an insider said I was jealous of Vera, so let me just take a moment and straighten that shit out."

"So what's your response?" Bridget asked.

Chaunci tilted her head to the side. "My response is hell-the-fuck no." She turned the wine bottle over her glass and only three drops plopped out.

Did I drink this whole bottle?

"Anyway," Chaunci continued. "Jaise may be kissing Vera's ass and Milan may be laid back and trying to be friendly, but I'm not scared of Vera. Her l'il 'I used to be a cripette' or whatever the hell routine she has, doesn't intimidate me. I will curse Vera out and take her ass down if I have to. And you can put all my money on that."

I hope I am not coming across as drunk as I feel. Damn, I need a V8.

"Vera seems to be very strong-willed," Bridget said. "And she doesn't back down from much. In a lot of ways you two are alike."

"Chile, please." Chaunci tooted her lips and waved her hand. "Her greatest wish is to be like me. But that's just not going to happen, now is it?" she said sarcastically. Motioning her hands like a scale she said, "Journalism." She lifted one hand high. "And hair grease." The other hand sank. "Not. Even. In the same league."

"Pardon me, Ms. Morgan." Dextra, Chaunci's Trinidadian au pair, stood in the doorway. "Kobi called. She say it's story time on de sky or some'ting like dat," Dextra said confused. "I asked her to hold and she say she would meet you on the computer."

Chaunci struggled to sound sober as she said to Dextra, "When she's at her dad's we do story time via Skype."

"Skype? What tis dat?" Dextra asked.

"It's a visual conversation on the computer. She sees me and I see her."

"Ai-yi-yi. You young people. Well, she's waiting for you and I'm going to be leaving now. I'll see you in a few days when Kobi returns."

"Goodnight, Antie." Chaunci waved.

"Goodnight, my dear." She walked out of the doorway and a few moments later closed the front door behind her.

"Dextra has been a part of our family since Kobi was a baby and we wouldn't trade her for the world." Chaunci did her all not to tilt to one side or the other as she walked toward her home office. Never before had walking this short distance in her apartment been a struggle. Knocking off an entire bottle of Chardonnay was not her intention. Her intention was to simply have a glass of wine with her dinner—two glasses at most—enough to chase away the loneliness that nested in her chest and the horniness that crept between her thighs.

Chaunci took a deep breath and turned on the computer. She logged onto Skype and in a few seconds Kobi appeared on the screen. She sat in the center of a pink canopy bed and was dressed in a hot pink tutu, a sleeveless Princess Tiana night shirt, and a tiara tilted on her head.

Her chin rested in her left palm as her eyes drooped, her top lip was tucked in and her bottom lip was poked out. "Hi, mommy," she said with a drag. "It's story time." She held up the book on her lap.

"Hi, baby." Chaunci paused. *Would you get your drunk ass together?* "Why do you look so sad?"

"No reason." Kobi flipped her book open. "I'm ready to read so that I can go to bed."

"What's wrong, Kobi? Tell mommy."

Tears filled Kobi's eyes and ran over her cheeks.

Chaunci's heart pounded and suddenly she felt sober again. "Kobi, look at me." Kobi complied and Chaunci continued. "Please, tell me what's wrong."

Kobi ran her fingers across her lips. "I have to learn to zip it. I've already said too much. And Shannon told me if I spilled the beans it would be big trouble. I don't want her trouble, Mommy. She knows karate."

Am I hearing right? Maybe I'm still drunk. I need a cup of coffee. "Kobi, you can tell Mommy anything."

"Mommy, you have to promise not to say a word." She folded her hands in a prayers position and shook them. "Please. I need to see my daddy again and Shannon told me if I opened my fat mouth that I wouldn't be able to visit them anymore. And Mommy, I don't want to be without my daddy anymore. Remember I used to cry at night because I wanted a daddy? Now I have one, I don't want to make him go away. I'm just going to be quiet and do whatever Shannon says."

"Wait a minute. Wait a motherfuckin—" Chaunci paused. *Woosaaaa* . . . She exhaled slowly. "Kobi, start from the beginning. What exactly happened?"

Kobi swallowed. Chaunci could see the hesitancy and fear on her face.

"It's okay," Chaunci said calmly. "You can tell Mommy anything."

"Mommy," Kobi sniffed. "Shannon's mean."

Chaunci's heart thundered. *Don't jump to conclusions.* "Why do you think she's mean?"

"She told me I had to go to bed. But Omari got to stay up and watch T.V. And mommy, Ms. Vera's daughter, Skyy, is over here and she and Omari were teasing me, saying I had a big mouth and that's why I had to go to bed." She sobbed.

Chaunci looked at the clock: 8:00 p.m. *Don't go flying over there. Relax.* She took a deep breath. *Now ask her where Idris is.* "Kobi, where is your daddy?"

"He and Shannon are out getting their party on. I think they're at a club."

"Who's there with you and the other two children?"

"This mean old lady name Aunt Cookie who told me that I was too grown."

"Why did she say that?"

"No reason at all. I just told her that a woman didn't have to settle for a man just because he was fine and that Ms. Shannon should learn that."

Chaunci blinked. "Why would you say something like that? Where did you get that from?"

"I heard you tell Ms. Milan that once. And I overheard Shannon complaining that my daddy was getting on her nerves and if he wasn't so fine she would teach him a lesson. I just called myself being helpful, Mommy. But Aunt Cookie told Shannon and now they both turned on me."

"You shouldn't have said that, Kobi."

"You're taking her side?"

"No. I'm always on your side, but right is right. Now tell me about the part where she said you should zip it or you won't see your daddy again."

"Because after Aunt Cookie told on me, Shannon said, 'You need to learn to shut up and zip it! I can't stand you. And if you keep talking, not only am I going to beat your behind, you will not be able to come over here again!'"

"Oh really?" Chaunci arched her brow. "And where was your daddy?"

"He just stood there."

"He just stood there!" Chaunci rose from her chair and paced before the computer. She turned back toward the computer screen. "I'm coming to get you."

"No, Mommy." Kobi's eyes widened. "Then Daddy will be mad at me and I won't see him again."

You're right because I'ma kill the motherfucker. "Kobi, nothing will come between you and your daddy."

"Shannon will, Mommy. She told me that. She said, 'I will come between you and your daddy.' Please Mommy, I want to stay."

Chaunci swallowed. *Think . . . Think . . . Think . . . Deep breaths.* "Okay, Kobi. I'm going to try it your way, but I will be there to get you in the morning."

"Okay, Mommy. I love you. We can read the story tomorrow when I come home, okay?"

"Okay," Chaunci said, trying her best not to reveal that she was still brewing inside. "I love you, too, and yes, we will read the story tomorrow."

Chaunci's computer screen went black and a few moments later her screen saver of Kobi's baby picture danced across her screen. *I'ma cuss this motherfucker out.* She picked up her phone and dialed Idris's cellphone.

No answer.

She paced. *He just stood there? Really, Idris?*

She dialed his number again.

His voice mail came on. She left a message. "This is Chaunci. I need to speak with you. It's important."

Chaunci turned toward the camera and she could see Bridget looking at her intensely. She turned away and just as she walked toward the window the phone rang. She scurried over to answer. It was Idris.

"Hello?"

"Chaunci?" Idris said, shouting. There was a ton of noise in the background. "Can you hear me?"

"Yeah," she said pissed. "I can hear you. Can you hear me?"

"Yeah, wassup?"

Be calm. "What . . ."—She took a deep breath—"the fuck . . ." inhale "is Kobi doing at your house," exhale "and you're out clubbin'?"

"Excuse me?"

"You heard me," she spat. "Like, seriously, Idris, you're almost forty years old and you're at a club with your wife while your daughter is at your house crying her eyes out? What the hell kind of shit is this? My child could've stayed the hell home if you weren't going to treat her right, and tell your wife that I will fuck her ass up over my child! And you better—hello? Hello?" *I know this motherfucker didn't just hang up on me?* Chaunci looked at her iPhone and the screen read, "Call disconnected." *This negro has lost his damn mind.*

Chaunci quickly dialed him back. No answer.

She called again. No answer.

And again. Straight to voice mail.

She paced the room.

"Chaunci," Bridget said. "We're going to rap it up for the night."

No response.

"I know you're too upset to talk about what just happened and I'm sure you want to race over to Idris's house and wait for him. And we would love to film that, but I know you're bigger than that and charging over to someone's house is not your style."

Nothing. Chaunci continued to pace.

"And besides, like Kobi said, they aren't there, anyway. They're at the very place we're headed."

Chaunci stopped in her tracks.

Bridget smirked. "The ballroom at the Metropolitan. The Moroccan room."

Chaunci resumed pacing.

Bridget continued. "Kobi had it wrong when she said a club. Shannon's hosting a fund-raiser for the homeless and pretty much everyone's there. Vera's there, Jaise is there. I could—"

Before Bridget could continue, Chaunci walked out of her home office and headed straight toward her walk-in closet. She slipped on a pair of four-inch Manolos and a beaded midriff jacket, which instantly dressed up the fitted True Religion jeans and black camisole she wore. She pulled her hair back into a ponytail, tucked her clutch beneath her arm and stormed out the door.

"Carl!" Bridget screamed as they hurried behind Chaunci. "Let's roll!"

Vera

Vera stood in her custom-designed dressing room, looking
in her trifold mirror and staring at Taj's beautiful reflection.
Her lips eased into a crescent moon as she admired her
husband. He was dressed in the smoothest Yves Saint Laurent
tuxedo she'd ever seen, and the sexy way his dreads draped over
his shoulders made her clit thump like an erratic heartbeat. No
matter her inner turmoil, they were soul mates, lovers beyond the
mortal realm of being in love. He could practically read her mind,
which is why she knew that he knew that she had some shit—
which he wouldn't like—to tell him.

She swallowed and diverted her eyes from his reflection.

Can he really read my mind?

Don't be ridiculous.

She resumed puckering her lips and dressing them with lipstick. The jazz band Art Of Noise played an uptempo beat
through the surround sound as Vera found her gaze wandering
back to Taj's reflection, where his eyes clearly asked her, "What's
the problem?"

"Nothing," she said beneath her breath. *And this isn't the time.* She quickly looked at the camera crew and smiled.

She stole another glance at Taj.

Is he even blinking? Her lipstick slipped from her hand and rolled onto her royal-blue cocktail dress. She looked at the small smudge it left behind and bit one corner of her bottom lip. Damn. *Would he look another way?*

She dabbed the smudge away with a baby wipe and then patted Angel perfume behind her ears.

Am I losing my mind?

She reached over to her all-glass vanity for her emerald-and-diamond choker and tried to fasten it around her neck. She failed and the jewels crashed against the glass, causing her to jump for fear of damage. She inspected the vanity. Nothing.

She held the necklace in her hand. She didn't want to ask for Taj's help because him getting too close might make her slip and say some shit.

Before she could decide what to do, Taj said, "Let me help you with that." Reluctantly, she handed him the necklace, struggling like hell to maintain a smile.

"Are you okay?" Taj asked, fastening the clasp.

"Yes," she said a little too quickly. "I'm fine."

Taj paused. "All right," he said as if he were saving the rest of his thoughts for later. "We need to talk, though."

"I know."

"No matter what, you know I love you. We haven't been right since the recital and I want to get things back together for us."

"I know. I do too."

Taj smiled. "You smell delicious." He slid his hands around her waist. "And you look delectable." He kissed her on one side of her neck.

Vera took a step back, but instead of letting her go Taj pulled her closer, and they locked eyes. She absorbed every inch of him and his gaze reminded her that he wasn't just a doctor. He was a doctor with Brick City roots and a South 14th Street swagger who not only knew her better than she knew herself, but when he got pissed or thought she was hiding some shit, he didn't hesitate to let his thuggism take the place of being politically correct.

Vera straightened his tie. "You look so handsome."

He paused. "And you look even better." He paused again. "You know I love you."

Why is he telling me that again? "I love you most—"

"Carl," Bridget interjected. "Cut the camera off."

"Why?" he asked, baffled.

"Because I need to know if you have a gun."

"A gun?" Carl said, taken aback.

"Yes, a gun!" Bridget screamed. *"Because I need to be put out of my misery!"* She pounded her fist on the heated marble wall. "What the hell is going on here?" She paced. "What. The. Hell. Is. Going. On. Here! Really, I need to know!" She placed her right hand like a sun visor over her eyes and spun around. "Are violinists and ballet dancers going to skip through here at any moment? Jesus, Mary, and Joseph! Somebody save me! I'm dying of boredom."

"Why are you carrying on, Bridget?" Vera asked, pissed.

"Because this is ridiculous! Do you need a script? If so, I have plenty!" Bridget snatched her briefcase off the edge of the chaise. "Which would you like?" She pulled out a pile of papers. "Something basic: financial problems, cheating, he doesn't make your love meter rise? Or are you looking for an Academy Award? If so, he needs to be gay. Or even better, you need to be gay. A Millionaire Wife on the down low! Nielsen ratings will soar through the roof!"

"You're going too far," Vera said.

Bridget yawned and patted her lips. "If I'd listened every time I was told that, I would've never had an affair with a priest. I'd still be a goddamn nun, a tight-ass virgin, counting rosary beads, all while losing my mind! So save your intimidation tactics for your costars. They don't work on Sister Mary-Francis. I mean, Bridget." She shook her head in disgust. "Is Milan going to be the star again this season? Je-sus! You need to kick it up a notch, Vera. Crip-walk or something. Or better yet," she said, as if a lightbulb had just gone off. "Why don't we chat about what's really been going on? Let's start with the interview you did yesterday?"

Vera gasped slightly and Taj's eyes landed on her mouth. "What's really been going on? Interview? What interview?" he asked.

"Nothing really going on except, you know," Vera hesitated. "We all give interviews that'll be aired during the show when the new season starts."

"And?" Taj pressed.

"And nothing," Vera said and Taj watched her as she bit her bottom lip.

"You're lying to me now?" he said more as a statement than a question.

"No. It just isn't the right time to talk to you about it."

"About what?"

Bridget snapped, "About how she wants to open a new salon in L.A., and maybe one in Atlanta. About how her salons here in New York are running themselves and are virtually unfulfilling. And about how she needs to do something besides cook for you,"—she pointed at Taj—"and play mommy all day, God forbid. She loves the kid, obviously, but she's a woman too. And blah, blah, blah, you get the picture. Simply put: She doesn't want to be your trophy wife."

"You said all that?" Taj said, taken aback, releasing Vera from his embrace.

Vera watched a road map of veins come alive in his neck. "Taj—"

"The cameras roll and suddenly you're brand-new? This is how we doin' it?"

"Taj—"

"Excuse me for cutting you off, Vera," Bridget said. "But Taj, she also wanted to talk to you about HSN's offer to market her hair products—the ones she's been selling in her salons." Bridget winked.

"I don't believe you just said that!" Vera spat in disbelief. "I should beat your ass!"

Bridget pointed her hands like guns. "And that would make for even better TV. Now, roll tape, Carl."

"You're a genius, Bridget." Carl smiled as he focused the camera. "A damn genius."

"Taj, can we talk about this later?" Vera said. "We don't want to be late for the charity event."

"No, we gon' talk about this shit right now." Taj's nostrils flared. "And what the hell is HSN?"

"Home Shopping Network," Bridget said. "Carl, get a close-up on Taj's face. His expressions are priceless. Hell, we might be able to do this episode in 3-D."

"Bridget, Bridget, Bridget!" Carl squealed.

Taj spat at Vera, "You back on that Home Shopping shit? So you've been running around here not picking up Skyy from camp, missing her dance recitals, and doing everything else other than talking to me, your husband. And instead of you being up front with me and here for our child, you're running around getting high off bullshit!"

Vera blinked. *Has this negro gone crazy?* "First of all, you don't let another chick, Bridget or anyone else, tell you some shit about me and get all huffy. And second of all, I don't appreciate you saying that I'm putting anything before our child!"

"That's not what I'm saying!" Taj snapped.

"Then what *are* you saying?"

"I'm saying that you seem to be talking to everybody else but me."

"Because everybody else listens!"

"Oh, I don't listen to you now?"

"Every time I've ever tried to talk to you about what I want to do, you change the subject. I am not your goddamn Susie Fuckin' Homemaker!" She pointed at her reflection in the trifold mirror. "And you are not about to turn me into some robotic bitch!" She looked around her crowded dressing room. "This is just too much!"

"Oh, I get it. Taj is the bad guy. The villain. Is that your role on this show? The victim?"

"I resent that."

"I tell you what. Since I've been telling you what to do and you wanna pretend that you've been listening, then this is what you *will do:* You *will keep* your ass home. No L.A. No Atlanta. And definitely no Home Shopping Shit. And I don't wanna hear any more about it. Now, unless you've got something else to get off your chest, I'm ready to go."

"And cut!" Bridget screamed in glee. "Perfect scene, people, perfect scene."

"Cut? Oh, hell, no," Vera snapped. "Ain't no cut unless somebody's getting cut the fuck up. Did you just tell me what the hell I *will* do? Yeah," she said, answering her own question. "I believe you did." She grabbed her purse and started to sort through it. "Let me see if I can help you find your goddamn mind, because you have lost that motherfucker." She pointed at Taj.

"Vera—" Taj tried to interrupt.

"Vera my ass. Don't you ever tell me what I will do! Since when did I sign up for you to be my goddamn boss? I agreed to marry you. I agreed to have a child with you. But I never agreed to give up who I was and what I wanted!"

"And I didn't ask you to."

"That's because you can't."

"Vera," Taj said sternly, as he looked around at Bridget and the camera crew salivating at their every word. "We can talk about this later. We need to go."

"Fuck that." She tucked her clutch securely beneath her arm. "This needs to be a solo night out." And before he could protest Vera stormed out of the room, swaying her hips in rage from side to side.

The Club

Chaunci walked into the Metropolitan, parted the velvet drapes, and strutted into the Moroccan ballroom. As she crossed the threshold and spotted Shannon, Vera, and Jaise, she knew then she was at war with the truth. The truth of her being jealous, and mad, and pissed that somehow love and happiness and contentment had gone on without her, while all of these bitches: Vera, Jaise, and Shannon, seemed satisfied.

Chaunci hated being jealous, especially since she couldn't stand Vera and Shannon, and Jaise simply pissed her off. She had to get rid of this nagging feeling because this was not the mission she intended.

This was to be a selfless mission that required her to be strong as steel, focused, and capable of taking Idris's ass to task and fucking him up—if need be—for leaving her baby crying while he and his wife were getting "their party on." Bastards.

With Bridget and a cameraman on her heels Chaunci swung her hips into overdrive, parted Idris's small circle of friends and associates, and tapped him on the shoulder. He quickly turned around and his eyes revealed a pissed surprise.

"When you hung up on me"—Chaunci placed one hand on her hip—"I wasn't done." She placed the other hand on the respective hip.

"What are you doing here?" Idris said in a low yet stern tone. He grabbed Chaunci lightly by her forearm and forced her to walk a few inches away from the group he'd been talking to.

"Didn't I just explain that to you?" She snatched her arm away. "And don't touch me again!" She brushed a nonexistent wrinkle from her sleeve. "Now, I tried being polite and calling you on your shit via the telephone, but you wanted to get it crunked and I don't do well with telephone bullies. So here I am. Now, as I was saying, I don't appreciate my child calling me crying hysterically, screaming about some nasty babysitter, a set of bad-ass kids—including your *stepson*—and how *your* wife told *my* child that she better learn to zip it, that she wouldn't be able to see you anymore, and that if she didn't learn to shut up she was going to beat her ass—"

Idris's jaw tightened as he raised his voice. "Shannon didn't—"

"The gold diggin' bitch did, and you know it. My child said that Shannon's ass was mean and I believe her—"

"You better—"

"No, you better check that bitch's mouth before I check her in the mouth. Now truthfully you ran off and married out of desperation and I guess she has your pussy-whipped-wussy-ass fooled, and that's cool, but you better make sure she treats Kobi Sarai Morgan right or I'ma bust her ass. Period." Chaunci pointed into his face.

"You are way over the top and completely out of line!"

Chaunci sucked her teeth. "I don't give a damn. Fuck the line." She spat as her words slurred, reminding her that she had had one too many tonight.

Across the room Vera wrinkled her brow as she stood talking to Shannon and Jaise. She pointed behind the cameraman who was filming. "Is that . . . ummm, Chaunci?" She paused. "Why is she flinging her arms in the air?" She paused again. "Is she arguing with Idris?"

All the women turned toward the action.

"Shannon," Vera said. "Is she really showing her ass over there?"

"You need to handle her," Jaise insisted.

"Oh, I will," Shannon said pissed.

"Well, let's go," Vera said and she and Shannon walked toward Idris and Chaunci.

Jaise looked into the camera and said, "I guess we don't need Al-Taniesha to see how new-money-*ghett-tow* rolls. No offense. I adore my new friends. I'm just making an observation." She shook her head as she strutted across the room.

"This chick has lost her damn mind," Shannon said as she approached Chaunci and Idris who were so engulfed in their argument that neither of them realized they were drawing a crowd of whispering onlookers with every passing second. "I really don't want to take my Jimmy Choos off and beat this hoe's ass, but I will."

"Chaunci," Jaise said, attempting to break up the argument. "I know you're much more of a lady than this. Let me speak to you for a minute—"

"When I'm done checking this motherfucker," Chaunci spat. "I'll get to you."

"Shannon," Jaise whispered. "Call security. Have her ass arrested."

"We don't call security," Shannon said, as she stepped in between Idris and Chaunci. "I am security. So Chaunci, you need to calm down and tell me what the problem is."

Chaunci looked Shannon over and snarled, "If you don't back your ass up—".

"Look." Shannon released a frustrated sigh. Her voice evident that she was attempting to be diplomatic, she said, "What. Is. Your problem?"

"Shannon," Idris said to his wife. "Don't argue with her. I'm going to have her escorted out of here." He looked toward the door and motioned for security to come near.

"Oh, no you didn't, motherfucker!" Chaunci screamed. "Why don't you tell your wife about how to treat your daughter right instead of trying to put me out!" She looked Shannon dead in the face. "You want to know my problem? You and this punk motherfucker are my problems—"

"What's going on?" One of the security guards asked as they approached the argument.

No one answered them and instead the spat continued. Shannon snapped, "Wait a minute—"

"I don't have any more goddamn minutes," Chaunci said. "So, I'ma handle this shit right now!"

Shannon interjected. "You need to—"

"No, what *you need* to do is stay in your damn lane and understand that you better not *ever* threaten my child!"

"What!" Shannon said in disbelief.

Idris shook his head. "She claims that Kobi called her—"

"What the hell is '*she claims*'?" Chaunci spat. "Tell her how our child called me crying hysterically about how your wife was in her face being mean and screaming about how she needs to learn to zip it, she wouldn't be able to see you again, and that she was going to beat her ass. Now, I'ma give you about two point five seconds to straighten this shit out or I'ma do it. Because the truth of the matter is Kobi doesn't know her that well and hell, you either. So let the replacement bitch know that I'm not the one." She looked Shannon over and then turned back to Idris.

Shannon chuckled in disbelief. "You have lost your mind! I am not that bitch who takes kindly to threats, so let me just *straighten you out*. I'm far from a replacement, bitch. By no means did I pop into your life, you popped into mine! Idris and I were a couple for five years and then all of a sudden, here you come, the return of the jilted college girlfriend who had a baby and kept her a secret."

Chaunci felt gut punched.

Shannon continued. "Idris and I are not fly by night. Yo' ass was fly by night! I was the one who broke off my relationship with my man, because I didn't want to be bothered with any baby-mama drama. But nevertheless, here you are."

"That's right. And when you mess with my baby, I will definitely have some drama for your ass."

"Trust me, you don't wanna go there with me. Now whatever went on between you two and why your relationship didn't work out is none of my business or my goddamn concern."

"Then what are you bringing it up for?" Chaunci said pissed. "And if you're the same chick that he told me about—when I was riding his dick—then all he did was compare you to me. Which means you were a fill-in for the five years you were together and now that you're married, you're still a fuckin' fill-in."

"Ladies, we need to break this up," one of the security guards said.

"Chaunci, you need to leave," Idris said.

"Negro, please." Chaunci spat. "When I'm done, I will leave. Now let's get back to the subject at hand—Kobi."

"Chaunci," Shannon said. "We all know that your jealous ass really isn't here because of Kobi, but since you'd rather pretend that this is truly your reason then hear me when I say this: when Kobi comes to my house I'm the mother there and she's too grown. Now, I didn't tell her she couldn't see her father but I did tell her that she needed to keep out of my conversation and that if she kept getting into it she'd be staying home when we went to Dorney Park next week, because I don't reward bad behavior."

"That's not your place," Chaunci said. "She has a father. He can handle the discipline."

"You don't make the rules for me!" Shannon screamed. "Now if you don't want your child spoken to, then what you can do to help her out is teach her how to stay in a child's place, because I don't deal with grown children."

"Like I said, her father can handle the discipline!" Chaunci spat.

"Ladies," the guard said. "We really can't have this in here. If you don't stop, we will have to physically escort you out of here."

"Shannon, let's just calm down," Idris said.

Shannon side-eyed Idris and continued. "Like *I said* and like I told her father, when Kobi is in my house she will abide by my rules. And when she's out of line, I'ma check her ass. Now, I was trying to give your child a pass. But since she's added lying to the mix, that's a whole other situation."

"And what the hell does that mean?" Chaunci asked.

"That means if she lies on me again I'ma tap her ass and I don't give a damn who doesn't like it. Now I don't know how you do it, but where I'm from kids get a backhand for the shit that comes out of their mouths. So what you better do is teach her some manners or I will take her and—"

Smack! Before Shannon could finish Chaunci reared her hand back and slapped her so hard that Shannon's neck jerked to the right and seemed to get stuck there. Cameras flashed and reporters buzzed as if it was a heavyweight fight.

Idris and Vera immediately stepped between the two women. But not before Shannon returned Chaunci's slap with a back hand. "Are you crazy?" Vera screamed.

"What the hell are you doing?" Idris yelled at Chaunci. "You can't come in here attacking my wife." He held Shannon back.

"Let her ass go!" Shannon said.

"Chaunci, if you don't leave now," Idris said, "I will be pressing charges."

"Zoom in, Carl!" Bridget screamed. "Housewives gone wild!"

Chaunci froze. She didn't expect to stand silent and not move, she expected to fling her arms in the air and allow her punches to fall wherever they landed, but something about the camera being pointed in her face, Idris holding Shannon back, and Bridget screaming like a Jerry Springer hype-man, took her breath away. She didn't need to be here, not like this. She needed to handle Shannon and Idris, but this type of ruckus and at this level could only lead to her blacking out and laying Shannon on the ground. But that would lead to jail and it wasn't worth it, so she attempted to collect herself by dusting her shoulders and tucking her purse. "I'm done. Because I've made my point."

"And you've met your damn match," Shannon spat as Chaunci turned toward the door and disappeared behind the velvet curtain with every reporter and clicking camera in tow.

"That was some down low, low-down, *and country*"—Jaise took a toke off her cigarette and flicked the ashes into the midnight breeze—"trailer. Park. Bullshit." She released a cloud of smoke and looked toward Carl, who was riding in Jaise's car, conducting an interview about what had happened earlier with Chaunci. "This was supposed to be the Millionaire Wives Club, not The Classless Hoes."

"So were you surprised by Chaunci's actions?" Carl questioned.

"Yes, I was quite surprised. We're supposed to be ladies at all times. At least that's how I was raised." Jaise mashed her cigarette into the ashtray. "But I believe Chaunci's from Murfree-ghetto-boro or something, so I guess that's how they do it down there. Real Clampett style." She nodded her head for emphasis. "A buncha damn Beverly Hoodbillies. Jesus. Chaunci ought to be ashamed of herself."

"So whose side were you on?"

"I was Team Shannon all the way. Anybody originally from low-income housing is not to be played with. I wouldn't even be seen on those sides of town, let alone mess with the people—with the exception of Vera, of course. Not that I have anything against the less fortunate." Jaise paused. "Carl, can you edit out that last comment. I wouldn't want anyone to think I'm not sensitive to the broke, I mean the poor."

"I'll have to talk to Bridget about that."

"Please." She smiled and hoped that he was done. She'd had enough to deal with and didn't want to waste another moment on Chaunci.

The autumn breeze blew into Jaise's face as she slid another cigarette into her mouth and lit it.

The driver filled the Rolls-Royce's sound system with Nina Simone's "Do I Move You?"

"Turn that up," Jaise said as her thoughts turned to her and Bilal's first date, when she'd sang her heart out to him. She was in a club full of people, yet she felt like the only one there. She pursed her lips and after she freed seductive *S*'s of smoke, she sang with the same fever and intense fire that she'd had that special night she sang for her man. The very night she knew she'd captured him.

"Do I soothe you? Tell the truth now/ The answer better be hell yeah . . ."

She sang from the bottom of her heart until the words led to tears and the tears led to flashbacks of the arguments they'd been having.

She stopped singing.

Wiped her tears.

Entertained memories and visions of the dismay, distance, and disconnect she'd seen in Bilal's eyes—a look that said he didn't know who or what they'd become.

And the truth of the matter was, she didn't know either. All she knew was that she wanted to find peace, because somehow it had been lost. And she needed to regain it because there was no way she could live like this.

Chain-smoking.

Overeating.

Crying.

Complaining.

Phony.

Not able to appreciate shit.

Not knowing her left from her goddamn right.

An attention whore, pimped by high drama, glitz, and riches, who would surely die a lonely-ass reality-TV vixen if she didn't get her shit together.

Jaise put out her cigarette as her car rounded the corner of her block. Pockets of her neighbors stood on their respective steps looking out into the street. "Oh, God," she said to no one in particular. "Mel Gibson must be roaming the neighborhood drunk and cussin' out Jews again."

She shook her head as her driver double-parked in front of her brownstone. She heard someone shouting, "I can't believe you gon' sneak that bitch over here! Riding around with her like I wouldn't see you!"

Bash! Clash! Boom!

Who the hell is that crazy heifer? Jaise stared out the window at the short woman with large breasts who swung a metal bat, bashing dents in the hood of a navy blue 2010 7 Series BMW parked in front of her house.

Is that my motherfuckin' car?

The raging woman continued. "Motherfucker, I'm tired of you fucking me and using me! You can't even pay child support, or see your daughter, but you can ride that bitch around!"

Bash! Clash! Boom! Glass flew into the street.

The deranged woman yelled, "Tell that bitch I said come outside, Jabril!"

Ja . . . . bril?

"Oh, hell the fuck no!" Jaise hopped out of her Rolls-Royce

and raced toward the action. "What the fuck are you doing? I bought that goddamn car! That's my goddamn car!"

"Ma, stay out of it."

Jaise turned to the left and Jabril stood there. "Don't tell me what the fuck to stay out of!" She snatched off her earrings. "This trick is fucking up my shit and I'm 'bout to whup her ass!"

"Bring it, bitch!" The woman swung the bat. "I ain't scared of you or your son!" That's when it registered that this was the same chick, Nicole, who'd had Jabril arrested for child support.

"What the hell is this bird doing back over here?" Jaise screamed.

"You just called my mother a bitch?" Jabril spat, and before Jaise could think straight Jabril reached over and caught Nicole's bat with one hand then backhanded Nicole with the other. She dropped like a stone.

Motherfuck! "Don't hit her again!" Jaise screamed at Jabril. "You lost your fuckin' mind? Get your ass in the house!" She tugged him toward the steps as a few of her neighbors inched closer to her home. Carl held the camera on one shoulder and raced toward them. "Jabril, let's fuckin' go!"

"Oh, you gon' slap me!" Nicole struggled to her feet. "And you know I'm pregnant."

"What?" Jaise said breathlessly, as all the wind flew from her body. She looked into Jabril's face and all she could see was Lawrence, swinging his arm in the air and slapping her across the room when she told him she was pregnant with Jabril. She took a step back. She did all she could to erase the flashback, but she couldn't shake it, and it left her with no choice but to pull her hand back and knock Jabril so hard in his face that a series of coughs flew from his mouth.

"Ma," Jabril held the side of his face. "What the fuck?" He tried to catch his breath.

Before Jaise could respond or snap out of the zone, Nicole

smacked Jabril, swinging her fists like windmills, and within seconds she and Jabril were wrapped in a full-fledged cyclone, shoving Jaise out the way and knocking her on her behind.

"Bril!" Christina yelled as she ran out of Jaise's house with her hair disheveled and her clothes in disarray.

Jaise rose to her feet and did a double take. "Where the fuck did you come from?" Before Christina could answer Jaise refocused her attention on the fight. She grabbed Jabril by the back of his white T-shirt and stretched it twice its size. She wrapped the hem around her fist and yanked. "Stop it!" she yelled, trying to break up the fight. "Stop it! Jabril, stop it! She's pregnant."

"She ain't pregnant!" he spat. "She's lyin'."

"So what if I'm lying? You don't put your hands on me!"

Jabril slapped Nicole again.

"Stop it!" Jaise screamed. "Y'all motherfuckers"—She grabbed Jabril by his waist—"Gon' go to jail fighting and shit!" she spat.

"I already called the cops!" Christina shouted as blue lights and sirens filled the night.

"Why *the fuck* did you do that?" Jaise panicked as five police cars screeched to a halt and the smell of burned rubber filled the streets. "Jabril, stop it!" Jaise screamed. "Stop it! You need to get your ass in the house!" As she pulled on him again, his elbow came up and swung back to fend off a blow from Nicole, but he caught Jaise in the mouth instead. She stumbled backward and came within inches of banging her head on the steps, but somehow kept her balance.

"What the fuck?" Bilal slammed his car door. He walked over and the look on his face said he was more than pissed. He was dressed in black dress pants and a cream button up. For a moment Jaise wondered where he was coming from.

He stepped directly between Jabril and Nicole, tossing Jabril out of the fight and onto the side of the damaged BMW. Bilal pressed his arm across Jabril's neck while giving Nicole a warning eye. "Stay your ass over there." He looked at Jabril. "I'm so fucking sick of you."

"Get off of me!" Jabril struggled to push Bilal away.

"You better calm your ass down," Bilal spat, unmoved by Jabril's attempts to push him away. "Or I'ma whup yo' ass and arrest you my damn self! Cops calling me and shit saying the locals on their way to my house again." He turned toward Jaise. "I've had enough of him!"

"Let him go!" Jaise screamed.

"Lieutenant," one of the officers yelled as he charged over. "Let him go. We got it from here."

Bilal peered at Jabril before he backed away.

"Now what the hell is going on?" the cop spat.

Nicole screamed, "That niggah beatin' on me and shit and I'm tired of tussling with this triflin' motherfucker! He gon' fuck around and I'ma shoot his ass. Out here beating on a woman and shit!" Her eyes cut over to Jaise. "Is that how you raised your son? To hit women?"

Jaise swiped blood from her lip. "Don't you worry about what the hell I do with my son," she snapped, not letting on that Nicole's comment caused her heart to crack. "You worry about how your li'l welfare check is going to pay for the damage you did to my damn car! Because I will be pressing charges against your ass!"

Jabril snarled, "I told that bitch—!" He stabbed his finger at Nicole.

"Don't call her a bitch!" Jaise spat. "Cause she is no more a bitch than *your* ass, slapping a goddamn woman. I should kick your fuckin' ass!"

"Enough with all the damn bitches!" Bilal barked. "Get to the point."

"I want that motherfucker arrested!" Nicole screamed. "Out here beating on me and shit! And I have witnesses and if they won't testify there's that camera over there!"

Jaise dropped her head. She had to be in the Twilight Zone. She had to be.

"And I . . . umm," Jabril sputtered. "I want her ass arrested too! Look what she did to my car! This is why I took that damn restraining order out, because she's fuckin' crazy! Out here destroying property and screaming loud enough to wake the fuckin' dead!"

"You did what?" Jaise said shocked. "When did this happen?"

Jabril didn't respond.

The cop turned to Nicole. "Is this true? Does he have an order of protection against you?"

"Yeah, and? So what? I got a restraining order on his ass too, but it didn't stop him from making a new wet spot in my bed this afternoon! Motherfucker is around here playing games and shit!"

Christina gasped. "What?"

Jabril turned to her. "Don't listen to her, you know she pulled a knife on me awhile back."

"A what?" Jaise said.

Nicole popped her neck. "And I'll pull that motherfucker again if you think you gon' keep using me and shit. I'm tired of this back and forth with you, Jabril. Really fuckin' tired."

Christina drew in a sharp breath. "I don't believe you were with her this afternoon. That's why you were late picking me up."

"Yeah, bitch, he was at my crib. We fucked. And what?" Nicole growled, "Silly ass."

"You're silly, bitch." Christina lunged at Nicole and hit her in the face.

Nicole tried to lunge back but instead hit one of the cops.

"All right, that's it!" an officer announced. "Everybody's under arrest!"

"Whoa, wait a minute," Jaise said. "Can we try and handle this another way?"

"I have no choice," the officer said, "but to take them in."

"Bilal," Jaise turned to him. "Can you talk to them? Please."

Silence.

"My kids!" Nicole screamed, as one of the officers pulled her hands behind her back and began to read her her rights.

"My daughter's in the car," Jabril said, in the midst of an officer handcuffing him.

"Kids?" Jaise said put off. "Daughter?" Jaise looked toward Nicole's car and three small children, the oldest no more than six and the youngest no more than two, were in the backseat.

"Are you two getting high?" Jaise said pissed and in complete shock. She looked Jabril dead in his eyes. "You on crack or some shit? Really. Are you? 'Cause that's the only goddamn thing that would make me understand why you've crumbled to shit." She looked at Nicole. "More than the damn police need to be called on you! A set of dumb motherfuckers trying to raise kids!" Jaise gawked at her neighbors, who stood around watching. "What the hell are you all looking at?"

She walked over to Nicole's car and opened a back door. She reached for the baby girl, who was the spitting image of her and Jabril, and took her out of her car seat. There was no way Jaise could be in denial anymore about this being Jabril's child. She knew at that moment that she was. Her heart told her there was no need for a blood test.

The baby smiled at Jaise and instantly melted her heart. Jaise squeezed the baby and smelled her hair. She kissed her softly on the forehead. After taking in that this was the first time she held her granddaughter, she extended her hand to the other children. "Come on, babies."

"No," the oldest child, a boy, whined. "My mommy said me, my brother, and sister not sposed to talk to strangers." Tears ran from his eyes and snot from his nose.

"It's okay, Nigel," Nicole said. "You can go with her."

"Let's go home, Mommy," he whined.

"I'll be home in the morning," she assured him.

A knot caught in Jaise's throat as she thought about smacking

Jabril in his fucking face again and then slamming Nicole a good one. The children cried and screamed, "Mommy!"

"Shh, it'll be okay," Jaise comforted them. "Now, come with me, please. It's okay."

Reluctantly, the children eased out of the car and clutched Jaise by the hand.

"Bilal," Jaise said. "Can you help me—"

"Not this time," Bilal said as he walked toward his car, got in, revved the engine and pulled off before Jaise could protest.

"Get the kids . . ." Jaise said as if someone had deflated the air out of her balloon.

Doing her best to swallow her embarrassment and shake the shame, Jaise walked over to Nicole and for the next few minutes jotted down information about who she needed to call to come and get the children, while the police gathered eyewitness accounts from the neighbors. Carl walked over to Jaise and zoomed the camera in. "Does this qualify for down low, low-down, and country?"

Jaise looked at Carl and shoved the camera out of her face.

Vera

The sultry sounds of Eric Roberson and the scent of Taj's hand-rolled Cuban cigar floated beneath his office door into the foyer like a trail of seduction as Vera locked their apartment door behind her. She clutched her keys to her chest and wondered what to do next. Her mind told her to make a point by going straight to bed.

Quietly.

No stopping.

No second-guessing.

Simply walk past Taj's office and give him all the time he needed to marinate on the way he'd been acting. But her heart and her horniness told her to drop it, that maybe she'd proven her point.

The reflection of the foyer's river-rock water feature danced in the adjacent all-glass wall as Vera slipped her stilettos off, held them in her hands, and stared into the indigo of the New York skyline. At least a million lights shimmered over the city as she internally debated how to end their argument without being the one to fold.

He doesn't listen.

He doesn't. She stared at the blinking red and green lights of the Empire State Building. *Let him wallow in his shit.*

She swallowed as she walked past Taj's office and into their master suite, closing the double doors behind her. "Fuck him," she mumbled to herself, her voice bearing a trace of uncertainty. "Do I love him? Hell yes. Am I going to be ruled by him? Hell no." She slipped her clothes off and headed for the shower.

She stood under the rainspout and as her hair melted to silk and beads of hot water rolled over her breasts and dripped off her nipples, she wished Taj was there to encircle them with his heated tongue. She loved the way he sucked her breasts: soft, sensual, yet with hard lollipop pulls.

As she closed her eyes and squeezed a nipple with one hand and made her way down her thigh with the other, the bathroom door opened and Taj leaned against the doorway. His silence spoke a million words, and his eyes followed with a million questions, none of which Vera answered.

Fuck him, her thoughts reminded her. *Fuck. Him.*

She could see Taj's eyes inching their way over her naked ass to the slither of hair covering her vagina to her double Ds to her face. "Seven years of marriage, thousands of sessions of making love and making up comes down to you going on TV and telling everybody in America what the hell you're supposed to tell me first?"

Silence.

Don't say shit. Fuck him.

"And then you come in the house," Taj continued. "And you don't say a damn thing to me. Nothing."

Fuck. Him.

"How the hell am I supposed to feel about that?"

More silence.

"You said I never listen. I'm listening."

Nothing.

"You're not going to say anything? So I guess we'll be up all night. 'Cause I feel like I don't know what's going on. But one thing I do know is that I love you. I'll be damned if I'm going to throw away what we got and all we've built for some TV bullshit. I love you too much for that." He lifted his shirt above his head, dropped his pants, and stepped into the shower. "Talk to me." He leaned against the marble wall. "Please."

Vera scanned Taj's delicious brown, muscular body, stopping, staring, and appreciating his immeasurable hard inches. Usually she wouldn't hesitate to slide down the shower's wall and take him into her mouth, sucking every thick and fat inch of him. She loved to lick the muffintop head that always had just the right amount of precum to tease her tongue. She loved the taste of him, the feel of his dick in her mouth, in her wetness, or simply rubbing against her skin. She loved it, and no matter how many times they made love he always topped the last time. And yeah, she wanted to give in to him, become one with him again, but she knew his hard dick being exposed like this was entrapment. A clear setup, and she knew it was only a matter of time before the desires of her pussy took over and fell for the shit. *Damn.*

"Talk to me. Please." He stood under the rainspout with her, his hands on her ass cheeks, rubbing and squeezing. Her hard nipples were pressed into his chest as he looked into her eyes. "Because I don't want you to ever think I don't hear you. Or listen to you. I love you, and right now I need you more than you'll ever know." He whispered as he placed kisses on her nose, her lips, and her chin. "Talk to me."

Just give in.

Fuck him.

Fuck. Him.

"Don't say 'fuck him,' " Taj whispered to Vera as he slowly slid to his knees.

Is he reading my mind again?

"Talk to me," he said as his wet tongue graced everything in its path: her nipples, her navel, her clit.

Unable to resist a moment longer as he lapped her pearl, she said, "I love you but you don't own me."

"I know." He licked. "And I love you more than I think you know." He licked again. "And this arguing—" He gripped her clit and sucked, and mopped up the lining of it, "—is not for us."

Vera pressed her hands into Taj's broad shoulders. "Taj—" She paused and dug her nails into his skin. Her wetness eased onto his lips like sticky gloss as he worked his fingers and tongue simultaneously.

"We gon' get this shit back on track." He stood up and backed her into the corner, where she quickly waltzed around him and switched positions, his back now pressed against the wall. "I didn't know you felt like you do, and I'm sorry. I've been way out of line."

She locked eyes with him and wrapped her legs around his waist. She glided onto his dick, guiding it into her heated sweetness. He carried her out of the shower—dripping a trail of water behind them—to their bedroom.

Taj laid Vera in the center of the bed and she quickly wrestled her way on top. She thought about making him apologize for his behavior while she rode his dick and led him to space. She placed a nipple in his mouth and thought of telling him, "Tell me you're sorry and you'll never do that shit again." She paused, caught up in the rapture of their erotic dance—tongue exchanges, strokes, sucks, nibbles, nipple pinches, and hard thrusts—and within an instant they'd switched positions. Now instead of her pinning his shoulders to the bed, she lay on her back with her legs wrapped around his neck. Sweat baptized both their foreheads, ran along the sides of their faces, down his chest, her breasts, and both their backs. Chilling sensations sent shock waves so intense Vera could swear her DNA had been rocked.

She bit her bottom lip and pain shot through it. "Ssssssss . . ." She pushed her breasts together and he licked her chocolate nipples as if milk were oozing through them.

Roll his ass over.

I can't.

She caressed her clit as her sugar walls melted like sweet butter over his dick. He pulled out, slid his fingers into her slit, and eased back down her belly. His tongue generously lapped her jelly. "Whose pussy is this?" He eased back up her stomach and entered her again.

"That's not the question." She took control and rolled back on top. "The question is, whose dick is this?" She squeezed her inner walls. Her thighs popped and slapped against his.

His eyes rolled to the back of his head and he grunted, "I love this fat pussy."

"That's not an answer," she said, as he lifted her off his dick, held her slightly in the air, and moaned. "Look at that shit." He squeezed the base of his dick and a few moments later they found themselves dancing again. He now had her positioned doggy-style, ass up, head down.

"Taj!" Vera panted.

"I'm here, baby." He pulled her ass onto his shaft, thrust into her, and made drum beats as he pounded her with all he had.

Vera's mouth fell open. *You're supposed to be riding this motherfucker.*

Fuck—fuck—fuck—damn—damn—damn—this shiiiiit—izzzzzz—goooooood. "Jeeeezus!"

Taj pounded and slapped her on the ass, her behind jiggled against his shaft, and her pussy popped and exploded all over his chocolate log.

"You didn't answer my damn question." He yanked her hair back, the way she loved for him to do. "Whose pussy is this?"

And you didn't answer my question, "Whose dick is this?"

"Answer me." He pounded.

You answer me!

"Dick got your tongue?" he said, and that's when it clicked that she'd been talking shit in her head but the only things escaping from her mouth were moans, groans, oohs, and ahhs.

"Don't I give you everything you want?"

"Oh, God!" *I don't want you to give it to me.* "Damn . . . ummm. . . . right there . . . right there . . ."

He bit her on the shoulder. "I love you." He pounded.

I love you too. "Fuck!"

"And you know this is your dick, but you haven't told me yet whose pussy this is."

It's mine. "It's yourzzzzz, baaaaaaby!" she screamed as he made a pathway through the back wall of her pussy.

"So why are you always talkin' shit when those cameras are around?" He pounded and slapped her ass cheeks. "You have to stop that."

I don't have to do a motherfuckin' thing but stay black and be a woman. "And cum," she hissed. "I'm *cummmmmin'*! Fuck." She tried to dance her way back on top of him so she could sit on his face and smother his mouth while he drank her nectar. But his dick, the shifting of his hips, and his movements, all halted her for the moment, turning her words to mush as he flipped her around, laid her on her back, tossed her legs to the sides of his neck and laced her pussy with a sea full of pearls.

She watched him collapse on top of her, his chest to her breasts, his head in the crook of her neck. "I don't own you," he said as he gathered her close. "But you belong to me."

She moaned softly, though she suspected his words had a double meaning. "I know you love me. I know you do. I love you too."

Jaise

Jaise stood in her butler's pantry as her granddaughter, Jaden, cooed in an antique highchair while the other two children, Nigel and Tabari, sat wired at the kitchen table. Jaise had been asked three times if they were on Cops, MTV Cribs, or Hell Date. The last time the children asked the question she gave up, pointed to Carl and said, "Ask him."

Now they were all over Carl, dancing, singing, and doing somersaults for the camera. Jaise tried not to complain. Hell, they'd just seen their mother carted off to jail along with Christina and Jabril. And Bilal had just run off to God knows where, so after they each shed a few tears, they all mourned in the best way they knew how: the children showed their asses and Jaise retreated to the pantry in search of something to eat.

She peeked into the kitchen where the boys had just pointed their hands like guns and told Carl to hand over his wallet. "What should we eat?" she asked, not knowing if they would answer the question or not. Predicting that they wouldn't answer, Jaise took out two cans of apples and said, "Homemade applesauce."

"Ms. Jaise," Nigel said. "You just cashed your WIC check?"

"My who?"

"Yo' WIC check, 'cause that's the only time we eat applesauce."

"Oh . . . kay." Jaise placed a hand on her right hip. "So what do you suggest?"

"Some cookies," Tabari said, pumping his fist at Carl. "Chocolate chip."

"I want some too." Nigel smiled. "Ms. Jaise, my babysister loves cookies."

"She does," Jaise said taking the ingredients she needed to make chocolate chip cookies from her pantry and placed them on her center island.

"Umm hmm." Tabari rubbed his tummy. "Me too." He quickly looked at Carl. "Didn't I tell you this was a stick up, you're not 'spose to move."

"Tabari," Jaise called. "Why don't you and Nigel help me make the cookies? And I tell you what, if you're still here and your grandmother hasn't come to get you, then you two can help me bake a cake for Mr. Bilal. His birthday is tomorrow."

"It is?" the boys said excitedly.

"I love birthday cake," Nigel said. "I love everything!"

"I see," Jaise said, praying the tears she felt clogging her throat and stabbing her in the chest wouldn't take flight, flee from her eyes, and ache their way through her mouth. Otherwise she knew she'd be no more good, and instead of standing here acting like Florida Evans, she'd be balled in the corner and crying into her knees. Jaise measured the ingredients and handed the boys what she needed them to dump into the bowl. The children were excited as they mixed their ingredients, scooped the batter out of the bowl and placed the mounds on the cookie sheet.

As the cookies baked, the boys chatted away about how their mommy made them cookies and how their grandmother, Linda, made the best spaghetti in the world. Jaise laughed at their corny jokes, and even sang a few songs with them, but then like unexpected bolts of lightning, thoughts of *I'm losing my man* crept up her back and slammed like raging cymbals into her mind.

You finally met the one . . . and it took you fourteen months, two days, five hours, thirty minutes, and about five point six seconds to fuck. It. Up!

"Ding!" The oven's timer went off and water sprung into Jaise's eyes. She wiped them with the corner of her apron as she slid the cookies out of the oven, put them on a plate to cool, and placed them in the center of the table.

"Can we have a glass of milk?" Nigel asked, as Jaise handed the baby a cookie.

"You sure can." She said, thankful her voice didn't tremble.

She poured the milk and her thoughts continued. *Welcome back to your element—misery, despondency, discouragement, where nothing goes right, relationships are a disaster, and men always leave you in tears.*

"Ms. Jaise," Nigel interrupted her thought. "Your bell's ringing."

"I betchu that's your grandma." She looked away from the boys and headed toward the front door. She stopped in the guest bathroom along the way and washed her face. The bell rang again as she patted her face dry and said, "Just answer the damn door. And pray like hell she is not another Al-Taniesha."

Jaise looked through the peephole to confirm her guests. A short, older woman who resembled Nicole stood there.

She looks like she may have some sense. Jaise opened the door. "Are you Linda?"

"Yes." The woman smiled. "Jaise?"

"Yes, I'm Jaise. Come in."

"Grandma!" Nigel and Tabari ran down the hall and hugged Linda around the waist. "Did you know that the cops came and took mommy away? Are we going to pick her up now, grandma?"

"Yes, I know about your mommy and no, we're not going to get her right now," Linda said. "Now, tell Ms. Jaise thank you," she instructed the boys.

"Thank you, Ms. Jaise," they said in unison.

"Where's the baby?" Linda asked.

"In here," Jaise said, walking toward the kitchen. "You can come with me."

Linda walked into the kitchen and looked at the clock. "Boy, you guys are up and eating cookies at one in the morning as if it's the afternoon."

Jaise chuckled as she took the baby out of her highchair. "I know." Jaise felt tears creeping up her spine. *Don't cry. You better not cry in front of this woman.*

"Are you okay?" Linda asked.

"Just a little upset," Jaise confessed. "That all of this had to happen."

"Girl, we can't do nothing with or about these kids." She sucked her teeth, as she reached for a napkin and wiped the baby's mouth. "I stopped worrying a long time ago. I did my best and after that I don't have any more to give. I am here for my grand-children but if Nicole wants to run after these no-good men and have baby after baby, there's nothing I can do. I'm done. I've raised her and now the rest is on her."

"My son." Jaise paused, her mind was set on telling Linda off about classing Jabril as a no-good man, but hell, that's what he was. Wasn't he? "Jabril is only nineteen," Jaise said. "It's not that easy for me to give up."

"Well, let him take you to the grave, honey. I mean you have to do what you think is best, but I'm finished."

Jaise arched her brow, for lack of knowing what else to do. She felt a little envious that Linda could let go so easily. "But Nicole's your daughter."

"And I love her," Linda said. "And it's not easy to watch your children do the things you told them not to do. Or watch them go through what you've already gone through. But hey, when they choose to do dumb shit, this is what they get."

She's right. "Maybe I can get the baby again sometime," Jaise said more as a question than a statement.

"I'm sure the baby would love that." Linda took the boys by the hand and held Jaden on her shoulder.

"Bye, Ms. Jaise," the children said as they skipped out the door.

"Bye, babies."

Shortly after the children and Linda were gone, Carl left behind them. Exhausted, Jaise flopped down on the sofa and just as she thought about how she could finally scream and no one would hear her, she decided against it, and instead closed her eyes and drifted to sleep.

The morning sun crept into the sky as Jaise stretched and Bilal opened the door, tossing his keys on the gossip bench in the entryway. Immediately the smell of old vodka filled the doorway as he walked into the living room.

"Bilal," Jaise said, not knowing if it was the right time to address his obviously drinking and driving, or ask him where he'd been all night. Deciding against it, she looked at the clock: six a.m. "Happy birthday, baby!" She attempted to hug him and he pushed her away.

"Oh, now," his voice slurred. "You wanna remember my birthday? Huh?" He blew his hot and drunken breath into her face. "Happy birthday, baby?" He mocked her. "After I sat there all night in that fuckin' restaurant waiting for you, and waiting for you. And then when I think you're calling me, it's a fellow officer telling me about your fucked-up son." He walked up close to her and pressed her into the wall.

"Bilal, you're drunk." She tried to push him back, but failed.

"I'm not drunk, I'm tired."

"Just relax. It's your birthday today, and right after you sober up, we're going to celebrate—"

"Celebrate what, Jaise?" He stepped back. "Ain't shit to celebrate. My fuckin' birthday was yesterday." He turned away and walked up the stairs, leaving her standing there.

Al-Taniesha

"Oh, my chile gotta go to jail for y'all to come to my crib?" Al-Taniesha put her hands on her hips. "Well, you ain't getting your ass up in here today."

"Who's that, Niesha?" Lollipop crowded the doorway with a plastic jheri curl cap on his head and a zebra-print towel wrapped around his body. He looked directly into the camera and screamed "Oh, no!" as he scurried behind Al-Taniesha. "How y'all come without calling and shit? We ain't cleaned up, catsuit ain't pressed. My hair ain't done. Oh, hell, nawl, you got to come back."

"Listen—" Bridget tried to say.

"No, you listen." Al-Taniesha pointed. "I was gung-ho on being a video vixen and taking this motherfucker by storm. And I've been on TV before: *Wife Swap, Divorce Court, Judge Joe Brown,* but none of them meant anything to me, not like *Millionaire Wives Club.* And I'm still down with the get down, ready to handle my scandal, and rep for my cause. And I'm not faking it for the camera like those bougie-ass bitches Jaise," her eyes popped out her head, "Milan, and Chaunci. I'm real as hell, but one thing that ain't going down is you ain't about to come up in here and embarrass my chile. Hell no."

"How do you feel about her getting arrested?" Bridget quickly asked.

"It's a motherfuckin' rite of passage. Shit, she a woman now. She went to jail 'cause she had to beat a bitch's ass. Hell, at least she got heart. But I tell you what." Al-Taniesha turned away from the camera and yelled over her shoulder, "Chrissy, what was that bitch's name?"

"Nicole!" Christina yelled back.

Al-Taniesha turned back to the camera. "Nicole, I'm Christina's mama." She stood back and let Carl and the camera get a full view of her floral housedress, her bare feet, and the red bandanna wrapped around her head. "And I will whup yo' ass! Believe that. Now if you wanna bring it, come to building 54, Lincoln Projects, apartment 27A. 'A' stands for ass-kickin'. And Jabril, Lollipop is gon' kick yo' ass too."

"Don't be puttin' me in that mess, Niesha," Lollipop tossed over her shoulder. "I ain't gettin' in no fight. Messin' up my face and shit."

Al-Taniesha turned from the door. "If that li'l negro comes over here and you don't kick his ass I'ma kick yours."

"Well, then, we gon' be rockin' and rollin'."

"When they leave, I'ma take care of you," Al-Taniesha spat.

"I know you will, baby," Lollipop growled. "I know you will."

Al-Taniesha gave a schoolgirl giggle, then turned back to the door. "Now go on, get." She flicked her hand. "Go on home. 'Cause I ain't got nothing for you, and your asses won't be getting up in here today! As a matter of fact, I quit. I'm done. You over at those bougie hos' houses but never once come and check for a real bitch until now."

"Oh, Al-Taniesha," Bridget said. "Don't be so dramatic. And let's not forget we do have a contract."

"Unless you plan on buckin' and beatin' my ass to make me fulfill it, don't come back here!" When Bridget didn't respond, Al-Taniesha slammed the door in Bridget and Carl's faces. "Motherfuckers!"

Camera

Chaunci

"Lonely does not equal desperate," Chaunci said as she'd turned away from the camera. She'd grown tired of looking in Bridget's and Carl's faces.

"I think so," Milan insisted.

"You have lost your mind." Chaunci chuckled as she cradled the phone between her neck and shoulder. As Carl walked around her desk and pointed the camera in her face, Chaunci turned toward her all-glass wall and watched one of the cleaning crew's custodians make his way down the aisle. "And I hope you didn't wave a banner in front of Kendu's friend saying you had a desperate girlfriend," she continued.

"Would you stop with the paranoia? I didn't do that."

"And is he an athlete, because you know I can't do another athlete."

"He's not an athlete," Milan said. "And you need to go somewhere besides work and home."

"I can handle my outings, thank you. And besides, I'm not that crazy about Kendu and now I should hook up with one of his friends? Oh, hell no."

Milan chuckled. "Watch it, Chaunci."

"You know I love you, girl, but you know I have my eye on Kendu."

"That's because you don't know how to get over shit. Now back to the date. Would you just do it for me?" Milan pleaded. "Just meet Emory tonight, have dinner, and if you don't like him, you don't have to see him anymore. And I promise I will never hook you up again, especially if you hate him, which you won't. I did tell you he was fine, right?"

"Fine is no longer a black man's selling point. Can I get honest, committed, good credit, responsible, likes kids, backbone, and someone that I can tolerate for longer than a week? I've been fucked literally and figuratively by Mr. Fine, okay?"

"Mad black woman, you need to let some of that shit go. Not every guy will turn out to be husband material."

"I'm not looking for a husband."

"Then what are you looking for, because I'm confused. First Idris isn't the one for you, but then he shows up married, and you're hurt. Now I'm trying to hook you up with a responsible man, who is handling his business, and you don't want to be bothered. Are you still in love with Idris?"

"No. I was mad as hell but I'm done with that shit."

"Then go on the date . . . please. It'll be fun."

Chaunci drew in a deep sigh. "Okay, Milan. But—" She paused as she watched the custodian sit on the edge of the desk he should've been cleaning; while his long and muscular arm with skin that reminded her of a freshly picked black grape, reached for her employee's desk phone and dialed a number.

"Oh. Hell. No." Chaunci spat.

"What?!" Milan said excited. "You just said you would go."

"No, yes, wait." Chaunci collected her thoughts. "I'll meet Kendu's friend tonight, but that's not why I said 'hell no.' I said it because I'm sitting here watching one of the cleaning guys—and he must be new, because I've never seen his lazy ass around here before—sit his fine ass—see Mr. Fine strikes again—on the edge of my employee's desk and yap on her phone."

"You have got to be kidding me."

"I wish!"

"That's insane."

"Does he not see me sitting here? And now he's using her pen and sticky pad."

"He needs to be dealt with."

"Yes, he does, so let me go and handle this slouch right now!"

"Okay, and don't forget the date's at eight thirty."

"I won't." *Click.*

Chaunci rose from her desk and walked over to the custodian, who was still on the phone. "Excuse you," she said sternly. "But what are you—?"

"Shhh . . . wait a minute. I'm on the phone." He pointed his index finger to the receiver.

Chaunci blinked. "Excuse you, but you need to—"

"Hold it," he said firmly. "I can't hear. Just relax for a minute." He held his index finger in the air.

"Relax?! Oh, hell no."

He ignored Chaunci and continued on with his conversation. "Simone, make sure you're there on time. Okay, I love you too." He hung up and looked at Chaunci. His eyes skipped all over her body, lingering upon her breasts and hips and then back to her face. "Can I help you with something?" he asked as he stood up, towering at least three inches over her.

She placed her hands on her hips and sized him up. He wore a blue jumpsuit with a stitched tag on the right breast pocket that read "Parker's Cleaning." His sleeves were pushed midway up his muscular triceps and his shadow goatee added an extra sparkle to his beautiful face.

Fine as hell, but obviously trifling as shit.

"Can I help you?" he repeated himself.

"Can you *help me*?" Chaunci said taken aback. "Yeah, how

about you *help me* by staying your ass off that desk, not using my company's phone, and doing your job like you're supposed to."

"I am doing my job," he said. "It's just that—"

"What? You're lazy? Trifling? Trying to get over?" Chaunci snapped.

"Look, I know it may have looked bad but I was talking to my—"

"I don't care who you were talking to. And put that sticky pad and pen back!"

"Look, I needed to use the pad to write down—"

"It doesn't matter. All that matters is you staying off my phone and not stealing my supplies!"

"Steal? I wasn't stealing."

"That's what they all say. Now what I expect is for this not to happen again or I'll make sure your days pushing that broom are numbered."

"Are you threatening me?"

"No, I'm making a professional promise."

"Look, I needed to use the phone because—"

"You should invest in a cellphone."

"First of all my cellphone died, otherwise I would've used it and I had to call—"

"I don't give a damn who you had to call!"

"I didn't ask you to give a damn. I was trying to offer you an explanation but since you obviously have a stick up your ass, because you keep cutting me off, then I'ma step to the side, push my broom, and be about my business."

Chaunci blinked not once but three times. "Oh, no." She blocked his path. "You don't speak to me like that!"

"Lady, let me finish what I have to do." He walked around her and turned the vacuum cleaner on.

"Lady?" Chaunci said pissed. She stormed over to him and turned off the vacuum. "I don't know what l'il federally funded program you came from but you need to get your mind right and your life in order!"

"Back up." He looked her over and once again turned the vacuum on.

"Obviously," Chaunci said, yanking the vacuum's plug from the socket and tossing it to the floor. "You don't know who I am. But I will be calling the cleaning company's owner in the morning and you will be fired!"

"Obviously," he snatched the cord from the floor and wrapped it around the vacuum. "You don't know who I am." He gathered his cleaning supplies and stacked them in his portable station. "Because you can't fuckin' fire me. I quit! And you don't have to call the owner. *I am* the owner. I was simply filling in because one of the guys called out, but to hell with it! Now what *you can do* is take your pretty ass, push your own damn broom, and clean your own nasty-ass office!" He gave her a once-over before he turned away and yelled out to his employees. "Josh, Dave, Robert, Kaareem!"

"Yeah!" they said in unison.

"Leave the garbage where you found it, get your stations and the rest of your shit, we're out of here!"

Chaunci was speechless. She stood in the center of the floor and watched the cleaning crew she'd contracted storm out the door leaving the day's rubbish behind. "Fuck it." She threw her arms in the air and walked into her office and grabbed her purse. "I can't deal with this shit right now. Don't clean the motherfucker," she said to no one in particular. "At this moment, I don't give a damn."

As she headed to the elevator bay and pushed the "Close" button, she looked into the camera and said, "This is not my fuckin' day."

Vera

This was the fairy tale she remembered.

Loving Taj freely.

No second-guessing.

No sideways glances at him.

No thoughts of where they'd be five years from now.

She could breathe again.

Finally.

"I've fucked up." Taj spoke with his lips pressed against Vera's forehead; the tone of his voice made his words feel like a confession. She tried not to show her surprise at his cursing on camera, especially since he usually prided himself on not saying much. "I just feel like there's so much I need to tell you."

They were in their dressing room as Taj got ready for work.

"Are you okay?" Vera asked him. "Or is that your version of good morning?" she said as he handed her his silk tie.

"I'm fine." He sat down on a chocolate leather ottoman. Vera stood before him and he placed his hands on her waist. She slid his tie around his neck. "It's just that I've turned into someone else. Someone who didn't listen to you or hear you."

She crossed the center of his tie and knotted it. "No marriage is perfect, Taj."

"No, but they're not all fucked-up either."

"Taj, why are you going to left?" She paused, waiting for an answer. When she didn't get one, she continued. "Let's just go from now."

"Maybe you're right."

"I know I am." She pinned his caduceus tie tack on his tie and said, "Taj, I have to be honest. I have to go for this HSN opportunity. I have to. I don't know where it will lead or if they'll even offer me what I want, but I can't let this pass me by. I can't. Now, I'm willing to delay opening the salons in L.A. and Atlanta, but right now I feel like that's all I can compromise on."

"I know how much seeing your hair products in stores means to you."

"It all means something to me. But I realize marriage is about compromise and honesty. So, I'm being honest in telling you what I'm going to pursue and what I'm willing to compromise on."

"Whatever you want, I'll support you."

Vera cradled Taj's face between her hands and kissed him. "You're the best husband in the world."

"Oh, no." Bridget butted her palm against her forehead. "Carl, wake me up when *As The World Turns* is over."

They ignored Bridget and continued.

"Of course I'm the best husband in the world." Taj tapped Vera on the ass. "I'm also the only person who'll admit that when you started making Volume I was concerned as hell." He walked into the kitchen and poured himself a cup of coffee.

Vera followed him and put her hands on her hips. "What do you mean, you were concerned?"

He chuckled. "Because, baby, they used to stink. Damn, I couldn't stand the smell."

"Be quiet. You know I had to perfect the scent." She laughed. "And thank God for Aunt Cookie letting me experiment on her."

"And Ms. Betty," Taj said, reminding Vera of his stepmother. "I'll never forget when she called me and said, 'Junior, that wife of yours has got something special on her hands. My hair is smelling a little strange but it's thick and growing.' "

Vera smiled. "And the scent is perfect now and it comes in coconut, apple, and berry scents." She turned to the camera as if she were recording an infomercial. "Get your jar, because supplies are limited."

Taj chuckled. "Vera——" His cell phone rang before he could finish his sentence. He patted his pockets as his eyes scanned the room. "Have you seen my phone?"

"No." Vera paused. "Yes, I have. I moved it this morning. You left it in the bathroom." She quickly ran into their adjoining bedroom. "I'll get it for you."

"No," Taj said, on Vera's heels. "Just let it go——"

"Hello?"

"——to voice mail."

"They hung up anyway." Vera shrugged and handed Taj his phone.

He kissed her. "I have to go. Make sure you call the attorney so he can handle the business part of HSN's proposal."

"Taj, the attorney is already on board."

He smiled. "Look at you. HSN won't know what hit 'em."

"No, they won't," Vera assured Taj as he walked toward the door and then quickly came back. "I love you. I'll be a little late coming in. I have to pull some long hours at the hospital."

"Okay." Vera looked into his eyes and for the first time in the ten years they'd been together she wondered if he was telling her the truth.

Taj walked out of the kitchen. Just as the front door slammed, Carl tapped a sleeping Bridget. "What? What? What?" she sputtered.

"It's over."

The Club

After a few hours of being filmed at two of her salons, socializing with her stylists, taking care of business in her offices, and shooting her weekly interview, Vera was thankful when Bridget announced that she and Carl had had enough and were leaving.

Now she could be at peace . . . whatever the hell peace was.

The sound of Mary J. Blige's sultry voice rose from Vera's Hermès bag as she sat in her Manhattan office at her computer Internet surfing. She pulled out her cell phone and checked the Caller I.D.: Jaise.

"Hello?"

"Vera?" Jaise said. "Hey, girl. How are you? Are you busy?"

"Hey, Jaise." Vera paused. "I'm well. And, umm, no, I'm not busy. I was actually finishing up at one of my salons. What's going on?"

"I wanted to invite you to dinner at Café Noir."

Really? "Oh, I haven't been there in forever and that food is *soooo* good."

"So we're on?" Jaise let out a sigh of relief.

"Sure. I'd love to meet you for dinner. What time?"

"Now."

Now? "Oh . . . kay. I'm on my way."

Click.

"Finally, somewhere to go," Jaise said as she sat in her SUV with a thin cloud of cigarette smoke easing from her lips. She'd been sitting in Central Park in her ivory Range Rover for hours, her mind filled with a million thoughts, and she didn't want to think anymore, because every thought centered on Bilal and Jabril, and she was sick and tired of those mind-wreckers.

She needed a break. Some time to be free. Free to screw up without Bilal breathing down her neck. Without wondering what Jabril was going to fuck up next. Free to stomp her pointed heels and her voluptuous hips down the crystal staircase of her life and for once, for once, not give a damn if it was shattering behind her.

She was tired of a few things and at this moment one of the things that tore up her nerves was knowing that she'd spent hundreds of tearful, knee-bent nights praying for a black man who had more to offer than a big dick, and now that she had one who was about his business, she had no idea what to do with him.

Vera hailed a cab and slid into the backseat. "Café Noir. 125th Street and Adam Clayton Powell Boulevard," she said to the cabbie as she watched the dance of New York City traffic. Her eyes brightened as the cab whipped by the building where her first salon used to be. Though it was now a bodega, she couldn't help but smile at the memories.

"I know you're getting ready to close." An unknown chocolate Zeus walked into Vera's salon as she flicked on the neon "Closed" sign hanging in the window. "And I can come back tomorrow. I will come back tomorrow. But I just wanted to know if you cater to dreads."

Vera's eyes eased over each and every inch of him, from his thick Bob Marley locks, pulled back and tucked beneath a rasta tam, to his navy hospital scrubs and white lab coat, with the hospital I.D. that read "Dr. Taj Bennett."

She tried to control her smile but couldn't. "It depends on whose dreads need catering to."

A one-sided grin of his full lips. "Mine."

"Sure. But you don't have to come back tomorrow. I'm open now." She flicked off the "Closed" sign and he removed his tam, his dreads falling to the small of his back.

She washed and then twisted the roots of his hair. Her eyes made love to every tight muscle that she imagined lay beneath his scrubs. And upon inspecting the mountainous shape in his pants, her mouth watered and her body wondered what it would feel like to absorb his middle.

After she finished his hair and he paid her, he stepped into her personal space. "Sistah," he said, "I truly hope you don't mind me saying this to you, but I think you're beautiful and I'd like to know if it's possible—and I'm hoping like hell it's possible—for me to take you out for dinner."

And dinner led to breakfast . . . and breakfast led to ten years . . . and ten years led to right now . . . this moment . . .

"We're here," the cabbie said in a thick East Indian accent as he double-parked and pointed to the shabby-chic sign that hung above Café Noir's doors. The café was in a hundred-year-old brownstone that in 1910 was a school where black women learned etiquette, how to speak French, and how to cook Creole food. A hundred years later it had been transformed into a full-fledged upscale Creole café.

Vera slid a twenty-dollar bill into the pocket of the cab's Plexiglas divider. "Keep the change."

Jaise walked into Café Noir's Victorian parlor, where the hostess curtsied and said, "Bienvenue, or welcome, if you prefer I speak in English."

Jaise forced herself to smile. "Merci."

The hostess grinned. "Parlez-vous français?"

"Oui." Jaise pointed to the table where she spotted Vera sitting. "Mon parti est juste la bas." She followed the hostess and greeted Vera with a tighter hug than either of them expected. "It's good to see you, girl."

"You too," Vera said.

"Pardon me," the hostess said to Jaise and Vera. "Permettez-moi apporter vous Mesdames vin?"

"Oui." Vera smiled. "Vin blanc, si'l vous plait."

Jaise's eyes grew bright and obviously impressed. "Même pour moi."

"Okay." The hostess nodded as she went to get their white wine.

Jaise smiled at Vera. "You speak French? I'm impressed."

"Merci beaucoup," Vera said, "But truthfully I understand it a lot better than I speak it. I studied French in college. It's a shame I don't use it more often. But you seem to be holding your own quite well."

"I grew up speaking French," Jaise said. "My father is Haitian, and he would only speak to us in French. Needless to say," she continued as their server placed glasses of wine on the table, "since Daddy was the one with the money I learned how to say, 'J'ai besoin d'une somme d'argent' real quick."

Vera cracked up. "Girl, you're a mess. My ass would've learned how to say 'I need some money' too."

"You know what I'm saying." Jaise chuckled as she picked up her glass of wine and sipped. She wondered if Vera could see the stress she was feeling. She wanted desperately to confess and lay this shit on somebody's shoulder, anybody's shoulder, so she could get it off hers. But she didn't know how to do that. Hell, she didn't even really know Vera. And, yeah, they'd hit it off the other night on Vera's yacht, and sure, Jaise had invited her to dinner, but that was a far cry from placing her business on the table.

"Are you ladies ready to order?" the waitress asked.

Vera quickly combed the menu. "What are you having, Jaise?"

"Crabmeat Ravigote and a side of dirty rice."

"Umm, sons délicieuses." Vera smiled. "I'll have the same."

After a few minutes, the waitress returned with their food. "Bon appetit." She smiled and walked away.

"So how's being on the show working out for you?" Jaise asked Vera, stuffing a bite in her mouth. "Are you ready to kick Bridget's ass yet?"

Vera dabbed at the corners of her lips as she chewed and swallowed. "Bridget is a hot mess. Oh, my God. I had no idea the producers acted like that. Seriously, when I watched the show last season I didn't see her on camera at all. No one knows all the shit she does behind the scenes."

"Her team edits the hell out of a show," Jaise said. "Yes, she is truly working behind the scenes like a damn overseer. Give it a minute, you'll be wanting to backhand her. Just sneak her real good, and then stand back clutching your Louis and holding your chest and say, 'Oh my, what happened to you?' "

Vera laughed so hard she almost choked. "Please, stop!" she howled. "Because I can imagine Bridget getting her ass kicked and somehow managing to say, 'Roll tape, Carl.' "

Jaise cried with laughter and nodded in agreement. "Yes, that's Bridget." She sipped her drink. "A mess."

They ate in silence, both wondering what to say next. Then Jaise took a chance. "Vera, can I ask you something?"

"As long as the answer doesn't end up in the tabloids," she joked.

Jaise smiled. "No, none of that."

"Then shoot."

Jaise chewed the corner of her lip. *Deep breath in. Deep breath out. Just say the shit.* "Have you ever been so stressed that all you wanted to do was run away and never look back?"

"Hell, yes," Vera nodded.

"Well, please tell me the secret of how you handle it," Jaise said.

"It depends on what I'm stressed about," Vera responded.

"Hell, where do I start?" Jaise said. "Because I'm stressed about a laundry list of shit. My Range Rover has a rip in the back of the passenger seat. I think my housekeeper has been stealing my loose change that's lying around the house. My sixty-year-old uncle recently decided he wants to be my aunt. My sister keeps having babies by a different Mr. Right every other year. My son fucks up every other day, and my husband doesn't understand that I can't stop being a mother simply because my son is nineteen with two kids." She tossed back the last bit of her wine.

"Damn," Vera said. "You need some Calgon."

Jaise chuckled. "Calgon? I'm about to sue their asses. I have dumped box after box and nothing. Absolutely nothing. And when I soak in that shit, not only do I get up smelling like the perfume aisle at Walgreens, I'm still in my hundred-year-old brownstone, soaking in an antique tub, dealing with the same ole shit. Damn, I need a cigarette," Jaise said, exhausted.

"Me too," Vera said. "I need one for you. And I don't even smoke."

"See, I told you. Stressed, honey."

"But you can deal with that. Park the Range Rover and buy a new one. Fire the maid. Let Uncle be Auntie if he wants to. Your sister, her children, and Mr. Right, that's on her, not your business. Your husband, try and work it out, and your son and the second baby, this may sound harsh, but that's for your son to deal with. He has to be a man and you have to let him be a man. Nineteen-year-olds are employable and child support can come out of their checks. Oh, and Calgon, yeah, sue their asses."

"I wish it was that simple," Jaise said.

"Do you think it's that hard, or do you think we make shit harder than it has to be?"

"Good question."

"Sometimes," Vera confessed, "I do things that I know should be simple, but it feels so damn complicated."

Jaise said, taken aback, "So this shit is not exclusive to me?"

"No, girl, they are not designer problems."

"Thank ya, Jesus." Jaise waved her hands. "So what's on your back?"

"Chile," Vera sipped her wine. "My husband thinks I work too much and he wants me to play soccer mom. And I'm not interested in that shit. I love my husband but he married the wrong woman if he was looking for Justine Simmons or June Cleaver. Shit."

"Why don't you tell him that?"

"I did. But the way I did it was fucked up." Vera shook her head.

"What did you do?"

"We had a screaming match on camera."

"Girl, don't you know the worst shit always happens on camera? Chile, please, try your son getting arrested twice. And right after you swore this season they would see you doing nothing more than cooking and humming a few tunes. I planned on coming so correct this season that I had an entire episode I wanted to do that showed me joining the church."

"The church?"

"Church. Every other word out of my mouth was supposed to be Jesus—not fuck this and fuck that."

Vera laughed so hard that tears fell from her eyes. "That is funny as hell."

"No, that's a mess. Vera," Jaise said with glassy eyes. "I'm a wreck."

Vera hesitated. "Why are you crying? What's going on?"

Jaise paused.

"Just say it," Vera encouraged. "It's cool. I'm a good listener."

Jaise hesitated. "How do I"—she paused—"tell my son that I'm tired of being his mother?"

Silence. Complete and utter silence.

Jaise took her napkin from her lap, held her head down and cried into it. "That makes me feel *sooo* fucked-up." Her voice ached.

Vera scooted as close as she could to Jaise. Jaise seemed stressed but she had no idea how broken she really was. She rubbed her back as Jaise continued. "I've been his mother since I was seventeen. *Seventeen. Eleventh grade.* And I just want out. I look at my son and I feel so guilty. Thank God he has a trust fund, because he would die on his own with no money. He can't keep a job. It's one trifling, ratty-ass girl after another. He wants to rap and do a buncha dumb shit. He's getting locked up every damn time I turn around, and it just makes me . . . so . . . sick. I try to retrace my steps to pinpoint where I fucked up. Because if my child is fucked-up, then that has to mean I fucked him up."

"Jaise, I'm sure you did your best."

"No, I didn't, and I know I didn't. I could've done better. I should've done better."

"We can only work with what we have. With what we know."

"I just wish I could pinpoint that moment . . . that moment when things took a turn. Was he eight, nine, ten? When did this happen? If I knew then maybe I could redo some things in his life. In my life."

"Everybody makes mistakes."

"Yeah, but when you fuck up your kid, you don't get to do that over again. And now I just want to throw in the towel and walk away . . . but I can't."

"He's nineteen, Jaise. It's okay to let go."

"But I can't let go, because if I turn my child loose and he's not ready for the world then what does that say about me? I have to save him."

"You can't keep saving him. You have to let him be a man."

"Vera," Jaise wiped her face. "Jabril wouldn't know how to be a man if I paid him to act like one."

"Where's his father?"

"I hope he's dead and in hell. But if he didn't get there yet I'm sure he's at home with his white wife making cream kids."

Vera laughed and she and Jaise wiped tears from their eyes. "Thank you." Jaise mustered a smile. "Thank you."

Vera smiled, continuing to wipe her eyes. "I'm here, Jaise."

"Okay." Jaise sniffed. "Enough of true confessions. We're Millionaire Wives."

"And what does that mean?"

"It means we can't be sitting here crying."

"Why not?" Vera asked.

"Because it'll wreak havoc on our makeup."

Chaunci

Chaunci wore a sexy black dress that stopped midway down her thighs and complimented her healthy cleavage. After the day she'd had she needed a drink, a nice conversation, and a relaxing night—so Henri's was the right place to be. It was a ritzy supper club in the heart of Harlem that played live instrumental jazz and served the world's best Chateau Briand with a special clam and garlic sauce. People came from all over the world to enjoy the romantic atmosphere, where the ceiling shimmered like a star-filled night. The tables were individual booths that could be enclosed by red velvet drapes for privacy, and the service was impeccable.

The hostess greeted Chaunci. "Good evening."

"Good evening." Chaunci smiled. "I have reservations for eight thirty. Party of two."

"Right this way, ma'am."

As Chaunci took her seat the hostess said, "Your server will be here momentarily. Would you like to start off with something to drink?"

"No, thank you. I'll wait."

"Very well." The hostess nodded and smiled, as she turned away.

Chaunci sat at the table, fighting off every thought that told her to cancel this date, go home, and suck down a gallon of ice cream. *Don't be pathetic.*

"So, Chaunci," Bridget said. "Tell the camera what you're thinking right now."

"That this has been the day from hell." Chaunci looked into the camera and parted her lips into a fake smile. "And that I can't believe I let Milan hook me up with this blind, excuse me," She looked at her watch. "With this late-ass, blind date."

Ring . . . Ring . . .

She looked at her cellphone. "This better be him. Hello?"

"Chaunci?"

"Yes, this is Chaunci."

"This is Emory."

"Hi . . ." She hesitated.

"I owe you an apology for my lateness," he said. "I had a rough evening at work and it delayed me getting out of my house on time. Now I'm playing bob-and-weave through New York City traffic."

"I understand that." Chaunci smiled.

"Understanding," he said. "I like that."

She chuckled. "I understand a few minutes. Not an hour."

"I wouldn't waste your time like that, which is why I'm calling. I'm only a few minutes away and I hope you don't mind but I called the restaurant and asked that the server bring you a bottle of Merlot while you wait. I promise on the next date I won't be late."

"Aren't you presumptuous?" she teased. "A second date?" She wondered why his comment made her blush.

"Based on everything Milan told me and from how sweet you seem and sound right now we definitely have a second date in the near future."

"In that case, I'd love to have Merlot."

"Well, if you'd love to have it, then I have to make sure you get it."

"Thank you. I'll see you in a few minutes."

"That you will."

Damn . . . Chaunci thought as she squeezed her inner thighs. *His deep voice made me horny as hell . . . maybe I am desperate . . . or maybe I just need Jesus . . .*

"Merlot, ma'am?" the waiter said as he placed a chilled bottle in the center of the table. He poured Chaunci a glass, smiled, and walked away. As she took a sip she said a silent toast. *Here's to the night getting better . . .*

Five minutes later, "The party of Chaunci Morgan, please," floated over Chaunci's shoulder.

"Right this way, sir."

That's him. She sucked in her stomach. *What am I doing and why the hell am I nervous?* She quickly popped a dinner mint into her mouth. *Relax.* She closed her eyes and said a quick prayer. "Please let this negro be sane."

She opened her eyes and to her surprise stood the same fine ass, six foot two, trifling mofo that she'd just fired hours ago, holding a bouquet of red roses. Only now instead of wearing a blue jumpsuit he was dressed in black Armani slacks and a lavender button up. He had the audacity to be even more beautiful than he was before: chestnut colored eyes that sparkled, beautiful dark mocha skin that reminded her of the actor Djimon Hounsou, and a strong African chief-esque presence, complimented by an edgy swagger. *Goddamn.*

"Oh hell no," they said simultaneously.

"Did you set this up?" Chaunci spat.

"Did I set this up—?" He said baffled.

"You knew who I was all the time!"

"How would I know that?!"

"I don't believe this. I'm soooo sick of men and their bullshit!"

Chaunci snapped and stood up. "There's no way in hell you didn't know who I was earlier today! This whole deal was a set up, you just wait until I call Milan and cuss her ass out. Ugg! I don't believe this. Oh I'm going to—"

"Shut. The. Hell. Up. Damn," he said exhausted. "What is your problem?" He stepped into Chaunci's personal space, his minty breath landing directly on her lips. "Really, sweetness, what's good with you, because you are way too beautiful and too sexy to be this over-the-damn-top. Like *I said* I didn't know who you were earlier today, but I know who you are now, which is why I'm leaving, but before I go I'ma hit you with this—I don't know what your ex did to piss you off, but you need to chill before you miss out on everything and everyone meant for you."

"And what does that mean? Don't tell me you think you're meant for me, Romeo?"

"The name is Emory and I know damn well I'm not meant for you, because you talk too damn much and have gotten on my damn nerves, fa sho'."

"Then that makes us even."

"It doesn't make us shit." He slapped the roses and a hundred dollar bill on the table. "That's for the wine. Have a good night." And he walked out, once again leaving her center stage.

Chaunci looked at the roses and then into the camera, pissed that he'd made her panties wet, and her nipples hard. "Fuck him!" she said as she grabbed her purse and stormed out the door.

The Club

*S*even o'clock . . . *He should've been here two hours ago,* Milan thought as she opened her apartment door and smiled at her guests: a few of Kendu's friends and some of his ex-teammates, who walked through the door bearing gifts and well wishes.

"Thank you for coming." She forced herself to smile, as she looked from her guests to the camera, and back again. "There's food everywhere and plenty of champagne. Now all we need is my fiancé and we can have an engagement party." She tried to joke but the humor fell flat. She walked over to the CD player and turned up the instrumental jazz music, hoping that it would drown out her thoughts. It didn't.

He's not coming.

Seven thirty.

The bell rang.

Please God.

Milan cut through the center of the buzzing crowd and opened the door. Chaunci.

"Hey, boo!" Chaunci said as she and Milan exchanged cheeks.

Chaunci handed Milan a bottle of champagne. "I'm sorry I ran late. I was finishing up some last-minute things at the office."

"It's Saturday, Chaunci. Why were you at the office?"

"Kobi's with Idris and I had some things to do."

"Which means you had nothing to do. I have to get you a boo."

"Oh, hell no you don't." Chaunci eyeballed the room. "Where's Kendu?"

"He didn't get here yet."

"What?" Chaunci said, shocked. "Where the hell is he?"

"I don't know." Milan shook her head as she tucked her hair behind her ears. "I've called him a thousand times and he hasn't answered."

Chaunci squinted. She was clearly confused. "What do you mean he didn't answer?"

"I've called every damn hospital in New York and New Jersey. Hell, I even called the damn police precincts."

"Well where is he? Did he know about the party?"

"He knew," Milan said as she walked toward the kitchen.

Chaunci and the cameraman followed behind her. "He better hurry his ass up and get here then," Chaunci said. "Or I'ma cuss his ass out like you need to."

Jaise gripped the steering wheel of her Range Rover with one hand as she raced up the West Side Highway with Vera in the passenger seat. "I don't know what possessed me to be seen at Milan's low-budget-ass hoedown." Jaise eased a cigarette into the corner of her lips.

"Low-budget?" Vera said.

"Exactly. Who's ever heard of having an engagement party where you're not only asking for monetary gifts but also telling your guests to make the checks out to your charity? What's the charity, Milan's rent?"

Vera laughed. "It's a charity for homeless women and children."

"How tacky."

"Tacky?" Vera said taken aback. "How is that tacky?"

"Because just last year Milan was homeless and now she wants to exploit it and capitalize off the shit, as if her man-stealing ass has ever spent a night in a shelter. Pathetic. What an attention whore."

"You really don't like her, do you?"

"And you do?"

"Not really, but I've run into worse. Chaunci is the one I can't stand."

"Yeah," Jaise agreed. "Chaunci's li'l country ass is a hot-barnyard-mess."

Vera laughed. "But Milan isn't as bad. And when she called to invite me I felt like she was trying to be nice."

"First of all, *calling* to invite people . . . what happened to written invitations that arrive by mail?"

"It's an informal party."

"Invites to an engagement party should always be formal."

"Everybody is different."

"Either do it all the way or sit your ass down. As far as I'm concerned Milan's living proof that you can take the hooker off the block but you can't take the block out of the hooker."

"What?"

"You did know she was from the projects."

"I'm from the projects."

"Yeah, Vera, but you were saved early in life." Jaise waived her hand. "Milan is just a natural-born 'round the way-hood-ho in my humble opinion."

"You did not just say that. There's no way in hell, with as much as you got going on in your life that you are really this bougie."

"Bougie?" Jaise said, taken aback. "I'm not bougie at all. I'm a little offended by that."

"I didn't mean to offend you, Jaise. But you seem a little . . . you know."

"What?"

"Bougie."

"I'm really not and what a lot of people don't know is that I come from real humble beginnings."

Vera batted her eyes, completely surprised. "Really?"

"Yes, which is why I don't discriminate. When I was a child, my neighbors received Section Eight and my sister and I played with them all the time."

"You have got to be kidding me." Vera cracked up laughing. "I can't even believe we're holding this conversation." She said more to herself than to Jaise.

"I'm so serious," Jaise insisted. "We liked to play with them, and sure, my mother made us wear gloves and a hospital mask when we went over there. But after she made us shower and shake our clothes out, we were fine. And she always let us go back the next day."

"Jaise," Vera said. "Don't tell anybody else that damn story."

"Why not?"

"Because it sounds crazy as hell and besides, the real reason you don't like Milan is because of your friend from last season, Evan."

"Well," Jaise hesitated. "That's part of it. I mean, shit. Evan was mentally ill, don't get me wrong, and I didn't really know everything that was going on, but Milan was having an affair with her husband and now they're together like that's cool and raising Evan's child, as if they're a family."

"First of all, Kendu is the only father Aiyanna's ever known and it's not his fault Evan lied about him being her child's biological father. What else was he supposed to do?" Vera asked.

"You have a point," Jaise conceded.

"And I may not have been on the show last season, but I watched it, and Kendu clearly told Evan he didn't want her but she wouldn't let go."

"Yeah, she needed a psychiatrist, not for her husband to have a damn sex kitten."

Vera laughed. "Just be nice for the night."

"I will. I have my purse packed with my own wineglass, plate, and cutlery. So I'm determined to enjoy myself."

"You are way over the top," Vera said as Jaise crept up the block. She pointed to a prewar brick apartment building. "This is it, and there's a parking space."

"Oh, hell no." Jaise blinked, as she whipped into the space. "She doesn't even have a doorman?"

"Jaise."

"What? I'm just admiring how they do it downtown, real ganglandish."

Boney James filled the air as Milan refreshed some hors d'oeuvres and Chaunci fixed a tray of champagne glasses for the guests. "Milan, I cannot get over you inviting Jaise and Vera. Hell, you might as well have invited Al-Taniesha."

"Oh, hell, no. I can't stand Al-Taniesha. She and that Lollipop gross me out."

"But Ms. Bougie-ass Jaise is cool? That bitch is so phony. And you know I can't stomach Vera."

"Don't worry about Vera," Milan said as she garnished her tray of shrimp and red pepper. "And maybe you should try and give Jaise a chance. I think she's trying to be nice." She dusted her hands.

Chaunci looked at Milan and then dead into the camera. "That bitch wouldn't know nice if it slapped her in the mouth."

"Just don't you slap her in the mouth."

"I won't. Just don't you expect me to say one word to those heifers." She picked up the tray of drinks.

"Chaunci, if you don't want to speak, then fuck it, don't," Milan said a little more abruptly than she intended. But she had other shit on her mind, like where the hell was Kendu and why hadn't he answered her calls. Chaunci's petty-ass catfight was not the dilemma she wanted to tackle at the moment.

"Oh . . . kay." Chaunci hesitated. "Maybe before you get really pissed and start cussing you should go into your bedroom and try calling Kendu again. I'll handle the hors d'oeuvres and champagne."

"Yeah, maybe I should," Milan said as the bell rang. "Maybe that's him."

"I'ma try to be respectable and keep my thoughts, views, and opinions to myself," Jaise told Vera as she pressed the bell, "but I can't promise you a thing." She curled her lip as she looked from side to side. "I swear Milan ought to be ashamed of herself living here."

"It's not a bad building. It's downtown. It's trendy," Vera said.

"It's ghetto. And besides, this is supposed to be Millionaire Wives Club, not Gold Diggin' Boos." Jaise rang the bell again. "I betchu this damn thing doesn't work."

"You need some Valium and a drink." Vera chuckled.

"That reminds me." Jaise searched through her purse. "I think I have a Zoloft in my bag. 'Cause if I see a roach I know I'm going to have a panic attack." She pressed the bell once more. "What's taking them so long?"

Finally the knob twisted and Milan stood there smiling. "Hey, ladies. I hope you weren't standing out here too long." She air kissed Vera and Jaise on both cheeks.

"Well, when you don't have a doorman, it's not as if anyone can announce that we're here."

Milan paused and her eyes clearly cussed Jaise out.

"We weren't out here too long." Vera cut across their awkward moment of silence and handed Milan a bottle of wine.

"Come in." Milan smiled.

"Hold tight to your bag," Jaise whispered to Vera as they followed Milan. "There are some shady looking motherfuckers in here."

Goddamn. Chaunci looked up and into the eyes of the brick wall that her tray of filled champagne glasses had crashed into. She knew she'd seen those eyes before, that face, someplace. She just couldn't pinpoint where.

But at this moment she didn't give a damn . . . or maybe she did. Maybe she cared enough to enjoy the warmth of his stare. Her gaze dropped from his eyes to his full seductive lips, thick neck, broad shoulders, and wide chest. He had an athletic build and was extremely tall, but she was too wrapped up in his smooth blackberry skin, to guesstimate how tall he was. All she knew was that he was the right height to hoist her into the air and fuck her.

I have lost my damn mind.

"I'm *soooo* sorry," she said as the glasses crashed to the floor and the champagne ran from the man's button-down polo to his slightly baggy jeans to his black leather Louis Vuitton sneakers. "I really am." She dabbed the champagne from his shirt, which now clung to the center of his chest.

Hard. Washboard. Six pack. Damn . . . And that's when it clicked. She knew exactly who this was. "Emory?" She said and her blush quickly faded into a frown. "Oh, hell no." She sighed. "I knew I forgot to ask Milan if you were invited, so I could've stayed my ass home."

"Then you'd be leaving home the best part of you," he said, his eyes reflecting her thick hips, her hard nipples, her face. He took the napkins from her hand and dabbed at the spill. He smiled and immediately she thought about breast-feeding him.

Why are the assholes always so fine?

"And besides, you wouldn't have stayed home." He stepped over the mess they'd made and into her personal space. "You were *supposed* to be here and I *needed* to be here."

"You needed to be here?" She took a step back.

He took a step forward. "I wanted to see you."

"For what?" She attempted to take a step back but was halted by the wall directly behind her.

He smiled. "You just gon' run to the end huh?"

Silence.

"Look," Emory continued. "We got off to a bad start—"

"You're right, we did. You quit and left me stranded for a cleaning service." Chaunci said pissed as she bent down and began cleaning up the mess.

"You fired me and you know it." Emory reached for the broom that one of the guests handed to him.

"I had no choice. You were completely out of line!"

"I had to call my daughter. My cell phone died and my child is only seventeen and I'm a single father. Now maybe you don't have any children, but understand this—"

"Technically, I don't have to understand shit. And perhaps you did have to call your daughter but you could've been a little more professional! And for your information, I do have a daughter. She's seven, thank you very much!" she said sarcastically as she took the dustpan of glass, walked into the kitchen, and dumped it into the recycle bin. Before she could turn around she felt her hand being tugged lightly.

"Let me speak to you for a minute." Emory gently pulled Chaunci into the guest bathroom and locked the door.

"Do I need to call the cops?" she asked, taking two steps back.

"Listen to me, I—"

"I don't have to listen to you!" She pointed into his face. "Now open the door."

"Look—"

"Let me tell you something—"

"Would you shut the hell up! Damn," Emory said exhausted. "You talk too fuckin' much. What the hell are you so defensive about? You're too pretty to be so damn angry."

"Oh, don't try and put this shit on me, and I am not angry. I just want out of this damn bathroom with you."

"You know what?" Emory opened the door. "You can leave. Because apparently you don't know how to accept an apology and you're too uptight to hear when someone thinks you're breathtaking. To hell with it. I'm a thirty-nine-year-old man and I'm not gon beg you to hear me out. Fuck it." And he walked out of the bathroom, leaving Chaunci standing there.

"And where the hell is Kendu?" Jaise whispered to Vera as they grooved lightly to the music.

"I was wondering the same thing." She pointed to Milan who was working her way around the room, making light conversation. "Milan is clearly upset."

"Maybe I should ask her."

"Leave it alone," Vera said. "I'm sure she feels bad enough."

"Yeah, maybe."

Nine thirty, Milan thought as one of Kendu's friends, Terrance, walked over to her. "Where's Kendu?"

Milan hesitated. "He had some business to finish up at ESPN. You know he starts tomorrow night." She forced herself to smile. "I'm so proud."

"Yeah," Terrance said awkwardly.

"Milan." Emory walked over to her. "Where's Kendu?"

"He'll be here soon." She walked away swiftly. She had to, otherwise the next person who asked her where Kendu was, was sure to get cussed out. Especially since if she knew where the hell he was, she would find his ass and kill him.

Tears filled Milan's eyes as she walked directly into Chaunci. "Are you okay?" Chaunci asked.

"I just need a minute."

"You still haven't heard from him?"

"No."

"Do you want me to send everyone home?"

"I don't give a fuck what they do," Milan said as the bell rang.

She walked swiftly toward the door and snatched it open. Finally, it was Kendu.

"Where the hell have you been?" Milan spat as she stood at her apartment door, staring at Kendu. His eyes were red and he had a slanted smirk on his face. "Are you drunk? Seriously, you not only show up here hours late but you're drunk? Where've you been, Kendu?"

"Milan, don't start."

"What do you mean, don't start?" She closed the door behind her, and they stood in the hallway.

"I'm not drunk. I had a couple of beers—"

"You smell like you had a damn case."

"Look, I'm sorry okay? I overslept and now I'm here." He reached for the doorknob and she knocked his hand away.

"It's not okay. I've been standing here for hours looking stupid and making up one excuse after the other for you and all along you were at home drunk?"

"I'm not drunk!"

"You need to stop saying that. Really you do, because if I feel for one minute that you were sober and this is the shit you pulled then someone will have to call the cops to get me off of you!" She opened the apartment door and announced. "Look who I found."

Everyone cheered and clapped. "Now the real party can begin," Milan said with no sincerity.

"Karma is a bitch," Jaise said to Vera as they stood and sipped their drinks. "I'm sure Evan's somewhere laughing her ass off."

"Let's go and say congratulations," Vera insisted. "And be nice."

"I will," Jaise said as they walked over to Kendu and Milan.

"Jaise," Kendu said as she approached. He hugged her. "I feel like it's been a million years since I last saw you."

"It has been," she said. "How's my godchild?"

"She's fine." Kendu smiled. "She's spending the summer with my father and stepmother in Florida."

"Nice," Jaise said.

"Have you met Vera?" Milan asked Kendu, trying her best to sound chipper.

"No." His grin slid to the side of his mouth.

"This is Kendu," Milan said.

"Congratulations on your engagement." Vera smiled. She looked at Milan. "Well, listen, we're going to get going. But it was nice meeting you, Kendu, and thanks for having us, Milan."

"Yes, everything was really nice," Jaise said. "Except for your little girlfriend who pretended to be busy all night so she didn't have to speak to us, but it's fine, cause I don't give a damn."

"Goodnight," Vera said, locking arms with Jaise and pulling her toward the door.

"Why is everyone leaving?" Kendu asked as Jaise and Vera closed the door behind themselves.

"Because they've been here all fuckin' night," Milan snapped and then walked away.

As Jaise and Vera stepped onto the elevator they looked at each other and said simultaneously, "His ass was drunk as hell."

One by one their guests left and by the time an hour had passed, the only one left was Chaunci. "I'ma leave now, okay?" Chaunci said to Milan. She quickly looked at Kendu and rolled her eyes. "Stop by tomorrow, Milan. And I'll treat you to lunch, okay?"

"Alright, girl."

"Are you going to be okay?"

"What you think is going to happen to her Chaunci?" Kendu said pissed.

"Won't shit be happening to her, Kendu. Or I'll be fucking your ass up." Chaunci kissed Milan on the cheek, stormed out the door, and slammed it behind her.

"Milan—" Kendu said.

"Don't say shit to me," Milan growled.

"What do you mean?"

"Do you want to call the wedding off?" Milan asked. The words ached her mouth as she spoke.

"Why would you say something like that?"

"Why do you think I asked you that? Maybe you not showing up until the last minute for our engagement party and then you're fuckin' drunk to top it off."

"Milan, listen to me," Kendu said, reaching for her hands. "I'm sorry. I am. I overslept. And I'm an ass for that. Forgive me?" He kissed her gently. "Please. I'm sorry. I fucked up and I promise it'll never happen again."

She stared at him. A million thoughts of how she needed to put his ass out flooded her mind. "One day sorry won't be good enough." She turned toward the bedroom door and left him standing there.

Chaunci

Chaunci felt awkward as she stepped out of the building and spotted Emory walking up the block toward his black Escalade. She thought about approaching him, but quickly shook off the feeling.

Should I?

No, he's too arrogant.

He apologized.

They all apologize.

Fuck it. She walked to the corner and hailed a cab. A few seconds later one pulled up to the curb. She opened the door and glanced one last time at Emory in the distance. *Shit.* "Go on," she said to the cab driver. "I forgot something." She slammed the door and hustled up the block behind Emory.

As he opened his driver's-side door and slid in, Chaunci rushed toward the passenger side and tapped on the window.

Emory jumped. He blinked and rolled the window down. "Where in the hell did you come from?"

"Let me just say this to you," she said quickly. "I resent you saying that I have a stick up my ass."

"I just called it how I saw it."

"Well that's not it. It's just that I don't have time for bullshit. I added a no-tolerance clause to my constitution a few months back."

"Sounds like we adopted the same clause."

"And maybe I could've," she paused. "I should've handled things differently and been a little more receptive and sensitive to what you had to say, but I was pissed off."

"And I wasn't?"

"You weren't as pissed as me."

"So is that why you followed me to my truck? To tell me you were more pissed off than me?"

"You know that's not why I followed you."

"How would I know that?" Emory said getting out of his truck and walking over to Chaunci. He leaned against the back door and gently pulled her by her belt loop in front of him. "I can't read your mind."

Chaunci swallowed. *Just say it.* "I followed you to say that I owe you an apology too. We got off on the wrong foot and I would like to . . . ummm . . ."

"Umm what?"

"Start again."

"Oh really?"

"Yes, really." Chaunci smiled.

"So where do we start?"

"At Henri's down the street," Chaunci said. "I didn't eat much tonight and I'm dying for their lobster in garlic cream sauce."

Emory's eyes roamed all over Chaunci and his smile lit up the night. "Let's go," he said.

"All right, let's go. But one thing," Chaunci said as she boldly cupped his face between her soft palms. "I've been wanting to do this since I laid eyes on you." And daringly she kissed him and he kissed her back. A long, passionate, and soul stirring kiss.

"Damn," Emory said, as their kiss ended. "Looks like we're off to a great start."

"Seems so," Chaunci said, as they walked hand in hand toward the restaurant.

Milan

"Milan." Someone called her name as she stood back and watched Bridget gather china and platinum silverware in Bloomingdales that would impress the camera and would add up to a ridiculously high mock total at the register. She turned her head toward the sound of her name being called again. "Milan." It was Samir.

"What are you doing here?"

"I'm lost. I'm looking for the women's department."

Milan squinted. "Women's department? You know what they say about football players," she joked.

"Yeah ai'ight," he said seriously. "Don't play with me. I'm here to give my personal shopper a list of things my mother likes. Tomorrow's her birthday."

"Nice. Be sure to tell her I said happy birthday."

"Why don't you come with me to tell her? She's having a small get-together." His eyes drifted to her left hand.

Damn. She shook her head. *I forgot my ring.*

"No. I can't, really. I have a . . . ummm . . . few things to do. Like getting married. I'm meeting Kendu here to do our registry."

"Okay." He nodded. "But let me ask you something: What happened to your ring?"

"Why? I left it home."

"Well if you were engaged to me and you didn't have on my ring I'd be pissed off."

"And if she was engaged to you, I'd be pissed off," Kendu announced as he walked up behind Milan. "This is the second time I've seen your friend." He spat. "Something you two wanna talk to me about?"

"What?" Milan was completely embarrassed.

"Listen, no harm, no foul, man," Samir said.

"Knott," Milan spat as Samir walked away. "What the hell was that?"

"You tell me."

"I know you don't think anything of that."

"I don't know what the hell to think. I'm just ready to go."

"Are you serious? We're supposed to be registering."

He didn't answer. Instead he walked out the door.

Chaunci

WBLS' Quiet Storm played softly as thunderous rain slid down Chaunci's wall of windows. She lay on the chaise in her bedroom looking up at the vaulted ceiling and wondering if she should keep her date with Emory or stand him up. They'd been seeing each other practically every day since Milan's engagement party a month ago. And up until this morning when she rolled over in bed and the first person on her mind was Emory—she felt frightened; as if she were losing control and needed to turn away.

You need to go. You told the man you'd meet him.

I'm not going.

She lay in a black spaghetti-strap minidress with a deep V cut at the neckline. The dress hugged every one of her curves and showcased her tight thighs as she held her cell phone to her chest.

Maybe . . .

You're choosing to be miserable.

Maybe . . .

Just go . . .

Uncontrollable heat hit Chaunci in the face as soon as she walked into Limin's, a small and tight reggae club in the heart of Flatbush in Brooklyn. Limin's wasn't a spot that Chaunci would have chosen for a date, but hell . . .

Tanya Stephens's *Gangsta Blues* blasted through the club's sound system as Chaunci walked over to the bar and ordered a drink. A few minutes into sipping her daiquiri and nodding her head to the music she spotted Emory and froze. He sat on the other side of the room, laughing, sipping a beer, and moving to the music.

Damn. Even in the dim lights of the club, he was fine.

"Looking for me?" She walked over and stood in front of him.

"When I woke up this morning," he said as they embraced. "And you were the first person on my mind. I realized that I've been looking for you for a long time."

Chaunci blushed and he looked her over, his eyes fucking her every step of the way.

Chaunci's hair spilled over her shoulders like water. The lip gloss she wore lit up her face. Boldly, Emory took the tip of his index finger and slid it from the center of her lips to her cleavage.

"What are you thinking?" Emory asked.

"You first," Chaunci said nervously. She hated that she was out of her comfort zone of being calm, collected, and in control, mostly because she knew feeling butterflies led to taking blind leaps of faith in shit like love and commitment and she wasn't sure she was ready for that. And not because she'd tried true love once and had been hurt by it, but because not until she'd met Emory did she realize she'd never tried true love at all.

"I'm wondering if you're scared."

"A little," she admitted.

"Why?"

"Because how do I know where this will lead. I don't want to be hurt."

"I don't want to hurt you, I want to love you. Are you willing to let me do that?"

"What are you saying?"

"I'm saying that I want to see you exclusively."

"Exclusively?" she said surprised.

"I'm selfish. I want you to myself."

"Interesting."

"Interesting?" He couldn't help but smile. "Aren't you selfish?"

"I'm torn."

"On what?"

"If I should stay or leave."

He pulled her close to him. "Choose one."

"I think I should leave."

"Really?"

"Yeah." She paused. "And I think you should come with me."

Chaunci walked into his apartment and, as forward as she usually was when it came to making love, she felt nervous, like an innocent schoolgirl with Emory.

What the hell is wrong with me? He flipped on his radio to the sound of Mint Condition's "Someone To Love" and the electric-blue equalizer lit up the room. Chaunci grabbed Emory's hand, locked his fingers between hers, and they began to dance.

"Just let go," Emory whispered in her ear as he unzipped her dress. "And let me take the lead."

They danced slowly and his hands roamed her body as he undressed her. He pushed the straps of her dress off her shoulders one at a time and placed kisses on them, softly moving his tongue up her neck to her bottom lip. "What are you thinking?"

"Is this for real?" She stroked the seat of his pants. His inches creased the side of his thigh.

"It's real, baby." They kissed passionately.

Chills ran through Chaunci's body as the firmness of her clit became liquid in his hands.

"Emory . . ." she moaned as they lay on the floor beneath the skylight. Slowly he sucked one nipple and then the other. The wet warmth of his lips sent her to another dimension.

He kissed her nipples as if he'd wanted to taste them all his life. He sucked the side of her neck as if her skin were candy. Then he kissed a trail down the center of her body to her pussy lips, where he opened her with his mouth.

Chaunci had never felt like this. She could swear she'd melted at least a hundred times. Never in all her years did she know that her clit could have convulsions.

After coming twice Chaunci rolled on top of him and licked the outline of his tattoos, including the one on his hand. Then she bit his nipples and kissed him all over his stomach, moving up slowly, lifting his smooth chest hairs with her tongue. Then she pressed her forehead against his and looked into his eyes.

"Let it go, babe." He turned her over and she lay in the missionary position. His dick had to be at least eleven inches, because she'd never felt anything like it. She could swear he'd gone into her stomach, causing her to rake her nails down his back and cry out his name.

"What's the problem?" He stroked her with all he had. The pleasure he provided confused her. She didn't know if she was coming or going.

"Wait," she panted, as he threw her legs to one side of his shoulder, "slow down."

"Oh, hell, no. I know you're not running from the dick." He pounded.

"N-no," she stuttered. "It's just so big."

"Get used to it, because after tonight this is my pussy."

"Emory!" she squealed, barely able to breathe. Their bodies danced, sweated, and soared. Chaunci clutched his back as she felt her dam preparing to explode.

He bit into one shoulder. The sting of his bite broke the dam and the river flowed.

"Don't fuck around," he said as he lined her sugar walls with pearls. "And fall in love with me."

Action

Vera

Today was the day and this was the moment Vera decided she could have it all. And anything she didn't have was simply because she didn't want it—or didn't need it.

She'd just returned from Florida, and she strutted through JFK airport wearing a black power suit, a white camisole, and five-inch Jimmy Choos. Her Gucci aviators crowned her face. She was on a mission. A takeover. HSN had not only offered her a distribution deal but also a live weekly segment to show the world why everyone needed Volume.

She did a slight two-step as she walked into the lobby. People were everywhere, running, crying, jumping into one another's arms, chauffeurs holding cardboard signs with clients' names on them. Vera spotted Carl with his camera as she walked toward the exit, hoping to see Taj.

"Yes!" She pumped her fist as she looked into the camera.

"Tell the camera why you're so excited," Carl greeted her.

"Because," she said with confidence, "I am living proof that a mother, a wife, and a hard-working woman can have it all."

"Really?"

"Yes, really."

"And what do you say to the opposition?"

"I say, to hell with whatever angry cave-bitch started the opposing rumor." She put her hand on her hips. "Because clearly, she has never met me." She snapped her fingers. "Thank you very much." She smiled as Carl faded to the background and she proudly took a seat next to the door and waited.

And waited.

And just as she thought that she'd watched what seemed like a million people come and go she realized she'd waited over an hour.

Where is he?

She pulled her cell phone from her purse and dialed Taj's number. No answer.

Try again. She did. Nothing. "Taj, honey," she said into his voice mail. "I'm at the airport waiting. Please hurry. See you soon. Love you."

Another hour of unanswered and unreturned phone calls. Vera tapped her fingers on the edge of her seat. It was at times like this that she hated filming.

Where is he?

Something happened.

Stop. Thinking. The. Worst.

He's fine. His phone probably died. You know he's the worst when it comes to charging his phone.

True.

Deciding she couldn't wait a moment longer Vera walked out of the airport, hailed a cab, and she, Carl, and the camera slid in.

"257 Fifth and Park, please," she said to the cabbie.

Vera turned her head away from Carl and toward the window. New York City traffic whipped by in blurry snippets as the taxi driver burned up the highway, only to be forced to slow down once he reached the surface streets.

Vera pulled her phone from her purse and tried Taj again. No answer.

Where is he?

He's fine. Just focus on getting some wine and making some love.

Friday-afternoon traffic was at a complete standstill. The cars moved like turtles, and blaring horns roared like lions. It was a jungle, a bumper-to-bumper mess that apparently caused hallucinations. At least Vera thought so, because she had to be mistaken when she thought she'd spotted Taj, sitting at an outdoor café with his face contorted and his finger pointed at a slender mahogany-colored woman who looked just as upset as he did, if not even more so.

That's not him, Vera thought as the cabbie danced through traffic, only to be halted by the next traffic light.

The light changed and they crept down another block.

That was him.

No, it wasn't.

The cabbie picked up a little speed but was then cut off by a biker and forced to slam on his brakes, missing the green light by milliseconds.

That was him. Vera quickly stuffed two twenties in the pocket of the Plexiglas divider. "I have to go!"

"I can't let you out in the middle of the street!" the cabbie yelled as Vera flew out, leaving the door open for Carl, who practically fell out behind her. They hopscotched through traffic as she made her way across the street. She had three blocks to go.

One block.

Relax. It could be a business meeting.

"I just feel like there's so much I need to tell you." Taj's voice drove nails into Vera's head as she thought about the night he miraculously became supportive of everything she wanted to do.

Two blocks.

"Excuse me," she could hear Carl say from behind as they squeezed through the thick mob of people crowding the block.

Three. Vera slowed down, almost as if her batteries were giving out. She spotted Taj. But instead of rushing toward him she slowly walked. Stood back. Watched his face. He was pissed. The woman he was with had tears swimming in her eyes.

Vera wanted like hell to be mistaken.

Prayed to be mistaken.

And wishing her intuition would flee, but it yanked her by the throat and whispered in her ear, "This is not a good thing." If it didn't flee, she was convinced she'd have to give in to the voice that told her to kill him.

Carl scurried behind Vera, finally catching up. She could hear him gasp as the rubber soles of his sneakers screeched.

Beads of sweat ran along the side of Vera's temples as she swept her hair out of her face.

The summer evening sun beat against her back as she looked into Taj's face and he looked into hers.

She could see him thinking about what he needed to say. She wanted to give him a moment. She knew Taj was the kind of man who chose his words carefully, but he was taking too fucking long.

"I'm Vera, Taj's wife." She turned to the woman, hating that they were sizing each other up. "And you are?" She held out one hand.

"Dion." She left Vera's hand dangling. "His son's mother."

Jaise

It was all a lie. All of it. Every day, from the wee morning hour when Jaise rose and ran her hands across their cold bedsheets to the midnight hour when she turned to Bilal and kissed him down his spine only to be greeted with nothing. Absolutely nothing.

No hard dick.

No kiss.

No suckling her breasts, which used to be his favorite thing to do.

Nothing. But then again, maybe his nothing really was something.

Suddenly and without warning her life had literally become lights, camera, action.

"Hi, sweetie." Jaise smiled at Bilal as he walked in the front door, tossing his keys on the kitchen island. "How was work?" she asked. Not giving him a chance to respond, she continued. "I'm sure you had a tough night. Are you hungry?" she asked in a rush. She didn't want too much time between her words because she couldn't take any chances on Bridget noticing Bilal's dryness, especially since most of their conversations had been reduced to how good dinner was and how he was working late again. "I made you a nice breakfast, darling."

Jaise wondered if she sounded like Paula Deen.

She smiled into the camera as she pointed to each dish. "Grits, bacon, cheese and eggs, freshly baked biscuits, and Grandma's molasses."

"Jaise—"

Don't let him talk. "Work was good, baby?"

"Jaise—"

"I know you must be tired." She placed his food in front of him.

"Jaise—"

"Coffee or orange juice?"

"Jaise!"

"What?" she said, startled, sucking her stomach in, her breath lodged in her chest. She hoped like hell she didn't just provide him a passageway to say something no one—not even Jaise— needed to hear.

She stared at him, her eyes pleading for him to be quiet, but she couldn't tell whether he'd caught on or not. All she knew was that he was no good at faking reality-TV style.

"I love you," he said.

She set a full plate of food before him. "I love you too, honey, but you need to eat so you can get some sleep. I'm sure they worked you like a dog at the station."

"Jaise." He reached across the table and grabbed her hands. "I didn't go to work."

You better not drop one single tear. "You know what they say." She forced a smile, sliding her hands from between his. "When you do what you love, you'll never work again in your life. Now eat."

"Goddamn, Jaise!" he screamed, pushing his plate away. "Listen to me. I don't want shit to eat! Fuck!" The plate crashed to the floor and the food flew across the room.

Jaise could hear Bridget whispering, "Focus, Carl, focus."

"How long are we gon' do this shit? I'm tired." Bilal shook his head.

"You worked all night. Of course you're tired. Now eat."

"Don't say that shit again! Look at me." He grabbed her tightly by the forearms, causing her body to shake and tears to drip from her eyes. "I'm tired and I can't do this shit anymore."

"Bilal—"

"Shut up!" he yelled at the top of his lungs. "Do you know where I was last night? I wasn't at work. I wasn't. I went out with someone."

"You did what?" She jerked her arms away from him.

"I went on a date. A fuckin' date!"

Jaise stumbled. She'd heard wrong, she must have. "You're cheating on me? I can't believe this." She lost her breath.

"What the hell did you expect to happen?" he snapped. "I didn't fuck her. I didn't, because the whole night I kept thinking about you. I love you, but you're so busy running around here with Jabril that you're pushing me away. Don't you see I'm five seconds from running out the fuckin' door?"

"So you cheat on me! That's the answer?"

"No, it's not the answer, but it's real and I did that shit. But what I realized is that I don't need another woman. I don't *want* another woman. I want my wife. I *need* my wife." The veins in his neck stood out and he pounded on the kitchen table. "I love you and I'm begging you to love me."

"You don't have to beg me to love you!"

"Then what do I have to do, Jaise? Because you couldn't possibly be in love with me. When's the last time we made love?"

"You don't turn to me!"

"Because you won't face reality!" Tears dripped from his face. "Do you know how I feel? There was a time when you were my best friend, my soul mate, but I don't even know you anymore."

"I'm doing the best I can! I can't be everything to everybody!"

"All I need you to be is my wife."

"I am your wife! But you expect me to stop being a mother."

"No, I expect you to stop breast-feeding a grown goddamn man! I need you. And you're so busy saving Jabril's ass that you'd rather die than let him be a man."

"I'm trying to teach him."

"You're his fuckin' problem. He's not a man because you don't want him to be!"

"That's not true!"

"You know what, Jaise? I didn't sign up for this shit. I signed up for a wife."

"And what the hell am I?"

"A stranger." He snatched his keys off the island. "Don't look for me in the morning, because I won't be coming back. I'm done."

Jaise stood in the center of the floor. She wondered if she'd just dreamed this scene. She looked around the kitchen at the food splattered on the floor. She could smell the lingering scent of Bilal's cologne. He'd been here . . . and he'd left . . .

She lost her balance. She fell to the floor. Tears slid down her neck.

$\mathcal{V}era$

Here was the plan: Give a great performance on camera, act like she could handle what had happened to her, and when Bridget left, lose her mind.

Vera walked toward Taj's home office and her plum Alexander McQueens clicked like mad drums as she walked what felt like the pathway to death.

Just listen to what he has to say. Listen for the reasons he's been living a lie and I've been living a lie. Listen for the reasons I saw him with another woman who announced that she was his son's mother. What son? Surely I heard wrong. Surely everybody heard wrong: the blogs, the gossip sites, the tabloids. It was all wrong. It has to be.

Vera sucked in a deep breath and flung the door to the office open.

Taj spun around toward her in his chair. His eyes were red with tears as he stood up and faced her. "Vera—"

"Taj," she said. A nervous smile crept onto her face and rattled her voice. "I, umm, wanted to talk to you for a minute."

He breathed a sigh of relief. "Yes, baby, let's talk, please. I don't want you to think I cheated on you. I didn't," he said in a hurry as if his time to explain was soon to expire.

As if she hadn't heard a word he said, she said, "I need to know if I heard correctly yesterday. If I saw correctly. Did I see you with another woman? Do you have another child? Or am I going crazy? Am I losing my mind?"

"No, Vera." He reached for her. "I should've said something to you, but I just found out and I didn't know how to tell you—"

"So it's true." *She could feel her original plan for handling this quickly going to hell.*

"Yes, but I need you to hear me out."

Suddenly Vera was in Oz. Or maybe it was space. Or maybe she'd floated to the dimension just beyond shocked, breathless, and anxiously restless. This was not how shit was supposed to end or, hell, begin again. Especially since she was willing to sacrifice a moment of sanity for a lie.

But he didn't lie.

He told the truth, and the truth had just rendered her lifeless.

"So I haven't lost my mind. It's you. You've gone fucking crazy," Vera said calmly. "Okay."

"Vera, please," Taj begged. "I have a lot I need to say to you. A lot needs to be said."

"You're right," she agreed. "A lot needs to be said." She paused. "So why don't you call up every fuckin' blog, newspaper, tabloid, and every-other-goddamn-body who has my ass blasted all over the Internet and explain to them why the *fuck* you have another baby. And how in the hell you, Dr. Perfect, lied to me and left me in the dark. And if you can't pull that out of your ass, Taj, then don't explain shit to me!"

Just stay calm, she thought.

I'ma stay calm.

Maybe I should leave.

Vera felt as if she walked on uneven stilts as she moved from Taj's office to their master suite. He followed her.

She felt her heart squeeze tightly beneath her breasts, and a pain shot up her arm.

"Vera, let me explain."

"Explain what?" She spun around toward him. "Explain to whom? I don't want to hear shit you have to say—" She paused. Tears choked her and snatched her voice. She swallowed and once again thought of dropping the argument. *Let it go.*

She turned toward the door to leave, and as she stepped over the threshold it hit her that her life had fallen apart. It had all crumbled on top of her. There was no way she could turn and walk away as if it was okay. No way in hell.

She whipped back into the room and over to their walk-in closet. The tears she'd fought to hold back snuck past the corners of her eyes and streamed along the sides of her nose.

"Maybe I'll go and stay in a hotel for a few days," Taj suggested. "Maybe I need to give you some space."

"Oh, now you wanna run off to your other family?"

"That's not what I'm saying. I just don't want you to be upset—"

"Okay, cool," she said calmly, walking to her closet. "Excuse me for being upset. Excuse me for caring that for ten years I've lived a goddamn lie. I'm so sorry that's pissed me off!" She yanked Taj's shirts from the satin hangers. Knocked his shoes off the racks, snatched his pants from the circular rod, and threw everything into an open suitcase on the floor. "You're right. I need some motherfuckin' space! So I need you to take all yo' shit!"

Vera hustled everything of Taj's from the hangers and shelves to the floor. She stood in the midst of the garment windstorm and tossed his clothes with such force and speed that it felt like a tsunami had come. "I'ma give yo' ass all the space you need!" She haphazardly grabbed the suitcase and dragged it down the hall toward the terrace.

"What are you doing, Vera?" Taj spat, as the veins in his neck seemed to connect with the veins in his biceps and rose under his skin like bolts of lightning. He followed the trail of clothes that fell from his suitcase down the hall. They flew past the maids and the nanny, who whispered and looked at them like they were crazy.

"Vera!"

"Don't call me, motherfucker." She dragged the suitcase. "Call Dion, call that bastard of yours. Call those motherfuckers! Is he a junior, Taj? Is he the junior who lived? Oh, you getting the fuck out of here!" Vera opened the terrace's French doors, ran to the edge, and dumped everything that belonged to Taj over the railing. It floated like parachutes in the wind.

"Have you lost your fucking mind?" Taj screamed.

"No." She raced back down the hall. "I'm sane! If I were crazy I'd be throwing *you* over the fuckin' ledge!"

She grabbed another handful of Taj's belongings and tossed them below. She huffed as she dusted off her hands, ran past him, and tripped out of one of her heels. She kicked the other off, regained her balance, and raced back to their bedroom. She collected more of his things and tossed them into the sky.

"You betrayed me, motherfucker!" She struggled to maintain her breath, and beads of sweat rolled down the sides of her face and her neck.

"Vera—"

"Since you think we need space, then out-motherfuckin'-side will give you all the space you need! Sleep under the goddamn stars!" She tossed the last few pieces.

Taj took a step back and for a moment Vera wondered if she'd gone too far, but fuck it. He'd forced her hand and made her take it there. And true story, as crazy as she knew it was, even in the midst of all this, she wanted to make it all go away.

But she couldn't.

She couldn't.

"Get out," she said, out of breath, her tears and sweat forming a mask over her face. "Get the fuck out!"

Taj didn't respond and Vera was too bogged down by the ache

taking up space in her belly to continue antagonizing him. She could feel the pain from her stomach rising to her throat.

Taj walked backward until he reached the living room and then he walked out the door. And as the elevator doors closed Vera fell to her knees and cried for what felt like forever.

Chaunci

Things were too perfect.

And Chaunci knew she was playing house a little too much, and too often. They had movie night, pizza night, Michael Jackson Wii night. And Kobi liked him. Actually she loved him.

And they made love every night without fail.

There was no way she could continue to function like this.

And it's not that she was head over heels in love, but she could feel herself giving in. And she couldn't. There was no way in hell she could lose that much control.

Emory stretched, he turned over, and kissed Chaunci. Her lips were stiff. "What's wrong, baby?" He stroked her back.

She sat up in bed, her bare back pressed to the headboard and the sheet pulled over her breasts. "I was thinking that maybe we should, umm—"

"Should what?"

"Stop seeing each other for a while."

Emory looked at Chaunci as if she had two heads. "Where the hell did that come from? That's what you want?"

"It's not about what I want," Chaunci said. "It's about what I know. And I know that this whole deal is moving too fast and we need to slow down."

He squinted and stared at her. He looked her over, then lifted her chin. "You in love with me?"

"Emory—" She was seconds from saying "yeah." "Let's just quit while we're ahead."

"Ahead of what?"

She sighed. "I just—"

"You're scared."

"No, I'm just not ready—"

"To face your fears."

"Would you stop cutting me off?"

"Then stop lying to me!"

"I'm not lying to you."

He tilted his head. "So you're telling me the truth?"

"Yes."

"Aight, then cool."

"Cool?" she said, taken aback.

"Cool." He sat on the edge of the bed and reached to the floor for his pants. He slid them on.

"That's all you have to say? Cool?" Chaunci couldn't believe this shit.

"What the fuck you want me to say, Chaunci?" He slid his T-shirt over his head. "That I'm in love with you and that I know you're in love with me, but you're punking the fuck out? Seriously, I don't have time for that. I know what I want. You have to get your shit together. And if you can tell me that you done and you don't want us to be together, then cool. I'm not about to beg you or try to convince you that I love you." He slid his shirt on. "If you can't see that I want to spend the rest of my life with you then you have a problem. 'Cause I'ma make sure you wear that shit."

"I just think—"

"Chaunci, that's the problem: you think too much." He slipped his sneakers on.

"I'm not saying that we can never be together. I'm just saying that right now doesn't seem to be the right time. We can always be friends."

"Have you lost your mind?" Emory asked. "Really? Have you? 'Cause there's no way in hell that you believe what you just said. I don't know who you're used to dealing with, but I know bullshit when I hear it." He walked out of the bedroom and a few moments later the apartment door slammed behind him.

Chaunci lay in bed, staring at the ceiling. "What the hell did I just do?"

Milan

Floacist's seductive, poetic voice seduced Milan into Shonda's Soliloquy, a poetry spot in the heart of SoHo where there was always a nightly crowd. People from all over the tristate area packed the place as if it were a tourist attraction instead of a local spot where lovers of words, literature, and a deep lyrical movement came together and grooved.

Shonda's was a world all its own: an industrial loft decorated with white leather couches, flickering tealight candles on petite tables, candelabra chandeliers hanging above the small planked stage, and an all-blue glass bar that lined an entire wall.

Milan eased into the spot with Bridget and Carl behind her. Her eyes scanned the crowd as she nodded to the music. She was there to meet Kendu and get his thoughts on renting Shonda's for her birthday party, but from the looks of things he had yet to arrive.

"Drink?" The bartender smiled as Milan slid through the crowd and leaned against the center of the bar.

"White wine, please."

Once she had her drink, she eased onto a barstool and turned toward the stage, where Floacist made love to the mic, performing her hit "Forever" with Musiq Soulchild. Milan found herself softly chanting the words to the seductive poem. Her nipples tingled as she thought about what it would be like to make love to this beat. She closed her eyes and sipped her drink. Her shoulders slowly rocked to the music.

Feeling herself slipping into a zone, she forced her lids to open and immediately her gaze locked onto a familiar set of warm chestnut eyes. "Samir." She smiled and immediately wondered if she was smiling too much.

Deciding that her grin was a little too wide, Milan cursed her dimples. "Umm, what a surprise seeing you here." She fanned her face, as the awkwardness caused her body heat to rise.

"Yeah," Samir said. "I was surprised to see you here too, especially since this isn't Saks." He laughed.

"Excuse you." She chuckled, doing her best to avoid his eyes. "I happen to love poetry. I actually write a little from time to time."

"Yeah?" His eyes roamed over her body.

She crossed her arms over her breasts, hoping to hide the imprint of her hard nipples. "I do have a few nights a week that I give bougie some time off, thank you very much."

"Really." He nodded. He looked her up and down before looking toward the door. "Here comes the legend."

"Where?" Milan said anxiously. She turned toward the door to see Kendu walking toward her.

"Damn, this place is packed," he said, placing one hand on Milan's waist while kissing her on the lips.

"You know Samir, right?" Milan said, hoping Kendu didn't catch the nervousness in her voice.

"Yeah, sure," Kendu blew him off. He nodded. "Wassup?"

"You got it." Samir smiled. "Later, Milan."

"Yeah, later."

"I don't like this spot," Kendu said to Milan as Samir walked away.

"Why?"

"I just don't."

She stared at him. *He's lying.* "So what are you saying? You want to leave?"

"Yeah." He turned his face from side to side. "That's exactly what I'm saying."

Milan's footsteps echoed down the block as she stormed behind Kendu to his truck. As she tried to cross the street behind him one of her heels got stuck in a grid. "Kendu!" she screamed as he continued to walk. "Kendu!" she screamed again, causing a few people to turn around and look, but Kendu continued on his way. Unable to catch his attention, she wiggled her foot free, and scurried after him. "What the hell is your problem?" she said, pissed, as she caught up to him. "And where the hell did you park?"

"I'm sick of your shit, Milan!"

She whipped her head toward him. He continued walking. "What?" she said from behind him, hurrying as if she were on a chase. "What the hell are you talking about? What did I do to you?" she said toward his back. "And slow down."

He stopped for a moment and faced her. "It's always some shit with you!" He started walking toward the truck again.

Milan felt like she'd been slugged. *He wants to argue. Why does he want to argue?* "I don't know what your problem is, but I didn't do shit to you!"

"Why is this motherfucker all up in your face? First my retirement dinner, Bloomingdales, and now this spot. How did he know you'd be here?"

Is he jealous?

"Is this where you been meeting his ass? Is he the new athlete?"

What? "Kendu," she said, exhausted, as they cut through a thick crowd and crossed another block. "What the hell are you talking about? I had no idea Samir would be there."

"The hottest goddamn athlete in the NFL just randomly shows up somewhere and ends up in your face. How does that shit sound? Crazy to me." He took off again.

"Would you slow the fuck down?" She ran after him.

"No." He took the keys for his Infiniti truck out of his pocket and turned off the alarm. "Get in."

"Hold it! Stop for a moment," Milan said breathlessly. "What the hell is going on?"

"You on some silly shit." He pointed at her.

"Knott, I didn't know Samir was going to be there. I didn't."

"Sure."

"Are you accusing me of being with him?"

"You said it. I didn't."

"Is that what you expect from me?" she asked in disbelief.

"I don't know what to expect. I don't. Hell, you cheated on Yusef, so I damn sure can't say what you'd do to me."

There was the right hook again. "I'd never cheat on you." *Why am I trying to pacify him? Why?* "And furthermore, I cheated on Yusef with *you*. Hell, *you* cheated on your wife too!"

"Well, I guess we're two cheating motherfuckers." He unlocked the truck's door and slid in. "Now I'm ready to go the hell home."

"Well, you go ahead." Milan nodded.

"There you go," Kendu snapped. "Would you just get your ass in the truck?"

"No." She shook her head. "I don't appreciate—"

"You don't appreciate what, Milan?" He pointed his left index finger at her. "What could you, Ms. Millionaire-fuckin'-Wife, not appreciate? Hell, you struck groupie gold when I asked you to marry me. What more do you want?!"

Milan choked back tears. She looked down at the bits of glass on the ground, a few pieces of shredded newspaper, and other litter.

She turned, but as she walked toward the curb it hit her that she'd been called a groupie by her man. Of everything he could've called her—his best friend, his lover—of all the words he had to choose, he picked "groupie." *Ain't this a motherfucker?*

Milan turned again and walked up to Kendu, her heels stabbing through the litter. She looked him directly in the face and struggled to restrain herself from smacking the shit out of him. "Groupie?" She shoved him, but he was too big for it to have an effect. "Groupie?" She pointed a finger in his face.

"Milan, go 'head," he warned.

"Groupie, motherfucker?" The tears she'd fought to hold back snuck past the corners of her eyes and streamed along the sides of her nose. "Groupie?" She could look at him and tell he was sorry he'd said that to her. But she also knew him well enough to know that once pride filled his chest there was no way he'd apologize. So fuck him. "Groupie, motherfucker? Really? Why don't you just say what this is really about? This is about you not wanting to marry me!"

"Did I say that?"

"Yeah, you did. You said it practically every day. And what did I do? I made excuses for you. Ran around here trying to plan a wedding in a rush, because I knew it wasn't what you wanted! But I wanted to hurry and do it, just in case you were serious. I'm soooo stupid."

"Milan—"

"And you are such a fuckin' coward!" Her heart pumped like a revved-up '57 Chevy. She stood at the corner and watched the traffic. She slid her engagement ring off her finger.

"Put your goddamn ring back on," he snapped.

"For what? You don't want to marry me. I'm just a fuckin' girlfriend with an ornament on her hand, waiting once again for yo' ass. But not anymore. Fuck you. I'm done. I've been waiting since I was nine, waiting while I was in college, waited while I watched you marry some crazy bitch who put a baby on you. Waited and waited and waited. No more. Fuck you!"

Sweat and tears ran down her face. She could look in Kendu's eyes and see that he knew she was telling the truth. And though her heart felt like it was being ripped to shreds, she knew she couldn't wait a moment longer. Waiting had only caused her a million moments of grief, despair, and regret over what she should and shouldn't have done. She'd had enough of waiting for Kendu to get his act together and for him to act "right" when he felt "right."

The truth of the matter was that she *didn't* want to wait for him to get his shit together. She just wanted it to happen. She was tired of pretending that she understood him when most of the time she didn't.

She *didn't* understand how a grown man could hold on to the hurt of being an abandoned little boy now that he was thirty-two and knew that shit happened, that motherfuckers weren't perfect, and that that included his mysterious-ass mama and daddy. And he knew that the opportunities he'd been afforded were a blessing that the average person only dreamed about. So whatever his problem really was, she didn't know and didn't care to decode. To hell with it. She wasn't his therapist.

And right now, Kendu could kiss her ass because there was no way she was going to push aside another day or even another moment of what she wanted because she was, yet again, waiting for this motherfucker to get his shit together.

"I'm done." She handed him his ring.

"You're done." He looked her over. "So what are you saying, Milan?"

She didn't answer him. She simply walked swiftly down the block, disappearing into a subway station with the camera racing behind her.

"Ma'am, is Jabril Williams here?" Two uniformed officers stood at Jaise's door with an elderly white-haired woman wearing a worried look.

Jaise stood at her front door with her granddaughter on her hip and her grandson crying and hugging her around the knees. Jabril had come home with his children, claiming he was dedicating this weekend to being a good father and doing more than paying child support. And when he left shortly after J.J. started crying, he said he was running to Walgreens for Anbesol, Tylenol, Pampers, and milk.

That had been three hours ago.

"I haven't seen him," she said. "And who's asking for him?" She looked at the old woman. *Lord, please don't tell me he's fuckin' this bitch too.*

"Do you know when he'll be returning?" one of the cops asked.

"Officer, with all due respect, why are you asking me these things?"

"Because my granddaughter," the elderly woman said, "called me a few nights ago and said she was living here."

"Living here?" Jaise said, shocked. "Your granddaughter?"

"Yes." The woman's voice trembled with tears. "And she's only fifteen. She's a runaway and she's involved with Child Protective Services. I'm her guardian, so I was hoping she'd be here."

"Oh, no, ma'am. I have no idea who you're talking about, and Jabril isn't here."

"Do you have a way to get in touch with him?" the officer asked.

"No," Jaise said.

"Well, if it was a family emergency," the cop said, "how would you get in touch with him?"

Jaise smirked. "Officer, he *is* the family emergency."

"Well, ma'am, if you see him, please ask him to give us a call."

"If I see him," she said, closing the door.

After making sure they were gone, Jaise hurried to dial Jabril's cell phone. Voice mail. "You know what, Jabril?" she said calmly. "I'm convinced that you have lost your damn mind. Yo' ass is going to get locked up fucking with these young girls. I tell you what, you just better get your ass home and come get your damn kids!"

Click.

The sun rose and shot rays of light into Jaise's living room. She hadn't been to sleep all night and felt like she was walking through space. She'd had enough. She couldn't take any more. Bilal was gone and, hell, for all intents and purposes, Jabril was gone too.

She sat with her thighs crossed and the ball of her right foot lightly tapping her Persian rug. The tip of her toes gently brushed the hand-sewn fibers out of place as she struggled to ignore the migraine crawling down the back of her neck.

Focus . . .

She leaned her head against the back of her oversized sofa, closed her eyes, and tried to move past the first line of her silent prayer—the same prayer she'd said since last night.

God give me strength now.

He didn't.

She opened her eyes and her gut ached as she looked over to her grandchildren, who were doing their own thing. Jaise couldn't even remember if they'd been to sleep.

J.J. dug in a potted plant, broke off leaves, and ate bits of dirt, while his sister repeatedly bumped into Jaise's antique bookcase with her walker. Yet Jaise never told them to stop or tried to redirect them. Instead she attended to her thoughts.

She eased to the edge of the sofa and reached for her mirrored cigarette case. She wrestled with the clasp—that only seemed to cause her grief at times like this—and caught a glimpse of her reflection. Her usually beautiful button eyes were now at half-mast and had been transformed into exhausted almonds.

She licked her dry lips and resumed wrestling with her cigarette case. Finally it opened. She slid a Virginia Slims between the center of her lips and held her vintage Zippo lighter to the tip. Moments later her cigarette came alive. The first pull felt like a fresh peppermint breeze, restoring her senses.

Jaise walked over to the closet and pulled out the double stroller—the one item Jabril had ever purchased for his children. She unfolded the stroller and locked the wheels. "Come on, J.J." She put him in the front of the stroller. "Come on, Jada." She placed her in the back. "We're going to sit on the stoop."

Jaise grabbed her cigarettes and pushed the children out the door.

Two hours later, Jabril pulled up, parked his car, and slowly walked toward the house.

"Ma." He looked at her strangely. "Why do you have my children out here like this?"

Jaise didn't answer. Instead she pulled the last cigarette from her pack and lit it. She took a strong toke as Jabril said, "Ma. Do you hear me?"

"You know what?" She took a hit. "I hear you and I see you. I see that you are one trifling no-account motherfucker. I've had it." She flicked the ashes from her cigarette. "I'm tired. I can't keep saving you. I can't."

"Saving me?" Jabril said, put off. "Ma, what are you talking about?"

"I've been trying to make up for one mistake after another after another." She took a puff. "But you keep fucking up. I can't do it anymore. I have to let you go. So I tell you what. Take your kids and get out!" she screamed at the top of her lungs. Then suddenly she got quiet and said, "Get out."

"Ma," Jabril said, shocked, "what are you doing?"

"Get. The. Fuck. Out!" she said matter-of-factly. "I've had enough and I don't have anything left to give you!"

"Ma!" he said as she pushed the stroller toward him.

"You have to go," she said.

Jabril stood frozen. "I don't have no place else to go, Ma. Chill."

"You have two baby mamas and a sorry-ass daddy. Take your pick. But staying here with me can't happen anymore. I'm done."

Jaise walked into the house and it took everything she had not to break down. She squeezed her eyes tightly. Never had she imagined that this would happen. She'd been left on her ass. She loved her son, but she had to let him go. She was the best thing and the worst thing that had happened to him.

Jabril pounded on the door and with every knock and muffled scream of, "Ma, let me in!" Jaise felt like someone had shot her in the chest. She pressed her back against the door. She knew that if she kept standing her knees would give way. So she slid to the floor and cried until all she could see was a sea of blur.

$\mathcal{V}era$

Vera stood, poised and picture perfect, in the center of her gourmet kitchen wearing five-inch stilettos, designer jeans, a Chanel tee, and eighty-inch double-strand pearls, wondering when she'd quit being true to herself for the sake of fame and fortune.

She hated stardom. Rewind that—she hated bad press, and she hated people in her business. Scratch that—she hated people in her bullshit.

There was a difference.

She wanted the media to pay attention to what she had to offer, and to how far she'd come in life from the piss-filled projects to Fifth Avenue. She didn't want or need them to care about why Taj had lied, because she didn't have an answer for that.

And no matter how many nights she cried, screamed, prayed, and ached until her body convulsed, and "Dear God" fell dryly from her mouth, she couldn't pinpoint when the true Vera had been taken. All she knew was that the around the way chick who didn't tolerate anyone's shit had been kidnapped and replaced by a pathetic bitch.

I'm his son's mother. Dion's voice slammed into Vera's thoughts and haunted her, creating a vision of Taj, his son, and Dion as one big, happy family. Vera blinked but the vision didn't leave. Instead it grew more intense. She could see them making love and laughing at her.

All these years, she thought as the vision slowly faded. *All these fuckin' years! I loved your ass. Shared my fears and my most intimate feelings. I thought for sure you could read my mind.*

You didn't love me.

You couldn't have loved me.

I've been stole on . . .

I've been sucker punched and made to stand here and take the beat down on TV.

Uncertain what to do but knowing that she needed to sit down, Vera sat at her kitchen desk and turned on her laptop. She meant to check her e-mail and then turn off the computer. Yet before she thought twice, she was painstakingly combing the blogs. She read article after article and opinion after opinion about her life. Her marriage. Her fight with Taj. The other woman. Taj's son.

Nothing about her salons or her million-dollar deal with HSN. Nothing about her surviving hell or her testament of how a little ghetto girl had grown to be a rich bitch who handled her business. Nothing. Just line after line about how her life was a facade.

And maybe it was.

Maybe she was a fake. A phony. Perpetrator. A make-believe top bitch who thought she knew it all. And all along there was someone else who knew more about her than she knew about herself.

Vera looked around at the people in her house—Carl, Bridget, her assistant—and she wanted to tell them all to get the fuck out.

But she couldn't.

She had enough egg on her face. And so here she stood, turning back toward the camera, wearing a stupid-ass Cover Girl smile, when she really wanted to find a corner and crumble.

"Good morning, Mommy." Skyy skipped into the kitchen, her shoulder-length ponytail swinging from side to side as her sandals tapped across the marble floor. She hopped up on a barstool and sat at the kitchen island. "Mommy," she said. "Were you crying last night? Are you sad?"

Vera looked at her, taken aback. "No, baby." She reached across the island, cupped Skyy's chin, and kissed her in the center of her forehead. "Your mommy's fine." She turned toward the camera. "This is the best part of my morning." Vera's lips curled into a smile. "Spending time with my daughter before camp." She fixed Skyy a bowl of cereal and handed it to her.

"How sweet." Bridget yawned. "Carl, wake me up when this is over."

"Mommy, where's my daddy?" Skyy said with a full mouth and a stream of milk escaping the right corner of her lips.

Vera paused. *What do I say? Think.* "He'll be here to see you soon."

"Is he working?" Skyy pressed.

Vera hesitated. A sack of marbles filled her throat. *Think.* "I'm not sure."

"Okay." Skyy stuffed her mouth. "I really need to see him."

Relax. She's a child. Your child. It'll be okay. "Why, baby?" Vera poured herself a cup of coffee.

"Because I wanna know why his underwear was hanging off the terrace."

Vera's eyes bugged. She thought she'd had the staff clean everything up.

Skyy went on. "His boxers." She smacked her lips. "His socks, everything was all over the place. I even saw a pair of his briefs hanging on the flagpole a few flights below."

"The flagpole?" Vera gasped.

"And, Mommy," Skyy continued as if she were telling the world's most exciting story. "I was so embarrassed because Alicia pointed out the underwear hanging there."

"Don't worry about that," Vera assured Skyy.

"Mommy, these kids in camp yesterday were saying bad things about you and Daddy."

"What were they saying?"

"I can't tell you."

Vera walked over and sat next to Skyy. "What do you mean, you can't tell me? You can tell me anything. You know that."

"But it might hurt your feelings and make you cry."

"I promise I won't cry." She stroked Skyy's cheek.

Skyy said, "Well, some kids told everybody that they heard my daddy has a love child and that my family is a stupid fake."

"What?" Vera said, feeling like a bomb had gone off in her stomach.

"They even said that you and Daddy could've never been happy, because if you were he wouldn't have had a love child and embarrassed you. I told them to stop lying! But they told me it was in all the blogs. What's a blog?"

"It's what someone thinks, written on their website."

"Oh. Okay. And I kept telling them to stop teasing me, but they wouldn't leave me alone."

"I'll speak to the camp counselor," Vera said and then she paused and stared at Skyy. In all her years living in the belly of the gutter and having a junkie for a mother, she'd never had to deal with anything as hurtful as looking her seven-year-old baby in the eyes, and knowing she had to tell her that their life as they knew it was over.

Vera bit her bottom lip. "You may hear certain things about me and your daddy, but I only want you to believe what I tell you. Okay?"

"Okay."

Vera hesitated. "Your daddy." She paused again. "Has a son." She swallowed and felt as if her throat had been slit.

Damn, damn, damn, don't cry. You can't cry. Swallow. Breathe. Handle it.

Vera wanted to press forward and say something encouraging to Skyy but she didn't know what, so she sighed, her throat trembled, and her words lingered.

"Daddy has a son? What's his name?"

"Aidan." Vera pushed her bruised heart from her mouth back into her chest. "He's uh, about your age, actually a little younger."

Skyy's brown eyes gleamed like chocolate jewels. "I have a brother! A little brother? Wow! And his name is Aidan. Mommy, ever since the baby died, I've always wanted one of those!" She jumped up from her seat and pumped her fist in the air. "Yay! Just wait until I tell Ciara this, and Mommy—" She looked at a teary-eyed Vera and paused. "You don't have to cry, Mommy. This is a good thing. I'm sure we'll love Aidan." Skyy nodded for emphasis. "Just tell Daddy to bring him home when I get out of camp so I can meet him! Oh." She rubbed her hands together. "I can't wait." She started to dance. "I can't wait for Daddy to get home!"

Vera stared at Skyy and watched her hips move in glee from side to side. "Skyy." She walked over and squatted beside her. "Daddy's not coming home."

Skyy's hips froze. "What do you mean?"

"He's going." Vera cleared her throat. *Just say it.* "To be living somewhere else. Not with us. It's just going to be me and you living here."

"Is Daddy still mad at me? Because I poured his cologne on Fluffy? I only did it because Fluffy was stinky. I'm sorry."

"No, baby. It has nothing to do with you. Your daddy loves you so much. He would never be mad enough to leave because of anything you did."

"Will I see him again?"

"Yes." Vera mustered a smile. "You'll be able to visit him on weekends and holidays."

Skyy squinted. "So we won't be a real family anymore?"

Vera's voice cracked, and her entire speech about how parents who didn't live together were still a family died in her mouth. Instead a moan slipped out. "I'm sorry, Skyy—" She leaned back against the cabinets, her thighs slapped on the marble floor, and she cried until her entire body rocked. She could feel Skyy's tiny arms wrapped around her, her small hands patting Vera on the back. This was not how it was supposed to go. Her daughter wasn't supposed to comfort her. What kind of backward shit was this?

"It'll be okay, Mommy." Skyy wiped Vera's tears. She slid onto Vera's lap. "My friend Ciara doesn't live with her daddy. And my friend Kayla, she doesn't even know her daddy. So it'll be okay." She wiped Vera's eyes. "You don't have to cry." She slid her arms around Vera's neck.

"I'm soooo sorry, Skyy. You deserve so much more than this."

"We'll be a family again, Mommy." Skyy assured her. "You'll see. I'ma have a talk with Daddy and he'll be back home. Just wait and see."

You need to get yourself together. This is crazy. Vera wiped her eyes, looked at Skyy, and forced herself to smile. "You're a good girl." She hugged her. "And I love you more than you'll ever know."

"I know, Mommy. I love you too." She stretched her arms out. "Like this much!"

A genuine smile lit up Vera's face. "And I love you more than that." She softly grabbed Skyy's face and blew bubbles against her cheeks.

"You're silly, Mommy!" Skyy laughed as Vera tickled her.

After a few moments of soothing laughter, Vera sniffed and said, "Okay, Miss Goofy, time to go." They rose from the floor. "And listen." She brushed Skyy's shorts set off. "I don't want you to be concerned about me or your daddy. If those kids say anything to you that's not nice, you let them know I'll be speaking with their mother, and you tell the counselor."

"The counselor doesn't listen, so if they say anything about my daddy, I'ma slam 'em." She took a karate stance. "Hi-yah!"

"No, you will *not*."

"Well, I'ma tell Aunt Cookie on them. Aunt Cookie said she fights kids."

"Skyy, behave."

"Okay, Mommy."

Vera kissed Skyy on the forehead. "Now, remember what I told you. No matter what you hear, you only believe what I tell you. And if you're not sure about something, you come to me and we'll talk about it. Deal?"

"Deal." Skyy hugged her as the doorbell rang.

"I bet that's the driver to take you to camp." Vera pressed the button on the security monitor and zoomed in on the front door. "It is."

"Okay, Mommy." Skyy grabbed her backpack, ran toward the door, then quickly ran back to Vera and hugged her around the waist. "I don't want you to cry anymore. Okay? Daddy will be back home. He loves us." She squeezed Vera and the bell rang again. "I gotta go, Mommy." And she skipped out the door.

Vera looked around the room at a sleeping Bridget, a teary-eyed Carl, and her assistant, who shot her a sad smile. For a moment, a split second of insanity, Vera thought about breaking down and crying again. Instead she walked over to her floor-to-ceiling kitchen window and stared out into the morning sunlight.

Curtains

Milan

Milan knew things would end like this.
She could feel it in her gut.
In her bones.
In her very being.

It was as if the ending had been whispered in her ear when she was nine and crushin' on this motherfucker, and when she was a teen and loving this motherfucker, and again when she grown and was his mistress and he was her maintenance man and she sacrificed her whole life to be with him.

If only she had stopped to listen at least once, then she would've been prepared when it turned out that all she'd have in the end would be . . . nothing.

Funky fresh, fly, dope . . . or you just a lyin' niggah?

She stood in the shower and leaned against the tile wall as beads of water beat against her body. Tears rocked her throat and pain kicked her in the chest. This was the last time she would love Kendu. It had to be. She had overdosed on his bullshit, was cracked out and trippin' over his unfulfilled promises. There were no more tears left. None.

The only problem she had now were the memories.

"You wanna be my girl?" Kendu had asked her when she was ten and he was eleven. He tossed a football in the air and she watched it twirl into his cupped palms.

"I don't know you like that." Milan popped her lips as pop rocks danced in her mouth.

"Yes, you do. You love me, girl." He tossed the football.

"You need to go see Coach Reid if you wanna play ball."

"That's where I'm going."

"Good, 'cause if you wanna talk to me I'ma need all your attention."

"All my attention? That must mean you gon' be my wife. And if you my wife then we gotta kiss."

"Ill."

"It's not nasty."

"Well, how you do it?"

"Like this." He grabbed her behind and shoved his tongue into her mouth.

She pushed his chest. "You don't be sticking your tongue in my mouth and grabbing my behind! I should get my brother to kick your ass!"

And she should've, because then she wouldn't be standing here twenty years later like a bumbling fool, crying and pounding on the shower wall.

Five minutes into her tears, Milan thought, *I have to get it together.* She wiped her eyes with the back of one hand.

Damn, I just wanna stop loving him. Now, at this moment.

She stepped out of the shower and onto the bath mat. After she dried off and oiled her skin, out of habit she reached for one of Kendu's oversized white T-shirts that he always left behind whenever he spent the night, and slipped it on.

She climbed into bed. It felt like she carried boulders on her back and nails were being shot into her chest, leaving her no choice but to curl into a fetal position and cry until all she could see was blackness.

Hours later, "Milan!" and a heavy pounding forced her out of sleep. She opened her eyes, and tears that she'd held hostage beneath her lids escaped down her cheeks. Just as she wiped them away, the pounding boomed through her apartment door. "Milan!"

She looked at the clock: 3 a.m. Maybe she was dreaming.

The pounding came again. It wasn't a dream.

"Milan!" It was Kendu.

Reluctantly she eased out of bed and walked to the door.

"Milan."

Open the door.

She placed one hand on the knob. Twisted it.

Don't.

She released the knob. The automatic locks clicked back into place.

"I need to talk to you," he said calmly on the other side of the door. "And I know you're there." He jiggled the knob. "This shit is getting old, Milan." She could hear the mixture of anger and pain in his voice. "Milan."

Silence.

"Fuck. It's been two goddamn weeks, Milan. Shit is getting old. Just come home."

No.

"Milan—"

He is not entitled to my love. That shit is a privilege.

"You're not answering my calls." She could hear his frustration. At any moment she knew he was going to scream. He continued. "You're not letting me in."

Here it comes.

"*Damnit,* Milan!" He pounded on the door. "Just let me talk to you!"

Maybe I should . . .

She placed one hand on the knob again. *If you talk to him, if you see him, you know you're going to give in.* She snatched her hand away and pressed her back against the door.

"Just hear me out," Kendu said hopelessly.

She sighed. *He sounds like he means it, like he gets the shit this time. Like he's changed.*

She turned back around and faced the door. *Nobody changes in two fuckin' weeks.* Suddenly she was dizzy.

I love him so much . . .

"I love you so much, Milan," he said.

Everything wasn't bad . . .

"I miss you, baby."

But where was it going?

"I just need to talk to you."

Nowhere.

"I know you're there."

And that's the problem: He knows you'll never go anywhere.

"Milan."

I know I'll regret this shit.

"Milan." He called her again.

Suppose he leaves and never comes back?

Yeah, suppose he does. Who gives a fuck? Stand. Up. For. Something! Just stop being a weak bitch for this motherfucker. Stop letting him play you. He's been playing since 1988. When the hell is enough enough?

I love him so fuckin' much . . .

"I'm sorry, baby."

Every apology doesn't have to be accepted.

Tears flooded Milan's face as she leaned back against the door. She could feel the vibrations of his fist slamming into the door as he called her name over and over.

She slid to the floor and brought her knees to her chest. She wanted desperately to open the door, let him in, make love, and forgive him, because for so long—no matter what had happened between them—his dick had been their mutual soothing stick.

But it couldn't be this time. This time she needed to deal with his bullshit and he needed to face it.

Kendu continued to bang. The last thing Milan remembered before her tearful and exhausted eyes closed, and the morning sun came up was Kendu whispering "I love you" into the crack of the door.

Chaunci

"Please, God," was all Chaunci could pray. No matter how she tried, no other words came to mind. And yeah, she'd grown up in the church. Surrounded by amen corners and church mothers who knew the right words to put together and lay on the altar so it wasn't that Chaunci couldn't spew a religious soliloquy. She could. She just hated the contradiction of praying out of habit and not desire.

And besides, how could she change her prayer midstream? She'd been praying all this time to be happy with who she was, and now she had to change and shake shit up by praying and asking God to change her, just when she thought He'd perfected the task?

Chaunci was supposed to be independent, take charge, and do her own thing. And she did. But somehow in the midst of her emancipation and becoming a strong black woman, she'd never given herself permission to love and be loved without fear. Which is why she was at Emory's office, reality-TV camera in tow. She leaned against the doorway and as Emory spun his chair toward her, she said, "Don't turn around. Please just let me speak. Listen." she paused. *Just say it.* "Scared as hell."

Pretty girls get lonely too. She hated that her mother's voice and piss-poor advice haunted her at the wrong times.

"All of my life I watched my mother cry at night because she was lonely, had been hurt, and made all the wrong decisions with men. I promised myself I would never be as weak as she was. So whenever I felt like I was about to lose myself in something, I ran from it, and that included love. I didn't know how to love a man and not compromise who I was.

"I could love my daughter unconditionally because she was an extension of me. But a man? Men. As fine and as pretty as they were, I watched them tear shit up all of my life, and I was scared of that."

Chaunci felt anxiety crawl up her back. She thought for a moment that she needed to turn around and leave, especially since Emory hadn't said one thing. *Finish.* She drew in a sharp breath and eased it from between her teeth. "I want to love you, Emory. I do love you, and I'm willing to let all of this animosity from my past go. I'm willing to let you love me. And I'm sorry for being such a bitch." She nervously chuckled. "I just hope you'll be able to see past it and we can get things back on track."

She watched Emory's chair turn around and her heart dropped. *What the hell?* She was beyond pissed. She placed her hands on her hips.

Dressed in a navy blue and greasy jumpsuit was one of Emory's workers. He wiped his eyes with the back of his hands, leaving streaks of grease and oil beneath his eyelids. "I would take you back if I could." He sniffed. "But I think we would need to get to know each other first." He walked over to Chaunci and extended his hand. "I'm Hank."

She left him hanging. "I don't believe this shit." She looked from side to side. "Where's Emory?"

"He just left. He let me use his computer to check my Black Planet account. I got a few honies hitting me up."

Chaunci had never been so embarrassed in her life. She looked into the camera and the only thing she could think to say was, "Shit happens."

She held herself together long enough to make it back to her apartment, sit in her living room, and give Bridget an interview of trash talking about her costars, with the exception of Milan. Instead she talked shit about Kendu. After she called him "sucker" and "dumbass" for hurting her girlfriend, the camera crew and Bridget were on their way out the door. "Thanks, Chaunci," Bridget said as she stood in the hallway. "You've certainly kicked things up a notch this season. I just hope it's enough. Otherwise you'll be replaced by Shannon."

Chaunci slammed the door in Bridget's face. No sooner had she walked away and headed toward her bedroom to sulk than her bell rang. "This goddamn Bridget." She snatched the door open. "Bridget."

"I look like Bridget?"

It was Emory.

"No, well, I don't know." *What the hell am I saying?* "What are you doing here?"

"Is that really what you want to say to me?" He looked her over.

No. "I came by your shop looking for you."

"Yeah?"

"Yeah. And I practically made love to one of your attendants."

Emory laughed. "Yeah, I saw that."

"And—" Chaunci paused. "What do you mean you saw that? You were there?"

"Yeah."

"Where were you? And if you heard me, why didn't you come out?"

"I'd left and when I came back you were there. So I listened. And I thought about what you had to say."

"And?"

"And I think maybe we should try again."

Jaise

Jaise listened to raindrops beat against her skylights as she lay faceup in bed and stared at the ceiling. She closed her eyes and ran her hands over the sunken spot that Bilal's body had spent the last year carving into the mattress. The coldness of her Egyptian sheets chilled her palms and felt cool to her thighs as she rolled into his spot, clutched his pillow, and buried her nose into his fading scent. She wondered what she'd do when it was all gone.

She desperately wanted to bury her need and desire for his touch, his nipple-sucks, his shaft pressed against her shaved middle, and his twelve inches of hardness sliding against her clit and slipping into her stream of thick cream. She mourned yesterday. She wished she could bring their good times back into existence. But she couldn't. They were memories, and the only thing alive, well, and showing its existence were their bad times. And the bad times were what had cut off her windpipe and stuffed her esophagus with pain.

A part of her knew—actually her whole existence more than knew—her fairy tale would turn tragic. Bilal was too good to be true, and the goodness, the fruitfulness of his kind of love wasn't meant for her life. She'd been fated for fucked-up circumstances and no-good motherfuckers. Who was she really? Who was she to have such a man love her unconditionally?

So maybe she'd willed him to leave her. Yeah, that was it. She'd envisioned that he would disappear from her life, because he'd become tired of the exact same thing she was tired of: her baggage.

Tears rolled over the bridge of her nose and sank into her pillow.

A few moments into embracing loneliness her phone rang. Jaise contemplated not answering, especially since her heart wanted it to be Bilal, but her Caller I.D. revealed that it was Jabril.

Be strong. Being firm doesn't mean you don't love him. And hell, no, he cannot come back.

Jaise wiped her eyes as she sat up in bed. "Hello?" she answered.

"Ma," Jabril said as if he were in a hurry.

"Yes, Jabril."

"Ma, seriously, I need to come home. I'm sorry about all the shit I've done. I can't take staying with Nicole and all these damn kids another day. I see what you and Bilal were trying to tell me."

"No, Jabril, you cannot come back."

"Ma, I know you're mad at me. But I know what to do. I need you."

"I know you need me, baby. You need me to let you be a man."

"Ma, what am I going to do?"

"You'll figure it out." And she hung up before the knotting in her stomach that told her this was her baby, the child she'd carried for nine months, pleading for her help on the phone forced her to give in. She prayed like hell she'd made the right decision.

What kind of mother throws her baby away?

You're not throwing him away. You're loving him.

And who's loving you?

Jaise shook her head. She looked around her bedroom and did

her all to chase the demons of memories away, but she couldn't. She reached on her nightstand for her cigarette case. She tried to pop the case open and fumbled with the clasp.

"What the fuck am I doing? What am I doing?" She swallowed. She knew she was a fool to have fucked up such a beautiful thing. He loved her. He loved her. And here she was, lying in bed, dead. Well, maybe she wasn't dead, but she was damn sure dying.

She tossed off her covers and got into the shower. She quickly dressed, grabbed her purse, and ran out the door, practically knocking down Bridget and the camera crew, who were standing on her stoop preparing to ring the bell.

"Where are you going?" Bridget screamed. "We have to film your final episode!"

"Fuck the episode," Jaise spat as she slid into her car. "I have to go get my man!"

Vera

Vera held the phone to her chest, took a deep breath, and dialed Taj's number.

"Hello?" he answered on the first ring.

"Taj," Vera said, stopping herself short of completing her sentence with "Hey, baby."

"Vera." He let out a sigh of relief. "It's so good to hear your voice. How are you?"

"I'm okay." She hesitated. "Listen, I wanted to invite you over for dinner tonight so we can talk." She closed her eyes. She knew him well enough that she knew he was nervously stroking his chin.

"Sure," he said. "I'd love that, because we really, really need to talk."

"Yes, we do."

He's stroking his chin again.

"I just want to explain," he said. "And I hope like hell that you understand how much I love you and that it's not what it looks like. I didn't cheat on you. I'm too in love with you for that. I—"

"Taj, baby, sweetie," Vera said calmly, "Let's not discuss this over the phone. Okay?"

"All right. What time do you want me to come over?"

"In an hour."

"I love you, Vera."

"I know you do." And she hung up, the sound of his voice replaying in her mind a little longer than she wanted it to.

Vera stood in her dressing room and slipped on a fitted sleeveless black Chanel dress that stopped midway down her thighs. She stepped into her magenta snakeskin Louboutins and proceeded to do her makeup to perfection. Her long sweeping lashes curled at the ends, and her lips were colored with a deep rich plum lipstick.

Her family, a few of her friends, her costars, and the camera crew were due to arrive at any moment, and she had to be sure everything was perfect and in its place. After all, this was her final episode of the season, and then she was done with reality TV.

Hell, she had to deal with *her* reality, a space she'd been avoiding until now. Because now she had no choice but to deal with the turn of events that had suddenly and without warning grabbed her by the jugular.

Ding-dong . . .

Vera looked at her watch. It was exactly an hour. Just as she came out of her dressing room and headed to the front door, she noticed that Bridget and the camera crew had arrived and were setting things up. The closer she got to the door the more she heard Taj's keys jingling and trying to twist in the lock. They were jammed.

A smile ran across her face and a slight snicker escaped from her lips as she thought about how she'd had the locks changed.

Taj pressed hard on the bell. A few moments later Vera opened the door and his presence filled the doorway. No matter how disappointed she was, there was no way she could ever deny his beauty. He leaned against the doorframe with one hand slipped in the side pocket of his navy blue linen pants. He wore a white linen button-down, with the top three buttons open, giving sneak peeks of his smooth chest hair.

Vera felt a rush of mixed emotions, wanting to be wrapped in his arms yet also wanting to slice his throat.

"You changed the locks?" He filled the doorway.

"I did."

"Don't you think that's a bit much?" He stepped into her personal space.

She took a step back. "Are we really going to rehash what's a bit much?"

"Yeah." He nodded. "I think we should."

Breathe . . .

Taj stroked his chin.

Breathe again.

"We'll talk about the keys another time." He slid the useless keys into his pocket and lightly pulled her into his arms.

Almost instinctively she melted into his embrace, and he buried his nose in her hair, taking long breaths of her scent. "You feel so good." He tightened his hold on her.

Feeling her eyes fill with tears, Vera backed out of his embrace. Taj tangled a pinky finger with one of hers before completely letting her go. "You look beautiful."

"Thank you." She blushed.

"What's all this?" He took a step back and observed the living room. There were linen-covered tables with caviar, shrimp, lobster tails, exotic cheeses, desserts, and buckets of chilled champagne. "You're having a party?" Taj asked, puzzled. "I thought we were going to talk."

"We are." She squeezed his hand. "We're celebrating a new turn in our lives."

Taj stared at Vera and she wondered if he was tapping into her thoughts, so she quickly turned away and poured herself a glass of champagne.

"So you want us to get through this?" Taj watched her closely.

"Yes." She made eye contact. "I do. I want this to end."

"Mrs. Bennett," Vera's assistant, Deborah, said as she walked into the room. She gave Taj a small wave. "Hello, Mr. Bennett."

He nodded. "Hello."

Deborah turned back to Vera. "Security called and said your guests have arrived."

Taj said. "What guests, Vera?"

"Those who are going to help us celebrate."

"I don't—"

"Taj, it's not that big a deal."

"Why do you keep cutting me off?" he snapped.

"Listen." She held his hand. "Sit back, relax, and enjoy the moment. Just be patient, okay? These are our family and friends. As a matter of fact—" She handed him a glass of champagne. "—have a drink."

Deborah opened the door and Vera's guests quickly filled the room. Jaise and Bilal were the first to walk in.

"Bilal," Vera said with surprise. She smiled and greeted him with a hug and a kiss on the cheek. "It's really good to see you." She pointed to Taj. "You know my husband, right?"

"Yeah." Bilal walked over to Taj as Vera and Jaise embraced.

"Long story," Jaise said as she and Vera exchanged cheeks. "But he's home."

"Hey, hey, now," Aunt Cookie announced as she walked into the room with Boyden beside her profiling. "Whatcha workin' wit? Aunt Cookie is in the building."

Shannon and Idris filled the doorway. Idris kissed Vera on the cheek and quickly made his way over to where Taj and Bilal were chatting.

Shannon and Vera hugged tightly. "Whatever you decide," Shannon whispered to Vera. "I'm here for you."

"And don't forget about us, now."

Vera looked up and standing there were her childhood friends Angie and Lee. "I didn't think you guys would make it." Vera cried as they fell into a group hug. She wiped her eyes and said, "It's so good to see you guys."

"You called and asked us to come," Lee said. "And there's no way we wouldn't be here."

"That's right," Angie said. "And just so you know I came up from Atlanta packing, okay? That's why I drove. Just in case we had to cap us a bitch, a kid, or a fine-ass doctor."

"Oh, my God!" Lee clutched her chest. "You had me riding in the car with you and a gun? You gon' mess around and go to jail. And I will testify against you. I can promise you that."

"Lee, would you calm down?" Shannon looked at her as if she were crazy. "It's not that serious."

Lee snapped, "Shannon, you're in New York. You're not riding shotgun with Annie Oakley."

"Would you two stop it so I can introduce you to my friend?" Vera interrupted. "Jaise, as you can see, these are my sister girl-friends, Angie and Lee."

Jaise smiled. "I feel like I already know you guys."

For the next hour everyone chatted and mingled. They ate, drank, and moved a little to the jazz grooving through the surround sound.

Vera glanced over at Taj and she could tell he was uncomfortable.

"Can I have everyone's attention?" Vera tapped her champagne glass with a fork, "Excuse me, excuse me."

"Shhh" floated around the room until everyone fell silent.

Vera walked to the front of the room and her guests gathered in a semicircle around her. "I want everyone to share a toast with me. So please grab a glass of champagne." Everyone complied.

Vera continued. "Taj, come here, please." She smiled and she could tell he was leery, yet he did.

Vera clapped her hands. "I have exciting news. We have a new addition to our family."

Jaise gasped. "Are you pregnant?"

"No, silly." Vera gave her a half smile.

"The reports and the blogs were true: Taj has a son." She smiled. "By his old high-school sweetheart."

"What are you doing?" Taj mumbled.

Vera continued. "And his name is Aidan. He's a little younger than Skyy. And from what I hear, he looks exactly like his daddy." She pointed to Taj. "He is such a proud papa. He has a boy and a girl."

"Vera—"

She turned to Taj. "Baby, you know I love you. I've loved you from the moment I laid eyes on you. You have been my everything and we've been through it all, but there are just some things in life I can not forgive."

"Vera—"

"No, baby, let me finish. I know you thought that maybe we would be able to get past this and the truth is, I did too, until I started thinking—that all of these years I thought that your ass was perfect. All-American doctor, saving the world, good ole boy. Superman. Coming to save me from myself."

"Vera, stop."

"Honey, listen to me. I have to tell you and let all of our friends know about how I thought I was the one fucked-up and fucking up." She looked toward her aunt Cookie. "Didn't you tell me that I needed to get it together? That I was working too much, Aunt Cookie. Isn't that what you said?" Vera turned back to Taj. "And I was soooo torn up and sick about the decisions I was making. My God, I thought I was just always doing something that you didn't approve of."

"Vera—"

"It was as if you were the American Dream and I was anti-American dream. But all along I was the one being fooled. You were an illusion, living proof that if it's too good to be true, it's a facade. And so—"

"Would you stop?"

"I've filed for divorce."

"What?" Taj looked at Vera as if he'd heard wrong.

"My Love," She clinked the tip of her champagne glass against his. "May we forever be friends."

Reunion

The Club

Millionaire Wives Club was a hit. The ratings for the second season were the highest the cable network had ever gotten for any show, making this one of the most highly anticipated reunions ever.

All the women were breakout stars, and the fans, blogs, gossip sites, and tabloids either loved them or hated them. There was not only the promise of a third season, but Bridget had already started perusing other major cities for a spin-off cast.

Jaise and Vera walked out onstage wearing five-inch heels and designer dresses that complemented their curves. They sat to the right of the host on a crisp white chenille sofa. Jaise crossed her legs at the ankles, while Vera crossed one thigh over the other.

Chaunci and Milan sat on an adjacent sofa. Chaunci was dressed in an olive-green strapless dress, and Milan wore a cream halter dress that lay perfectly over her thick thighs.

"Lights, camera, action!" the director yelled from backstage. "We're live."

"Welcome to the reunion of Millionaire Wives Club, season

two," said the host, who'd dyed his hair the wrong shade of red for his complexion. "I'm Don McBride and I'll be your host this evening."

"Hello, Don," the women said simultaneously as the studio audience clapped.

"Good to see you, ladies." He turned toward Vera. "Why don't we start with you?"

Vera smiled. "Let's start with me."

"Can you tell us how you and Taj are? I mean, my gosh, you really took the season out with a bang. Are you guys divorced?"

"No," Vera answered. "We're not. We're working on getting our lives back in order."

"Is he back home?"

"Almost. We're taking things slowly. But I'm sure he'll be back home soon."

"Were you able to recover all his clothes that you threw off the terrace?"

Vera and the audience chuckled. "I think he's replaced those."

"Well, all of America wants to know what happened."

Jaise held Vera's hand while she took a deep breath. "When Taj and I were dating, shortly after we had our daughter, we broke up for a few months. And he, umm, spent a night with an old fling. And eight years later, she heard that I was on TV and Taj was this famous oncologist, and she came calling. Especially after she found out her son wasn't her ex-husband's child. But that has nothing to do with Aidan. He had a right to know his father."

"So Taj really didn't cheat on you?"

"No."

"How's your relationship with Aidan?"

"He's part of our family. He's adorable. We love him and Skyy loves her brother. He comes to our house. Is every day great? No. Is this an adjustment? Yes. But we'll make it."

"Sounds like you're on the right track." Don smiled as he looked into the studio audience. "How about we take our first question of the evening?" He pointed to a short Latino woman with blonde hair. "What's your question?"

"Hi, my name is Jessi and my question is for Vera. Are you still working on selling your hair products on HSN? Because I can't find them."

"Yes, we'll debut our line next month. So look out for Volume."

"Thank you, Jessi," Don said as he turned to Chaunci. "So, Chaunci, what's going on with you? Any new prospects?"

Chaunci smiled. "If you're asking if I have a boyfriend, the answer is yes. Emory and I are doing okay."

"So you're over Idris?" Don pried.

"I've *been* over Idris."

"Then there's a chance you and Vera will become friends?"

"Hell, no," Chaunci snapped.

"Team Shannon." Vera smirked.

"I'm sure we'll be seeing that on a T-shirt." Don chuckled. "Let's move on to our next question from the studio audience." He pointed to the audience and two women, both wearing red bandanna dresses, stood up. "Hey, y'all. I know you remember me. I'm Roz."

"And I'm Trena." She snapped her fingers and looked directly into the camera. "Hey, Money, hey, baby. Don't even let those C.O.s stress you about that extra time they placed on your bid, 'cause if a mofo needs to be shanked, then you gon' have to shank his ass! At least you got heart, baby."

"That's my boy." Roz smiled.

"Okay," Trena said. "Now, here's my question. Chaunci, were you jealous of Vera this season?"

Chaunci cleared her throat. "No, I—"

"Well, then, what the hell was wrong with you?" Roz interjected. "I was looking at the TV like, is this heifer trippin'? Vera should've handled you on a number of occasions. And the way you treated Emory, girl, a mess. And, Vera, I was with you, girl, when you called that fool Taj out. Acting like he's so high and mighty. I would've jumped dead in his shit too and then taken a crowbar and beat dat ass."

"You ain't nevah lied," Trena agreed. "His ass would've needed a doctor!"

"Only one question, please," Don said.

"These ain't questions, these is comments," Roz carried on. "And Milan. Damn, you put all that work into Kendu and what did you get in the end?"

"Not a damn thing," Trena said. "Thank you, that's all we have to say." And the women took their seats.

Don looked completely caught off guard, but since this was live TV he had to gather himself on the air. "Okay, well, let's move to you, Jaise. How's Jabril?"

"Well, Jabril isn't perfect—"

"At least you're being honest this reunion," Chaunci cut her off.

"Yeah, really." Milan sneered. "Because last year you made him out to be America's dream kid."

"How about this?" Vera interrupted. "It's her damn story and her damn son. And if she wants to twist shit, how about that's her business? You bitches lie, show your ass, and do all sorts of dumb shit. Shall we rehash it? Otherwise back the hell up."

"Click, click, boom!" Bridget yelled from backstage.

"Oh, you're really going a little too far," Chaunci spat at Vera.

"That's all you ever say," Vera snapped. "I meant to go that far."

"You know what I say." Jaise waved her hand. "All's fair in love and bitch slaps. Now, can I continue?"

"Yes," Don said. "Jaise, please continue. Also, can you tell us what's changed for you?"

"Well, Don, I learned that I had to let my son go and be a man, which is the hardest thing in the world to do. I had to see that there was a difference between being a mother and being a smother, a codependent. And I was truly holding him back."

"How's he doing now?"

"Believe it or not." She shot a look at Milan and Chaunci. "Jabril is in the firemen's academy." Her face lit up. "He lives in Brooklyn in a studio apartment. He pays his own rent and his child support. He's really trying to get his life together."

"Great," Don said. "Now we have another question from our audience." He pointed.

"Hi, I'm Keisha and I wanted to know how things are between you and Bilal."

"Bilal and I are closer than we've ever been. Our first year was hell. It was. And I know that I played a major part, but things are back on track and I have my priorities in order."

"So does your son still come first in your life?" Don asked. "I'm sure everyone wants to know."

"I love my son and I will not apologize for that. And I can't say that I'll never help him again, because that would be a lie. But I'm not sure if I can answer whether my son continues to come first. But what I *can* say is that my husband and I are one, and my son is my son, and umm—"

"Here y'all motherfuckers go again!" Al-Taniesha screamed as she stormed onstage wearing a lavender sequined skirt suit with a large-brim hat and veil. Lollipop walked slowly behind her wearing a long black robe and white priest collar, holding a bible in one hand.

"No cussin', Niesha," Lollipop said. "No cussin'."

"Oh, excuse me." Al-Taniesha fanned her face. "Got me cussin' and shit. And here I am saved."

"Al-Taniesha," Don said, flabbergasted. "I had no idea you'd be here."

"Because nobody invited me. If it wasn't for Bridget, I wouldn't have known the reunion was being recorded. And, see, this is why I quit the show, because of favoritism. These heifers all up on TV showing their asses and because I had some class and didn't want to do that, I couldn't get any airtime. So I said, 'Al-Taniesha

Chardonnay Richardson, you better step to the side and quit before you been done cut a bitch.' Forgive me, Jesus. What I meant to say was, I didn't appreciate that again."

"So, umm, what are you two doing now?" Don asked, doing his best to collect himself.

"Well, we have got a special calling over our lives." Lollipop clutched his bible. "Thank ya."

"Sho' do." Al-Taniesha waved her hand. "Amen."

Lollipop continued. "And I am now Bruh Pastah Lollipop, head of the collection plate, I mean, the congregation of Heathen No More Tabernacle."

"And I'm first lady of Heathrow, Hallelujah—what is it again, Lollipop?"

"Heathen."

"First lady of Heathen No More Tabernacle." Al-Taniesha snapped her fingers. "As you can see, we're doing our own thing and we don't need these hoes, I mean, these heathens to be successful. But they are welcome to come to the tabernacle." She pointed at the other women. "Because lawd knows they need somebody to pray for 'em."

"Wow, well." Don reached for a glass of water on the table next to his chair. "This has really been quite an unexpected turn of events. I don't even know where to go from here." He paused. "Oh, yeah, umm, Milan." He looked toward her. "I believe we still need to catch up with you. How are things?"

"Things are okay, Don. Life is different," Milan said, while Chaunci patted her hand.

"So I take it that you and Kendu aren't back together?"

"No." Milan did all she could to hold her tears at bay and sound sure of herself.

"Do you still love him?"

Milan hesitated. Tears filled her throat. She looked up at the ceiling, then back toward Don. "It gets better every day." She mustered a smile.

"Well, I need to know the secret." Kendu stood up and walked down the center of the aisle. All eyes immediately fell on him and instantly the audience started buzzing.

Kendu continued. "I need to know the secret of how it gets better every day because for me it gets worse." He continued to walk until he was at the front of the stage staring at Milan. "I don't know what the hell to do. And I sat at home, watching this shit and I kept looking at you, Milan, and thinking I have to go and get her. I gotta try one more time. Because I've been in hell for the past six months and I'm lost without you. All I wanna do is love you, Milan. But if I can't and you won't let me love you then tell me how to get over that shit. Tell me."

"Well down at the Heathen No More Tabernacle," Lollipop said. "We offer classes entitled Flesh Be Still."

"Milan," Kendu walked on stage, ignoring Lollipop. "Tell me. Tell me how to do it." Tears filled his eyes as he kneeled before her. "I think about you every day. I've called you a thousand times, written you a million letters and you won't talk to me. Talk to me, Milan. Tell me. I promise you if you tell me you don't love me, or better if you tell me how to stop loving you then I'll try. But as of right now, today, I'm fucked up."

Tears ached Milan's throat as she said. "You take me for granted."

"I'm not perfect. I'm not and I fuck up. I do dumb shit. I get scared—"

"Scared of what?" She rolled her eyes to the ceiling. She had to do something to stop tears from spilling, but judging by the way they were filling her bottom lids nothing would stop them.

He continued. "Scared that you'll never come back. I've never loved as much or as hard as I love you. It's like I breathe you. Milan, tell me do you still love me? Because if you don't, I promise I'll walk away. I'll leave here today and deal with the bed I made."

Milan swallowed. She desperately wanted to lie but she couldn't. "I still love you," she whispered.

"Then marry me."

"What?"

"Marry me right now, at this very moment. Right now."

"Knott—"

"Marry me." He kissed her. "Marry me. You make me a better man. You make me want more. I'm no good with this shit, Milan. Just say you'll marry me, right now."

"How am I going to marry you right now, Knott? I need time to think."

"No, you don't. Let's just do it."

"All you need is a preacher," Lollipop said as he cleared his throat.

"And I'm working on the license right now!" Bridget screamed with a phone held to each ear. "And Carl, I hope you're getting close-ups! Ratings will shoot through the roof. Milan!" She screamed. "I smell a spin-off!"

"I haven't even said yes." Milan wiped tears from Kendu's eyes.

"Oh, girl," Jaise said. "Would you tell this damn man yes?"

"Knott." Milan paused.

"Say yes," he whispered.

Milan cupped his face and pressed her lips against his. "Yes."

He stood up and took Milan by the hands. "I love you," he mouthed as sweat formed on his brow.

Chaunci, Jaise, and Vera walked into the audience, leaving Milan and Kendu onstage as the ceremony began.

"Are we really doing this?" she mumbled to him.

"Hell, yeah." He grinned. "We're taking it back to our roots. Ghetto, baby."

Milan laughed. "This is why I'm madly in love with you. You just have a way with words."

"Let's get it on." Lollipop stood up and looked toward the audience. "I bring you greetings from the Heathen No More Tabernacle, where you are welcome to send donations for one of our many charities. We take credit cards, debit cards, Family First cards, Visa, Mastercard, and we are working on American Express.

"And now that we've got that out of the way, let's handle this here. We are gathered here today to unite this fine, oversized chocolate bar, who looks like my cellmate from back in the day, Nephew."

"Nephew!" Al-Taniesha screamed. "Why are you bringing up Nephew?"

"Would you get to the point?" Kendu said.

"I am. I am." Lollipop continued. "Okay. We are gathered here today to unite Milan Starks and Kendu Jackson."

"Who the hell is Kendu Jackson?" Kendu frowned. "It's Malik. I know you watch football, man."

Lollipop grumbled. "That's what I meant to say, Malik. Kendu Malik and Milan Starks. We are gathered here today to witness them becoming one. Now, who gives this woman to this man?"

"We do." Bridget bolted onto the stage. "We do."

"Rings, please." Lollipop said.

Milan replied. "We don't have any—"

"Here you go." Kendu slid two rings from his pocket, one for him and one for Milan. "I came prepared, baby."

Milan smiled as Lollipop prayed over the rings and handed the respective rings to each of them. Kendu held Milan's hand and as he slid her ring onto her finger, he said, "Milan, I always knew that you would be my wife. I always knew it, from the moment I laid eyes on you on the playground and did my best break-dancing move to impress you to the moment we first made love. There was something about you that made me always want to risk it all to be with you. So here I am, promising to love, honor, and cherish you forever."

"This is so beautiful," Bridget whispered. "I need a tissue."

Milan wiped the tears that streaked Kendu's face with her thumb. She placed his band on his finger. "I never knew where we were going or where we would end up. All I knew is that I loved you so much and that I always wanted to be with you, forever. You are my best friend, the perfect lover, everything I have ever wanted and needed. And from this day forward I promise to love, honor, and cherish you forever."

"And by the power vested in me by the Heathen No More Tabernacle and the state of New York, I hereby declare you husband and wife." Lollipop turned to Kendu, "You may get busy with your bride."

"Carl!" Bridget cried. "Come over here, please. I need somebody to hold me."

Acknowledgments

First and foremost I thank my Lord and Savior Jesus Christ, who died so that I would have everlasting life!

To my mother and father for always being there.

To my husband for dreaming up crazy characters with me.

To my children who really think I'm superwoman.

To my family: Whitaker, Parker, Robinson, Britt, and Lassiter, thank you for all of the love and support, there's no way I could do any of this without you!

To Keisha Ervin for being my friend and most of all my reality TV partner! I wish you nothing but the best.

To Danielle Santiago, here's to your comeback.

To K'wan and Charlotte for encouraging me to write a part two to *Millionaire Wives Club*.

To my friend and brother, Dywane Birch, thanks so much for always being there and most of all thanks for keeping it real at all times.

To Adrianne Byrd, you are the funniest person I know. You have an amazing amount of talent, are a wonderful friend, and I wish you nothing but the best!

To my lifetime BFFs Kenya, Sharonda, and Val, love you dearly my sistah-girl-friends!

To my agent Sara Camilli, thank you for being so wonderful.

To Porscha Burke, I'm sooo excited to be working together again! Here's to the future!

To my One World family, thank you for patience, your time, and your talent. I may have written the manuscript but together we made this a book.

To each bookstore, website, bookclub, and to everyone who has ever supported me in my career thank you for all that you've done.

And saving the best for last the readers, hands down I have the best readers in the world! Thank you so much for supporting me in all of my literary ventures. I'd love to hear from you. Please email me at tushonda111@aol.com.

One love,
Tu-Shonda

TU-SHONDA WHITAKER is the *Essence* bestselling author of *Millionaire Wives Club, The Ex-Factor, Flip Side of the Game,* and *Game Over.* Under the pseudonym Risque she wrote the One World erotic novels *Smooth Operator, Red Light Special,* and *The Sweetest Taboo.* She received the Ella Baker and W.E.B. Dubois International Award for fiction writing. She lives in New Jersey with her husband and their three children.